The Lone Ranger and Tonto Fistfight in Heaven

Reservation Blues

Indian Killer

The Toughest Indian in the World

Smoke Signals (a screenplay)

The Business of Fancydancing

I Would Steal Horses

Old Shirts & New Skins

First Indian on the Moon

The Summer of Black Widows

One Stick Song

For Diane, Joseph, and David

For Christy

Contents

Love—bittersweet, irrepressible—
loosens my limbs and I tremble.

—Sappho

THE SEARCH ENGINE

O n Wednesday afternoon in the student union café, Corliss looked up from her American history textbook and watched a young man and younger woman walk in together and sit two tables away. The student union wasn't crowded, so Corliss clearly heard the young couple's conversation. He offered her coffee from his thermos, but she declined. Hurt by her rejection, or feigning pain—he always carried two cups because well, you never know, do you?—he poured himself one, sipped and sighed with theatrical pleasure, and monologued. The young woman slumped in her seat and listened. He told her where he was from and where he wanted to go after college, and how much he liked these books and those teachers but hated those movies and these classes, and it was all part of an ordinary man's list-making attempts to seduce an ordinary woman. Blond, blue-eyed, pretty, and thin, she hid her incipient bulimia beneath a bulky wool sweater. Corliss wanted to buy the skeletal woman a sandwich, ten sandwiches, and a big bowl of vanilla ice cream. Eat, young woman, eat, Corliss thought, and you will be redeemed! The young woman set her backpack on the table and crossed her arms over her chest, but the young man didn't seem to notice or care about the defensive meaning of her body language. He talked and talked and gestured passionately with long-fingered hands. A former lover, an older woman, had probably told him his hands were artistic, so he assumed all women would be similarly charmed. He wore his long blond hair pulled back into a ponytail and a flowered blue shirt that was really a blouse; he was narcissistic, androgynous, lovely, and yes, charming. Corliss thought she might sleep with him if he took her home to a clean apartment, but she decided to hate him instead. She knew she judged people based on their surface appearances, but Lord Byron said only shallow people don't judge by surfaces. So Corliss thought of herself as Byronesque as she eavesdropped on the young couple. She hoped one of these ordinary people might say something interesting and original. She believed in the endless nature of human possibility. She would be delighted if these two messy humans transcended their stereotypes and revealed themselves as mortal angels.

"Well, you know," the young man said to the young woman, "it was Auden who wrote that no poem ever saved a Jew from the ovens."

"Oh," the young woman said. She didn't know why he'd abruptly paraphrased Auden. She wasn't sure who this Auden person was, or why his opinions about poetry should matter to her, or why poetry itself was so important. She knew this coffee-drinking guy wanted to have sex with her, and she was considering it, but he wasn't improving his chances by making her feel stupid.

Corliss was confused by the poetic non sequitur as well. She thought he might be trying to prove how many books he'd skimmed. Maybe he deserved her contempt, but Corliss realized that very few young men read poetry at Washington State University. And how many of those boys quoted, or misquoted, the poems they'd read? Twenty, ten, less than five? This longhaired guy enjoyed a monopoly on the poetry-quoting market in the southeastern corner of Washington, and he knew it. Corliss had read a few poems by W. H. Auden but couldn't remember any of them other than the elegy recited in that Hugh Grant romantic comedy. She figured the young man had memorized the first stanzas of thirty-three love poems and used them like propaganda to win the hearts and minds of young women. He'd probably tattooed the opening lines of Andrew Marvell's "To His Coy Mistress" on his chest: "Had we but world enough, and time, / This coyness, Lady, were no crime." Corliss wondered if Shakespeare wrote his plays and sonnets only because he was trying to get laid. Which poet or poem has been quoted most often in the effort to get laid? Most important, which poet or poem has been quoted most successfully in the effort to get laid? Corliss needed to know the serious answers to her silly questions. Or vice versa. So she gathered her books and papers and approached the couple.

"Excuse me," Corliss said to the young man. "Was that W. H. Auden you were quoting?"

"Yes," he said. His smile was genuine and boyish. He had displayed his intelligence and was being rewarded for it. Why shouldn't he smile?

"I didn't recognize the quote," Corliss said. "Which poem did it come from?"

The young man looked at Corliss and at the young woman. Corliss knew he was choosing between them. The young woman knew it, too, and she decided the whole thing was pointless.

"I've got to go," she said, grabbed her backpack, and fled.

"Wow, that was quick," he said. "Rejected at the speed of light."

"Sorry about that," Corliss said. But she was pleased with the young woman's quick decision and quicker flight. If she could resist one man's efforts to shape and determine her future, perhaps she could resist all future efforts.

"It's all right," the young man said. "Do you want to sit down, keep me company?"

"No thanks," Corliss said. "Tell me about that Auden quote."

He smiled again. He studied her. She was very short, a few inches under five feet, maybe thirty pounds overweight, and plain-featured. But her skin was clear and dark brown (like good coffee!), and her long black hair hung down past her waist. And she wore red cowboy boots, and her breasts were large, and she knew about Auden, and she was confident enough to approach strangers, so maybe her beauty was eccentric, even exotic. And exoticism was hard to find in Pullman, Washington.

"What's your name?" he asked her.

"Corliss."

"That's a beautiful name. What does it mean?"

"It means Corliss is my name. Are you going to tell me where you read that Auden quote or not?"

"You're Indian, aren't you?"

"Good-bye," she said and stood to leave.

"Wait, wait," he said. "You don't like me, do you?"

"You're cute and smart, and you've gotten everything you've ever asked for, and that makes you lazy and dangerous."

"Wow, you're honest. Will you like me better if I'm honest?"

"I might."

"I've never read Auden's poems. Not much, anyway. I read some article about him. They quoted him on the thing about Jews and poems. I don't know where they got it from. But it's true, don't you think?"

"What's true?"

"A good gun will always beat a good poem."

"I hope not," Corliss said and walked away.

Back in Spokane, Washington, Corliss had attended Spokane River High School, which had contained a mirage-library. Sure, the books had looked like Dickens and Dickinson from a distance, but they turned into cookbooks and auto-repair manuals when you picked them up. As a poor kid, and a middle-class Indian, she seemed destined for a minimum-wage life of waiting tables or changing oil. But she had wanted a maximum life, an original aboriginal life, so she had fought her way out of her underfunded public high school into an underfunded public college. So maybe, despite American racism, sexism, and classism, Corliss's biography confirmed everything nearly wonderful and partially meritorious about her country. Ever the rugged individual, she had collected aluminum cans during the summer before her junior year of high school so she could afford the yearlong SAT-prep course that had astronomically raised her scores and won her a dozen academic scholarships. At the beginning of every semester, Corliss had called the history and English teachers at the local prep school she couldn't afford, and asked what books they would be reading in class, and she had found those books and lived with them like siblings. And those same teachers, good white people whose whiteness and goodness blended and separated, had faxed her study guides and copies of the best student papers. Two of those teachers, without having met Corliss in person, had sent her graduation gifts of money and yet more books. She'd been a resourceful thief, a narcissistic Robin Hood who stole a rich education from white people and kept it.

In the Washington State University library, her version of Sherwood Forest, Corliss walked the poetry stacks. She endured a contentious and passionate relationship with this library. The huge number of books confirmed how much magic she'd been denied for most of her life, and now she hungrily wanted to read every book on every shelf. An impossible task, to be sure, Herculean in its exaggeration, but Corliss wanted to read herself to death. She wanted to be buried in a coffin filled with used paperbacks.

She found W. H. Auden's *Collected Poems* on a shelf above her head. She stood on her toes and pulled down the thick volume, but she also pulled out another book that dropped to the floor. It was a book of poems titled *In the Reservation of My Mind,* by Harlan Atwater. According to the author's biography on the back cover, Harlan Atwater was a Spokane Indian, but Corliss had never heard of the guy. Her parents, grandparents, and great-grandparents were all born and raised on the Spokane Indian Reservation. And the rest of her ancestors, going back a dozen generations, were born and raised on the land that would eventually be called the Spokane Indian Reservation. Her one white ancestor, a Russian fur trapper, had been legally adopted into the tribe, given some corny Indian name she didn't like to repeat, and served on the tribal council for ten years. Corliss was a Spokane Indian born in Sacred Heart Hospital, only a mile from the Spokane River Falls, the heart of the Spokane Tribe, and had grown up in the city of Spokane, which was really an annex of the reservation, and thought she knew or knew of every Spokane. Demographically and biologically speaking, Corliss was about as Spokane as a Spokane Indian can be, and only three thousand other Spokanes of various Spokane-ness existed in the whole world, so how had this guy escaped her attention? She opened the book and read the first poem:

The Naming Ceremony

No Indian ever gave me an Indian name
So I named myself.
I am Crying Shame.
I am Takes the Blame.
I am the Four Directions:
South, A Little More South,

Way More South, and All the Way South.
If you are ever driving toward Mexico

And see me hitchhiking, you'll know me
By the size of my feet.
My left foot is named Self-Pity
And my right foot is named Born to Lose.
But if you give me a ride, you can call me
And all of my parts any name you choose.

Corliss recognized the poem as a free-verse sonnet whose end rhymes gave it a little more music. It was a funny and clumsy poem desperate to please the reader. It was like a slobbery puppy in an animal shelter: Choose me! Choose me! But the poem was definitely charming and strange. Harlan Atwater was making fun of being Indian, of the essential sadness of being Indian, and so maybe he was saying Indians aren't sad at all. Maybe Indians are just big-footed hitchhikers eager to tell a joke! That wasn't a profound thought, but maybe it was an accurate one. But can you be accurate without profundity? Corliss didn't know the answer to the question.

She carried the Atwater and Auden books to the front desk to check them out. The librarian was a small woman wearing khaki pants and large glasses. Corliss wanted to shout at her: Honey, get yourself some contacts and a pair of leather chaps! Fight your stereotypes!

"Wow," the librarian said as she scanned the books' bar codes and entered them into her computer.

"Wow what?" Corliss asked.

"You're the first person who's ever checked out this book." The librarian held up the Atwater.

"Is it new?"

"We've had it since 1972."

Corliss wondered what happens to a book that sits unread on a library shelf for thirty years. Can a book rightfully be called a book if it never gets read? If a tree falls in a forest and gets pulped to make paper for a book that never gets read, but there's nobody there to read it, does it make a sound?

"How many books never get checked out?" Corliss asked the librarian.

"Most of them," she said.

Corliss had never once considered the fate of library books. She'd never wondered how many books go unread. She loved books. How could she not worry about the unread? She felt like a disorganized scholar, an inconsiderate lover, an abusive mother, and a cowardly solider.

"Are you serious?" Corliss asked. "What are we talking about here? If you were guessing, what is the percentage of books in this library that never get checked out?"

"We're talking sixty percent of them. Seriously. Maybe seventy percent. And I'm being optimistic. It's probably more like eighty or ninety percent. This isn't a library, it's an orphanage."

The librarian spoke in a reverential whisper. Corliss knew she'd misjudged this passionate woman. Maybe she dressed poorly, but she was probably great in bed, certainly believed in God and goodness, and kept an illicit collection of overdue library books on her shelves.

"How many books do you have here?" Corliss asked.

"Two million, one hundred thousand, and eleven," the librarian said proudly, but Corliss was frightened. What happens to the world when that many books go unread? And what happens to the unread authors of those unread books?

"And don't think it's just this library, either," the librarian said. "There's about eighteen million books in the Library of Congress, and nobody reads about seventeen and a half million of them."

"You're scaring me."

"Sorry about that," the librarian said. "These are due back in two weeks."

Corliss carried the Auden and Atwater books out of the library and into the afternoon air. She sat on a bench and flipped through the pages. The Auden was worn and battered, with pen and pencil notes scribbled all over the margins. Three generations of WSU students had defaced Auden with their scholarly graffiti, but Atwater was stiff and unmarked. This book had not been exposed to direct sunlight in three decades. W. H. Auden didn't need Corliss to read him—his work was already immortal—but she felt like she'd rescued Harlan Atwater. And who else should rescue the poems of a Spokane Indian but another Spokane? Corliss felt the weight and heat of destiny. She had been chosen. God had nearly dropped Atwater's book on her head. Who knew the Supreme One could be so obvious? But then again, when have the infallible been anything other than predictable? Maybe God was dropping other books on other people's heads, Corliss thought. Maybe every book in every library is patiently waiting for its savior. Ha! She felt romantic and young and foolish. What kind of Indian loses her mind over a book of poems? She was that kind of Indian, she was exactly that kind of Indian, and it was the only kind of Indian she knew how to be.

Corliss lived alone. She supposed that was a rare thing for a nineteen-year-old college sophomore, especially a Native American college student living on scholarships and luck and family charity, but she couldn't stand the thought of sharing her apartment with another person. She didn't want to live with another Indian because she understood Indians all too well. If she took an Indian roommate, Corliss knew she'd soon be taking in the roommate's cousin, little brother, half uncle, and long-lost dog, and none of them would con-tribute anything toward the rent other than wispy apologies. Indi-ans were used to sharing and called it tribalism, but Corliss suspected it was yet another failed form of communism. Over the last two cen-turies, Indians had learned how to stand in lines for food, love, hope, sex, and dreams, but they didn't know how to step away. They were good at line-standing and didn't know if they'd be good at anything else. Of course, all sorts of folks made it their business to confirm Indian fears and insecurities. Indians hadn't invented the line. And George Armstrong Custer is alive and well in the twenty-first cen-tury, Corliss thought, though he kills Indians by dumping huge piles of paperwork on their skulls. But Indians made themselves easy tar-gets for bureaucratic skull-crushing, didn't they? Indians took numbers and lined up for skull-crushing. They'd rather die standing together in long lines than wandering alone in the wilderness. Indians were terri-fied of being lonely, of being exiled, but Corliss had always dreamed of solitude. Since she'd shared her childhood home with an Indian mother, an Indian father, seven Indian siblings, and a random assort-ment of Indian cousins, strangers, and party crashers, she cherished her domestic solitude and kept it sacred. Maybe she lived in an aca-demic gulag, but she'd chosen to live that way. She furnished her apartment with a mattress on the floor, one bookshelf, two lamps, a dining table, two chairs, two sets of plates, cups, and utensils, three pots, and one frying pan. Her wardrobe consisted of three pairs of blue jeans, three white blouses, one pair of tennis shoes, three pairs of cowboy boots, six white T-shirts, thirteen pairs of socks, and a week's worth of underwear. Her only luxuries (necessities!) were books. There were hundreds of them stacked around her apartment. She'd never met one human being more interesting to her than a good book. So how could she live with an uninteresting Indian when she could live with John Donne, Elizabeth Bishop, and Langston Hughes?

Corliss didn't want to live with a white roommate, either, no matter how interesting he or she might become. Hell, even if Emily Dickinson were resurrected and had her reclusive-hermit-unrequited-love-addict gene removed from her DNA, Corliss wouldn't have wanted to room with her. White people, no matter how smart, were too romantic about Indians. White people looked at the Grand Canyon, Niagara Falls, the full moon, newborn babies, and Indians with the same goofy sentimentalism. Being a smart Indian, Corliss had always taken advantage of this romanticism, but that didn't mean she wanted to share the refrigerator with it. If white folks assumed she was serene and spiritual and wise simply because she was an Indian, and thought she was special based on those mistaken assumptions, then Corliss saw no reason to contradict them. The world is a competitive place, and a poor Indian girl needs all the advantages she can get. So if George W. Bush, a man who possessed no remarkable distinctions other than being the son of a former U.S. president, could also become president, then Corliss figured she could certainly benefit from positive ethnic stereotypes and not feel any guilt about it. For five centuries, Indians were slaughtered because they were Indians, so if Corliss received a free coffee now and again from the local free-range lesbian Indiophile, who could possibly find the wrong in that? In the twenty-first century, any Indian with a decent vocabulary wielded enormous social power, but only if she was a stoic who rarely spoke. If she lived with a white person, Corliss knew she'd quickly be seen as ordinary, because she was ordinary. It's tough to share a bathroom with an Indian and continue to romanticize her. If word got around that Corliss was ordinary, even boring, she feared she'd lose her power and magic. She knew there would come a day when white folks finally understood that Indians are every bit as relentlessly boring, selfish, and smelly as they are, and that would be a wonderful day for human rights but a terrible day for Corliss.

*　*　*

Corliss caught the number 7 home from the library. She wanted to read Harlan Atwater's book on the bus, but she also wanted to keep it private. The book felt dangerous and forbidden. At her stop, she stepped off and walked toward her apartment, and then ran. She felt giddy, foolish, and strangely aroused, as if she were running home to read pornography. Once alone, Corliss sat on the floor, backed into a corner, and read Harlan Atwater's book of poems. There were forty-five free-verse sonnets. Corliss found it interesting that an Indian of his generation wrote sonnets, while other Indians occupied Alcatraz and Wounded Knee. Most of the poems were set in and around the Spokane Indian Reservation, so Corliss wondered again why she'd never heard of this man. How many poetry lovers were among the Spokanes? Fifty, thirty, fewer than twenty? And how many Spokanes would recognize a sonnet when they saw it, let alone be able to write one? Since her public high school teachers had known how much Corliss loved poetry, and had always loved it, why hadn't one of them handed her this book? Maybe this book could have saved her years of shame. Instead of trying to hide her poetry habit from her friends and family, and sneaking huge piles of poetry books into her room, maybe she could have proudly read a book of poems at the dinner table. She could have held that book above her head and shouted, "See, look, it's a book of poems by another Spokane, what are you going to do about that?" Instead, she'd endured endless domestic interrogations about her bookish nature.

During one family reunion, her father sat around the living room with his three brothers. That was over twelve hundred pounds of Spokane Indian sharing a couch and a bowl of tortilla chips. Coming home from school, Corliss tried to dash across the room and make her escape, but one uncle noticed the book under her arm.

"Why you always reading?" he asked.

"I like stories," she said. It seemed to be the safest answer. Indians loved to think of themselves as the best storytellers in the world, and maybe they were, but did they need to be so sure of it?

"She's reading those poems again," her father said. "She's always reading those poems."

She loved her father and uncles. She loved how they filled a room with their laughter and rank male bodies and endless nostalgia and quick tempers, but she hated their individual fears and collective lack of ambition. They all worked blue-collar construction jobs, not because they loved the good work or found it valuable or rewarding but because some teacher or guidance counselor once told them all they could work only blue-collar jobs. When they were young, some authority figure had told them to pick up a wrench, and so they picked up the wrench and never once considered what would happen if they picked up a pencil or a book. Her father and uncles never asked questions. How can you live a special life without constantly interrogating it? How can you live a good life without good poetry? She knew her family feared poetry, but they didn't fear it because they were Indian. The fear of poetry was multicultural and timeless. So maybe she loved poetry precisely because so many people feared it. Maybe she wanted to frighten people with the size of her poetic love.

"I bet you're reading one of those white books again, enit?" the first uncle asked.

"His name is Gerard Manley Hopkins," Corliss said. "He wrote poems in the nineteenth century."

"White people were killing Indians in the nineteenth century," the second uncle said. "I bet this Hopkins dude was killing Indians, too."

"I don't think so," Corliss said. "He was a Jesuit priest."

Her father and uncles cursed with shock and disgust.

"He was a Catholic?" her father asked. "Oh, Corliss, those Catholics were the worst. Your grandmother still has scars on her back from when a priest and a nun whipped her in boarding school. You shouldn't be reading that stuff. It will pollute your heart."

"What do you think those white people can teach you, anyway?" the third uncle asked.

She wanted to say, "Everything." She wanted to scream it. But she knew she'd be punished for her disrespect of her elders. Because she was Indian, she'd been taught to fear and hate white people. Sure, she hated all sorts of white people—the arrogant white businessmen in their wool suits, the illiterate white cheerleaders in their convertibles, the thousands of flannel-shirted rednecks who roamed the streets of Spokane—but she knew they represented the worst of whiteness. It was easy to hate white vanity and white rage and white ignorance, but what about white compassion and white genius and white poetry? Maybe it wasn't about whiteness or redness or any other color. Corliss wasn't naive. She knew racism, tribalism, and nationalism were encoded in human DNA, and we'd all save our own child from a burning building even if it meant a thousand strangers would die, and we'd all kill in defense of our wives, husbands, brothers, sisters, parents, and children. However, she also wanted to believe in human goodness and mortal grace. She was contradictory and young and confused and smart and unformed and ambitious. How could she tell her father and uncles she read Hopkins precisely because he was a white man and precisely because he was a Jesuit priest? Maybe Hopkins had been an Indian killer, or a supporter of Indian killers, but he'd also been a sad and lonely and lovely man who screamed to God for comfort, answers, sleep, and peace. Since Corliss rarely found comfort from her family and friends, and never found it in God, but continued to want it and never stopped asking for it, then maybe she was also a Jesuit priest who found it in poetry. How could she tell her family that she didn't belong with them, that she was destined for something larger, that she believed she was supposed to be eccentric and powerful and great and all alone in the world? How could she tell her Indian family she sometimes felt like a white Jesuit priest? Who would ever believe such a thing? Who would ever understand how a nineteen-year-old Indian woman looked in the mirror and sometimes saw an old white man in a white collar and black robe?

"I've got to go," Corliss said. "I've got homework."

"Give me that book," the second uncle said. He took the book from her, opened it at random, and read, "'Glory be to God for dappled things— / For skies of couple-colour as a brinded cow.'"

All of the men laughed.

"What the hell does that mean?" the third uncle asked.

"It's a poem about a cow," her father said. "She's always reading poems about cows."

"You can't write a poem about a cow, can you?" the first uncle asked. "They're ugly and stupid. I thought poems were supposed to be pretty and smart."

"Yeah, Corliss," the second uncle said. "You're pretty and smart, why are you wasting your time with poems? You should be studying science and math and law and politics. You're going to be rich and famous. You're going to be the toughest Indian woman around."

How could these men hate poetry so much and respect her intelligence? Sure, they were men raised in a matriarchal culture, but they lived in a patriarchal country. Therefore, they were kind and decent and sensitive and stupid and sexist and unpredictable. These husbands were happily married to wives who earned more money than they did. These men bragged about their spouses' accomplishments: *Ha, my woman just got a raise! My honey makes more money than your honey! My wife manages the whole dang Kmart, and then she comes home and manages us! She's a twenty-first-century woman! Nah, I ain't threatened by her! I'm challenged!* Who were these Indian men? What kind of warriors were they? Were Crazy Horse and Geronimo supportive of their wives? Did Sitting Bull sit with his wife for weekly chats about the state of their relationship? Did Red Cloud proudly send his daughter out to fight the enemy? Corliss looked at her father and saw a stranger, a loving stranger, but a stranger nonetheless.

"And I'll tell you what," her father said. "After Corliss graduates from college and gets her law degree, she's going to move back to the reservation and fix what's wrong. We men have had our chances, I'll tell you what. We'll send all the tribal councilmen to the golf courses and let the smart women run the show. I'll tell you what. My daughter is going to save our tribe."

Yes, her family loved and supported her, so how could she resent them for being clueless about her real dreams and ambitions? Her mother and father and all of her uncles and aunts sent her money to help her through college. How many times had she opened an envelope and discovered a miraculous twenty-dollar bill? The family and the tribe were helping her, so maybe she was a selfish bitch for questioning the usefulness of tribalism. Here she was sitting in a corner of her tiny apartment, pretending to be alone in the world, the one poetic Spokane, and she was reading a book of poems, of sonnets, by another Spokane. How could she ever be alone if Harlan Atwater was somewhere out there in the world? Okay, his poems weren't great. Some of them were amateurish and trite, and others were comedic throwaways, but there were a few poems and a few lines that contained small bits of power and magic:

The Little Spokane

My river is not the same size as your river.
My river is smaller and colder.

My river begins in the north
And rushes to find me.
My river calls to me.
I swim it because it is water.
Water doesn't care about anybody
But this water cares about me.

Or maybe it doesn't care about me.
Maybe the river thinks I'm driftwood
Or a rubber tire or a bird or a dead dog.
Maybe the river is not a river.
Maybe the river is my father.
Maybe he's smaller and colder than your father.

Corliss had swum the Little Spokane River. She'd floated down the river in a makeshift raft. She'd drifted beneath bridges and the limbs of trees. She'd been in the physical and emotional places described in the poem. She'd been in the same places where Harlan Atwater had been, and that made her sad and happy. She felt connected to him and wanted to know more about him. She picked up the telephone and called her mother.

"Hey, Mom."

"Corliss, hey, sweetie, it's so good to hear your voice. I miss you."

Her mother was a loan officer for Farmers' Bank. Twenty years earlier, she'd started as a bank teller and had swum her way up the corporate fish ladder.

"I miss you, too, Mom. How is everybody?"

"We're still Indian. How's school going?"

"Good."

All of their conversations began the same way. The mother-daughter telephone ceremony. Corliss knew her mother would soon become emotional and tell her how proud the family was of her accomplishments.

"I don't know if we tell you this enough," her mother said. "But we're so proud of you."

"You tell me every time we talk."

"Oh, well, you know, I'm a mother. I'm supposed to talk that way. It's just, well, you're the first person from our family to ever go to college."

"I know, Mom, you don't need to tell me my résumé."

"You don't need to get smart."

Corliss couldn't help herself. She loved her mother, but her mother was a bipolar storyteller who told lies during her manic phases and heavily exaggerated during her depressed times. Those lies and exaggerations were often flattering to Corliss, so it was hard to completely resent them. According to the stories, Corliss had already been accepted to Harvard Medical School but had declined because she didn't feel Harvard would respect her indigenous healing methods. You couldn't hate a mother full of such tender and flattering garbage, but you could certainly view her with a large measure of contempt.

"I'm sorry, Mom. Listen, I picked up this book of poems—"

"Corliss, you know how your father feels about those poems."

"They're poems, Mom, not crack."

"I know you love them, honey, but how are you going to get a job with poems? You go to a job interview, and they ask you what you did in college, and you say 'poems,' then what are your chances?"

"Maybe I'll work in a poem factory."

"Don't get smart."

"I can't help it. I am smart."

Corliss knew she was smart because her mother was smart, but she also knew she'd inherited a little bit of her mother's crazies as well.

Why else would she be calling to talk about a vanished Indian poet? The crazy mother–crazy daughter telephone ceremony!

"So did you call to break my heart," her mother said, "or do you have some other reason?"

"I called about this book of poems."

"Okay, so tell me about your book of poems."

"It's written by this guy called Harlan Atwater. It says he's a Spokane. Do you know him?"

Her mother was the unofficial historian of the urban Spokane Indians. Corliss figured "historian" and "pathological liar" meant the same thing in all cultures and countries.

"Harlan Atwater? Harlan Atwater?" her mother repeated the name and tried to place it. "Nope. Don't know him. Don't know any Spokanes named Atwater."

"His book was published in 1972. It's called *In the Reservation of My Mind*. Do you remember that?"

"I don't read books much."

"Yes, I know, Mom. But you're aware there are inventions called books and inside some of those books they have things called poems."

"I know what books are, smart-ass daughter."

"Okay, then, have you heard of this book?"

"No."

"Are you sure?"

"Yes, I'm sure."

"I thought you knew every Spokane."

"I guess I don't. Have you looked him up on the Internet?"

"How do you know about the Internet?"

"I'm old, Corliss, I'm not stupid."

"Oh, jeez, Mom, I'm sorry. I don't mean to be such a jerk. It's just, this book, is pretty cool. It's getting me all riled up."

"It's okay. You're always riled up. I love that about you."

"I love you, too, Mom. I got to go."

"Okay, bye-bye."

Corliss hung up the telephone, grabbed her backpack and coat, and hurried to the campus computer lab. She was too poor to afford her own computer and was ashamed of her poverty. Corliss talked her way past the work-study student who'd said the computers were all reserved by other poor students. She sat at a Mac and logged on. Her user name was "CrazyIndian," and her password was "StillCrazy." She typed "Harlan Atwater, Native American poet, Spokane Indian" into the search engine and found nothing. She didn't find him with any variations of the search, either. She couldn't find his book on Amazon.com, Alibris.com, or Powells.com. She couldn't find any evidence that Harlan Atwater's book had ever existed. She couldn't find the press that had published his book. She couldn't find any reviews or mention of the book. She sent e-mails to two dozen different Indian writers, including Simon Ortiz, Joy Harjo, Leslie Marmon Silko, and Adrian C. Louis, and those who responded said they'd never heard of Harlan Atwater. She paged through old government records. Maybe he'd been a criminal and had gone to prison. Maybe he'd been married and divorced. Maybe he'd died in a spectacular car wreck. But she couldn't find any mention of him. The library didn't have any record of where or when the book had been purchased. The Spokane Tribal Enrollment Office didn't have any records of his existence. According to the enrollment secretary, who also happened to be Corliss's second cousin, there'd never been an enrolled Spokane Indian named Atwater. Corliss was stumped and suspicious. Every moment of an Indian's life is put down in triplicate on government forms, collated, and filed. Indians are given their social security numbers before the OB/GYN sucks the snot and blood out of their throats. How could this Harlan Atwater escape the government? How could an Indian live and work in the United States and not leave one piece of paper to mark his passage? Corliss thought Harlan Atwater might be a fraud, a white man pretending to be an Indian, seeking to make a profit, to co-opt and capitalize. Then again, what opportunistic white man was stupid enough to think he could profit from pretending to be a Spokane Indian? Even Spokane Indians can't profit from being Spokane! How many people had ever heard of the Spokane Tribe of Indians? Corliss felt like a literary detective, a poetic gumshoe, Sam Spade with braids. She worked for hours and days, and finally, two weeks after she first came across his book, she found an interview printed in *Radical Seattle Weekly*:

Harlan Atwater grew up in Wellpinit, Washington, on the Spokane Indian Reservation in eastern Washington State. His work has appeared in *Experimental Rice, Seattle Poetry Now!*, and *The Left Heart of Love*. The author of a book of poems, *In the Reservation of My Mind*, he lives in Seattle and is currently a warehouse supply clerk during the day while writing and performing his poems long into the night.

How did you start writing?

Well, coming from a culture where the oral tradition is so valued, and where storytelling is an everyday and informal part of life, I think I was born and trained to tell stories, in some sense. Of course, this country isn't just Indian, is it? And it's certainly the farthest thing from sacred. I am the child and grandchild of poor Indians, and since none of them ever put pen to paper, it never occurred to me I could try to be a poet. I didn't know any poets or poems. But a few years ago, I took a poetry class with Jenny Shandy. She was on this sort of mission to teach poetry to the working class. She called it "Blue Collars, White Pages, True

Stories," and I was the only one who survived the whole class.
There were ten of us when the class started. Ten weeks later, I
was the last one. Jenny just kept giving me poetry books to read.
I read over a hundred books of poems that year. That was my
education. Jenny was white, so she gave me mostly white classi-
cal poets to read. I had to go out and find the Indian poets, the
black poets, the Chicanos, you know, all the revolutionaries. I
loved it all, so I guess I'm trying to combine it all, the white clas-
sicism with the dark-skinned rebellion.

How do your poem ideas come to you?

Well, shoot, everything I write is pretty autobiographical,
so you could say I'm only interested in the stuff that really happens. There's been so much junk written about Indians, you
know? So much romanticism and stereotyping. I'm just trying to be authentic, you know? If you look at my poems, if you
really study them, I think you're going to find I'm writing the
most authentic Indian poems that have ever been written. I'm
trying to help people understand Indians. I'm trying to make
the world a better place, full of more love and understanding.

How do you know when an idea is worth pursuing?

Well, I don't mean to sound hokey, but it's all about the elders, you know? If I think the tribal elders would love the idea,
then to me, it's an idea worth turning into a poem, you know?

What is your process like for working on a poem?

It's all about ceremony. As an Indian, you learn about these
sacred spaces. Sometimes, when you're lucky and prepared, you
find yourself in a sacred space, and the poems come to you.
Shoot, I'm putting ink to paper, you could say, but I don't al-

ways feel like I'm the one writing the poem. Sometimes my whole tribe is writing the poem with me. And I feel best about the poems when I look out in the audience and see a bunch of Indian faces. I mean, the best thing to me is when Indians come up to me and say, "Hey, man, that poem was me, that was my life." That's when I feel like I'm doing the best work.

What writers have influenced your work, and whom do you admire now?

Well, I could name a dozen writers, a hundred poets, I love and respect. But I guess I am most influenced by the natural rhythms of the world, you know? Late at night, I go outside and listen to the wind. That's all the wisdom I need. I mean, I love books, but shoot, most of the world's wisdom is not contained in books.

There is a lot of humor in your poems, often in the face of tragedy. Where does your sense of humor come from?

My grandmother was the funniest person I've ever known and the most traditional. She was a sacred person in our tribe and told the dirtiest jokes, you know? So, obviously, I grew up with the idea the sacred and profane are linked, you know? I guess you'd say my sense of humor is genetic.

Do you consider yourself a radical?

I believe in the essential goodness of human beings, and if that's being radical, then I guess I'm a radical. I believe human beings would rather hop in bed with each other and do tender things to each other than run through the jungle and shoot each other. If that's a radical thought, then I'm a radical. I believe that poetry can save the world. And shoot, that one has always been a radical thought, I guess. So maybe I am a radical, you know?

What do you think will happen to American Indians in the future?
Well, shoot, my grandfather, he was a shaman, he used to tell me that tribal stories foretold the coming of the white man. "Grandson," he'd say to me, "we always knew the white man was coming. We knew the exact date. We knew he'd eat all the food in the house and poop on the living room carpet." My grandfather was so funny, you know? And he'd tell me that the tribal stories also foretold the white man's leaving. "Grandson," he'd say, "we always knew the white man was coming, and we've always known he was leaving." So, what's the future of Indians? Well, someday soon, I think we're going to have a lot more breathing room.

Corliss was puzzled by the interview. Harlan Atwater seemed to be an immodest poet who claimed to be highly sacred and traditional and connected to his tribe, but his tribe had never heard of him. He seemed peacefully unaware of his arrogance and pretension. Most important, Corliss's mother had never heard of him. No Spokane Indian had ever known him. Exactly who were this mythical grandmother and grandfather who'd lived on the reservation? Who was Harlan Atwater? And where was he? He must be a fraud, and yet he was funny and hopeful, so maybe he was a funny, hopeful, and self-absorbed fraud.

Corliss kept searching for more information about Atwater. She found him listed in the 1971 edition of *Who's Who Among American Writers*. There was a Seattle address and phone number. Corliss picked up the phone and dialed the number. Naturally, it was pointless. That number was thirty-three years old. The phone rang a dozen times. What kind of American doesn't have an answering machine or voice mail? But after ten more rings, as Corliss wondered why in the hell she let it ring so long, she was surprised to hear somebody answer.

"Hello," a man said. He was tired or angry or both or didn't have any phone manners. He sounded exactly like a man who wouldn't have an answering machine or voice mail.

"Yes, hello, my name is Corliss Joseph, and I—"

"Is this a sales call?"

She knew he'd hang up if she didn't say the exact right thing.

"Are you in the reservation of your mind?" she asked and heard silence from the other end. He didn't hang up, so she knew she'd asked the right question. But maybe he was calling the police on another phone line: *Hello, Officer, I'm calling to report a poetry stalker. Yes, I'm serious, Officer. I'm completely serious. I am a poet, and a lovely young woman is stalking me. Stop laughing at me, Officer.*

"Hello?" she asked. "Are you there?"

"Who are you?" he asked.

"I'm looking for, well, I found this book by a man named Harlan Atwater—"

"Where'd you find this book?"

"In the Washington State University library. I'm a student here."

"What the hell do you want from me?"

Excited, she spoke quickly. "Well, this used to be Harlan Atwater's phone number, so I called it."

"It's still Harlan Atwater's phone number," the man said.

"Wow, are you him?"

"I used that name when I wrote poems."

Corliss couldn't believe she was talking to the one and only Harlan Atwater. Once again, she felt she'd been chosen for a special mission. She had so many questions to ask, but she knew she needed to be careful. This mysterious man seemed to be fragile and suspicious of her, and she needed to earn his trust. She couldn't interrogate him. She couldn't shine a bright light in his face and ask him if he was a fraud.

"Your poems are very good," she said, hoping flattery would work. It usually worked.

"Don't try to flatter me," he said. "Those poems are mostly crap. I was a young man with more scrotum than common sense."

"Well, I think they're good. Most of them, anyway."

"Who the hell are you?"

"I'm a Spokane Indian. I'm an English literature major here."

"Oh, God, you're an Indian?"

"Well, mostly. Fifteen sixteenths, to be exact."

"So, fifteen sixteenths of you is studying the literature of the other one sixteenth of you?"

"I suppose that's one way to put it."

"Shoot, it's been a long time since I talked to an Indian."

"Really? Aren't you Indian?"

"I'm of the urban variety, bottled in 1947."

"You're Spokane, enit?"

"That's what I was born, but I haven't been to the rez in thirty years, and you're the first Spokane I've talked to in maybe twenty years. So if I'm still Spokane, I'm not a very good one."

Self-deprecating and bitter, he certainly talked like an Indian. Corliss liked him.

"I've got so many things I want to ask you," she said. "I don't even know where to begin."

"What, you think you're going to interview me?"

"Well, no, I'm not a journalist or anything. This is just for me."

"Listen, kid, I'm impressed you found my book of poems. Shoot, I only printed up about three hundred of them, and I lost most of them. Hell, I'm flattered you found me. But I didn't want to be found. So, listen, I'm really impressed you're in college. I'm proud of you. I know how tough that is. So, knock them dead, make lots of money, and never call me again, okay?"

He hung up before Corliss could respond. She sat quietly for a moment, wondering why it had ended so abruptly. She'd searched for the man, found him, and didn't like what had happened. Corliss was confused, hurt, and angry. Long ago, as part of the passage into adulthood, young Indians used to wander into the wilderness in search of a vision, in search of meaning and definition. Who am I? Who am I supposed to be? Ancient questions answered by ancient ceremonies. Maybe Corliss couldn't climb a mountain and starve herself into self-revealing hallucinations. Maybe she'd never find her spirit animal, her ethereal guide through the material world. Maybe she was only a confused indigenous woman negotiating her way through a colonial maze, but she was one Indian who had good credit and knew how to use her Visa card.

Eighteen hours later, Corliss stepped off the Greyhound in downtown Seattle and stared up at the skyscrapers. Though it was a five-hour drive from Spokane, Corliss had never been to Seattle. She'd never traveled farther than 110 miles from the house where she grew up. The big city felt exciting and dangerous to her. Great things happened in big cities. She could count on one hand the amazing people who'd grown up in Spokane, but hundreds of superheroes had lived in Seattle. Jimi Hendrix! Kurt Cobain! Bruce Lee! What about Paris, Rome, and New York City? You could stand on Houston Street in Lower Manhattan, throw a rock in some random direction, and hit a great poet in the head. If human beings possessed endless possibilities, then cities contained exponential hopes. As she walked away from the bus station through the rainy, musty streets of Seattle, Corliss thought of Homer: "Tell me, O Muse, of that ingenious hero who traveled far and wide after he sacked the famous town of Troy." She was no Odysseus, and her eight-hour bus ride hardly qualified as an odyssey. But maybe Odysseus wasn't all that heroic, either, Corliss thought. He was a drug addict and thief who abused the disabled. That giant might have been tall and strong, Corliss thought, but he still had only one eye. It's easy to elude a monster with poor depth perception. Odysseus cheated on his wife, and disguised himself as a potential lover so he could spy on her, and eventually slaughtered all of her suitors before he identified himself. He was also a romantic fool who believed his wife stayed faithful during the twenty years he was missing and presumed dead. Self-serving and vain, he sacrificed six of his men so he could survive a monster attack. In the very end, when all of his enemies had massed to kill him, Odysseus was saved by the intervention of a god who had a romantic crush on him. If one thought about it, and Corliss had often thought about it, the epic poem was foremost a powerful piece of military propaganda. Homer had transformed a lying colonial asshole into one of the most admired literary figures in human history. So, Corliss asked, what lessons could we learn from Homer? To be considered epic, one needed only to employ an epic biographer. Since Corliss was telling her own story, she decided it was an autobiographical epic. Hell, maybe she was Homer. Maybe she was Odysseus. Maybe everybody was a descendant of Homer and Odysseus. Maybe every human journey was epic.

As she walked and marveled at the architecture, at the depth and breadth and width of the city, Corliss saw a homeless man begging for change outside a McDonald's and decided he could be epic. He was dirty and had wrapped an old blanket around his shoulders for warmth, but his eyes were bright and impossibly blue, and he stood with a proud and defiant posture. This handsome homeless man was not defeated. He was still fighting his monsters, and maybe he'd someday win. If he won, maybe he'd write an epic poem about his journey back from the darkness. Okay, so maybe I'm romantic, Corliss thought,

but somebody is supposed to be romantic. Some warrior is supposed
to go to war against the imperial forces of cynicism and irony. I am a
sentimental soldier, Corliss thought, and I am going to befriend this
homeless man, no matter how crazy he might be.

"Hello," she said to him.

"Hey," he said. "You got any spare change?"

"All I've got is a credit card and hope," she said.

"Having a credit card means somebody knows you're alive. Somebody cares if you keep on living."

He smelled like five gallons of cheap wine and hard times.

"Listen," Corliss said. "McDonald's takes credit cards. I'll buy you
a Super Value Meal if you tell me where I can find this address."

She showed him the paper on which she'd written down Harlan
Atwater's last known place of residence.

"Okay," he said. "I'll tell you where that is. You don't have to buy
me no lunch."

"You give me directions out of the goodness of your heart. And
I'll buy you lunch out of the goodness of my heart."

"That sounds like a safe and sane human interaction."

Inside, they both ordered Quarter Pounders, french fries, and
chocolate shakes, and shared a small table at the front window. A
homeless old man and a romantic young woman! A strange couple,
but only if you looked at the surface, if you used five senses. Because
she was Indian, displaced by colonial rule, Corliss had always been
approximately homeless. Like the homeless, she lived a dangerous
and random life. Unlike landed white men, she didn't need to climb
mountains to experience mystic panic. All she needed was to set her
alarm clock for the next morning, wake when it rang, and go to class.
College was an extreme sport for an Indian woman. Maybe ESPN2
should send a camera crew to cover her academic career. Maybe she
should be awarded gold medals for taking American history and not

shooting everybody during the hour and a half in which they covered five hundred years of Indian history. If pushed, Corliss knew she could go crazy. She was a paranoid schizophrenic in waiting. Maybe all the crazy homeless Indians were former college students who'd heard about manifest destiny one too many times.

Corliss and the homeless white man ate in silence. He was too hungry to talk. She didn't know what to say.

"Thank you," he said after he'd finished. "Thank you for the acknowledgment of my humanity. A man like me doesn't get to be human much."

"Can I ask you a personal question?" she asked.

"You can ask me a human question, yes."

"How'd you end up homeless? You're obviously a smart man, talking the way you do. I know smart doesn't guarantee anything, but still, what happened?"

"I just fell out of love with the world."

"I understand how that goes. I'm not so sure about the world myself, but was there anything in particular?"

"First of all, I am nuts. Diagnosed and prescribed. But there's all sorts of nutcases making millions and billions of dollars in this country. That Ted Turner, for example, is a crazy rat living in a gold-plated outhouse. But I got this particular kind of nuts, you know? I got a pathological need for respect."

"I've never heard of that condition."

"Yeah, ain't no Jerry Lewis running a telethon for my kind of sickness. The thing is, I should have been getting respect. I was an economics professor at St. Jerome the Second University here in Seattle. A fine institution of higher education."

"That's why you're so smart."

"Knowing economics only means you know numbers. Doesn't mean you know people. Anyway, I hated my job. I hated the kids. I hated my colleagues. I hated money. And I felt like none of them respected me, you know? I felt their disrespect growing all around me. I felt suffocated by their disrespect. So one day, I just walked out in the campus center, you know, right there on the green, green Roman Catholic grass, and started shouting."

Corliss could feel the heat from this man's mania. It was familiar and warm.

"What did you shout?" she asked.

"I kept shouting, 'I want some respect! I want some respect!' I shouted it all day and all night. And nobody gave me any respect. I was asking directly for it, and people just kept walking around me. Avoiding me. Not even looking at me. Not even acknowledging me. Hundreds of people walked by me. Thousands. Then finally, twenty-seven hours after I started, one of my students, a young woman by the name of Melissa, a kind person who was terrible with numbers, came up to me, hugged me very close, and whispered, 'I respect you, Professor Williams, I respect you.' I started crying. Weeping. Those tears that start from your bowels and roar up through your stomach and heart and lungs and out of your mouth. Do you know the kind of tears of which I'm speaking?"

"Yes, yes," she said. "Of course I do."

"Yes. So I started crying, and I kept crying, and I couldn't stop crying no matter how hard I tried. They tell me I cried for two weeks straight, but all I remember is that first day. I took a leave of absence from school, sold my house, and spent my money in a year, and now I'm here, relying, as they say, on the kindness of strangers."

"I am kind because you are kind. Thank you for sharing your story."

"Thank you for showing me some respect. I need respect."

"You're welcome," she said. She knew this man would talk to her for days. She knew he'd fall in love with her and steal everything she owned if given the chance. And she knew he might be lying to her about everything. He might be an illiterate heroin addict with a gift for gab. But he was also a man who could and would give her directions.

"Listen," she said. "I'm sorry. But I really have to get moving. Can you tell me where this address is?"

"I'm sorry you have to leave me. But I understand. I was born to be left and bereft. Still, I made a human promise to you, and I will keep it, as a human. This address is on the other side of the Space Needle. Walk directly toward the Space Needle, pass right beneath it, keep walking to the other side of the Seattle Center, and you'll find this address somewhere close to the McDonald's over there."

"You know where all the McDonald's are?"

"Yes, humans who eat fast food feel very guilty about eating it. And guilty people are more generous with their money and time."

Corliss bought him a chicken sandwich and another chocolate shake and then left him alone.

She walked toward the Space Needle, beneath it, and beyond it. She wondered if the homeless professor had sent her on a wild-goose chase, or on what her malaproping auntie called a dumb-duck run. But she saw that second McDonald's and walked along the street until she found the address she was looking for. There, at that address, was a tiny, battered, eighty-year-old house set among recently constructed condominiums and apartment buildings. If Harlan Atwater had kept the same phone number for thirty-three years, Corliss surmised, then he'd probably lived in the same house the whole time, too. She wasn't searching for a nomad who had disappeared into the wilds. She'd found a man who had stayed in one place and slowly become invisible. If a poet falls in a forest, and there's nobody there to hear him, does he make a metaphor or simile? Corliss was afraid of confronting the man in person. What if he was violent? Or worse, what if he was boring? She walked into the second McDonald's, ordered a Diet Coke,

and sat at the window and stared at Harlan Atwater's house. She
studied it.

Love Song

I have loved you during the powwow
And I have loved you during the rodeo.
I have loved you from jail
And I have loved you from Browning, Montana.
I have loved you like a drum and drummer
And I have loved you like a holy man.
I have loved you with my tongue
And I have loved you with my hands.

But I haven't loved you like a scream.
And I haven't loved you like a moan.
And I haven't loved you like a laugh.
And I haven't loved you like a sigh.
And I haven't loved you like a cough.
And I haven't loved you well enough.

After two more Diet Cokes and a baked apple pie, Corliss walked
across the street and knocked on the door. A short, fat Indian man
answered.

"Who are you?" he asked. He wore thick glasses, and his black hair
needed washing. Though he was a dark-skinned Indian, one of the
darker Spokanes she'd ever seen, he also managed to look pasty. Dark
and pasty, like a chocolate doughnut. Corliss was angry with him for
being homely. She'd hoped he would be an indigenous version of
Harrison Ford. She'd wanted Indiana Jones and found Seattle Atwater.

"Are you just going to stand there?" he asked. "If you don't close
your mouth, you're going to catch flies."

He was fifty or sixty years old, maybe older. Old! Of course he was that age. He'd published his book thirty years ago, but Corliss hadn't thought much about the passage of time. In her mind, he was young and poetic and beautiful. Now here he was, the Indian sonneteer, the reservation bard, dressed in a Seattle SuperSonics T-shirt and sweatpants.

"Yo, kid," he said. "I don't have all day. What do you want?"

"You're Harlan Atwater," she said, hoping he wasn't.

He laughed. "Dang," he said. "You're that college kid. You don't give up, do you?"

"I'm on a vision quest."

"A vision quest?" he asked and laughed harder. "You flatter me. I'm just a smelly old man."

"You're a poet."

"I used to be a poet."

"You wrote this book," she said and held it up for him.

He took it from her and flipped through it. "Man," he said. "I haven't seen a copy of this in a long time."

He remembered. Nostalgia is a dangerous thing.

"You don't have one?" she asked.

"No," he said and silently read one of the sonnets. "Dang, I was young when I wrote these. Too young."

"You should keep that one."

"It's a library book."

"I'll pay the fine."

"This book means more to you than it means to me. Otherwise, you wouldn't have found me. You should keep it and pay the fine."

He handed the book back to her. He laughed some more.

"I'm sorry, kid," he said. "I'm not trying to belittle you. But I can't believe that little book brought you here."

"I've never read a book of Indian poems like that."

She started to cry and furiously wiped her tears away. She cried too easily, she thought, and hated how feminine and weak it appeared to be. No, it wasn't feminine and weak to cry, not objectively speaking, but she still hated it.

"Nobody's cried over me in a long time," he said.

"You know," she said, "I came here because I thought you were something special. I read your poems, and some of them are really bad, but some of them are really good, and maybe I can't always tell the difference between the good and the bad. But I know somebody with a good heart wrote them. Somebody lovely wrote them. And now I look at you, and you look terrible, and you sound terrible, and you smell terrible, and I'm sad. No, I'm not sad. I'm pissed off. You're not supposed to be like this. You're supposed to be somebody better. I needed you to be somebody better."

He shook his head, sighed, and looked as if he might cry with her.

"I'm sorry, kid," he said. "But I am who I am. And I haven't written a poem in thirty years, you know? I don't even remember what it feels like to write a poem."

"Why did you quit writing poems?" she asked. She knew she sounded desperate, but she was truly desperate, and she couldn't hide it. "Nobody should ever quit writing poems."

"Jesus, you're putting me in a spot here. All right, all right, we'll have a talk, okay? You've come this far, you deserve to hear the truth. But not in my house. Nobody comes in my house. Give me fifteen minutes, and I'll meet you over to the McDonald's."

"I've already been in that McDonald's."

"So?"

"So, I don't like to go to the same place twice in the same day. Especially since I was just there."

"That's a little bit crazy."

"I'm a little bit crazy."

He liked that.

"All right," he said. "I'll meet you down to the used-book store. You can see it there at the corner."

"You read books?"

"Just because I quit writing doesn't mean I quit reading. For a smart kid, you're kind of dumb, you know?"

That pleased her more than she'd expected. He was still a smart-ass, so maybe he was still rowdy enough to write poems. Maybe there was hope for him. She felt evangelical. Maybe she could save him. Maybe she'd pray for him and he'd fall to his knees in the bookstore and beg for salvation and resurrection.

"All right?" he asked. "About fifteen minutes, okay?"

"Okay," she said.

He closed the door. For a moment, she wondered if he was tricking her, if he needed a way to close the door on her. Well, he'd have to call the cops to get rid of her. She'd camp on his doorstep until he came out. She'd wait in the bookstore for exactly seventeen minutes, and if he was one second later, she'd break down his front door and interrogate him. He was an out-of-shape loser and she could take him. She'd teach him nineteen different ways to spell matriarchy.

She hurried to the bookstore and walked inside. An elderly woman was crocheting behind the front desk.

"Can I help you?" the yarn woman asked.

"I'm just waiting for somebody," Corliss said.

"A young man, perhaps?"

Why were young women always supposed to be waiting for young men? Corliss didn't like young men all that much. Or old men, either. She was no virgin. She'd slept with three boys and heavily petted a dozen more, but she'd also gone to bed with one woman and French-kissed the holy-moly out of another, and hey, maybe that was the way to go. Maybe I'm not exactly a lesbian, Corliss thought, but I might be an inexact lesbian.

"Is there a man waiting at home for you?" Corliss asked and immediately felt like a jerk.

"Oh, no," the yarn woman said and smiled. "My husband died twenty years ago. If he's waiting for me, he's all the way upstairs, you know?"

"I'm sorry," Corliss said and meant it.

"It's okay, dear, I shouldn't have invaded your privacy. You go on ahead and look for what you came for."

On every mission, there is a time to be strong and a time to be humble.

"Listen, my name is Corliss Joseph, and I'm sorry for being such a bitch. There's no excuse for it. I'm really angry with the guy I'm supposed to be meeting here soon. He's not my boyfriend, or even my friend, or anything like that. He's a stranger, but I thought I knew him. And he disappointed me. I don't even think I have a right to be angry with him. So I'm really confused about—Well, I'm confused about my whole life right now. So I'm sorry, I really am, and I'm usually a much kinder person than this, you know?"

The yarn woman was eighty years old. She knew.

"My name is Lillian, and thank you for being so honest. When your friend, or whatever he is, arrives, I'll turn off my hearing aids so you'll have privacy."

Who would ever think of such an eccentric act of kindness? An old woman who owned a bookstore!

"Thank you," Corliss said. "I'll just look around until he gets here."

She walked through the bookstore that smelled of musty paper and moldy carpet. She scanned the shelves and read the names of authors printed on the spines of all the lovely, lovely books. She loved the smell of new books, sure, but she loved the smell of old books even more. She thought old books smelled like everybody who'd ever read them. Possibly that was a disgusting thought, and it certainly was a silly thought, but Corliss felt like old books were sentient beings that listened and remembered and passed judgment. Oh, God, I'm going to cry again, Corliss thought, I'm losing my mind in a used-book store. I am my mother's daughter. And that made her laugh. Hey, she thought, I'm riding in the front car of the crazy-woman roller coaster.

She knew she needed to calm down. And to calm down, she needed to perform her usual bookstore ceremony. She found the books by her favorite authors—Whitman, Shapiro, Jordan, Turcotte, Plath, Lourie, O'Hara, Hershon, Alvarez, Brook, Schreiber, Pawlak, Offutt, Duncan, Moore—and reshelved them with their front covers facing outward. The other books led with their spines, but Corliss's favorites led with their chests, bellies, crotches, and faces. The casual reader wouldn't be able to resist these books now. Choose me! Choose me! The browser would fall in love at first sight. Corliss, in love with poetry, opened Harlan Atwater's book and read one more sonnet:

Poverty

When you're poor and hungry
And love your dog
You share your food with him.
There is no love like his.
When you're poor and hungry
And your dog gets sick,
You can't afford to take him
To the veterinarian,

So you have to watch him get sicker
And cough blood and cry all night.

You can't afford to put him gently to sleep
So your uncle comes over for free
And shoots your dog twice in the head
And buries him in the town dump.

How could he know such things about poverty and pain if he had not experienced them? Can a poet be that accomplished a liar? Can a poet invent history so well that his audience is completely fooled? Only if they want to be fooled, thought Corliss, knowing she was exactly that kind of literate fool. For her, each great book was the Holy Bible, and each great author was a prophet. Oh, God, listen to me, Corliss thought, I'm a cult member. If Sylvia Plath walked into the bookstore and told her to drink a glass of cyanide-laced grape juice, Corliss knew she would do happily do it.

Precisely on time, Harlan Atwater opened the door and stepped into the bookstore. He'd obviously showered and shaved, and he wore a navy blue suit that had fit better ten years and twenty pounds earlier but still looked decent enough to qualify as formal wear. He'd replaced his big clunky glasses with John Lennon wire frames. Corliss felt honored by Harlan's sartorial efforts and was once again amazed by Lillian as she smiled and turned off her hearing aids.

"You look good," Corliss said to Harlan.

"I look like I'm trying to look good," he said. "That's about all I can do right now. I hope it's enough."

"It is. Thank you for trying."

"Well, you know, it's not every day I'm the object of a vision quest."

"Everything feels new today."

He smiled. She didn't know what he was thinking.

"So," he said. "Do you want to hear my story?"

"Yes."

He led her to a stuffed couch in the back of the store. They sat together. He stared at the floor as he talked.

"I'm not really a Spokane Indian," he said.

She knew it! He was a fraud! He was a white man with a good tan!

"Well, I'm biologically a Spokane Indian," he said. "But I wasn't raised Spokane. I was adopted out and raised by a white family here in Seattle."

That explained why he knew so much about Spokane Indians but remained unknown by them.

"You're a lost bird," she said.

"Is that what they're calling us now?"

"Yes."

"Well, isn't that poetic? I suppose it's better than calling us stolen goods. Or clueless bastards."

"But your poems, they're so Indian."

"Indian is easy to fake. People have been faking it for five hundred years. I was just better at it than most."

She knew Indians were obsessed with authenticity. Colonized, genocided, exiled, Indians formed their identities by questioning the identities of other Indians. Self-hating, self-doubting, Indians turned their tribes into nationalistic sects. But who could blame us our madness? Corliss thought. We are people exiled by other exiles, by Puritans, Pilgrims, Protestants, and all of those other crazy white people thrown out of a crazier Europe. We who were once indigenous to this land must immigrate into its culture. I was born one mile south and raised one mile north from the place on the Spokane River where the very first Spokane Indian was ever born, and I somehow feel like a nomad, so Harlan Atwater must feel completely lost.

"Maybe you're faking," she said. "But the poems aren't fake."

"Do you write?" he asked.

"Only academic stuff," she said. "I'm kind of afraid of writing poems."

"Why?"

"No matter what I write, a bunch of other Indians will hate it because it isn't Indian enough, and a bunch of white people will like it because it's Indian. Do you know what I mean? If I wrote poems, I'd feel trapped."

Harlan had been waiting for years to talk about his traps.

"I started writing poems to feel like I belonged," he said. "To feel more Indian. And I started imagining what it felt like to grow up on the reservation, to grow up like an Indian is supposed to grow up, you know?"

She knew. She wasn't supposed to be in college and she wasn't supposed to be as smart as she was and she wasn't supposed to read the books she read and she wasn't supposed to say the things she said. She was too young and too female and too Indian to be that smart. But I exist, she shouted to the world, and my very existence disproves what my conquerors believe about this world and me, but since my conquerors cannot be contradicted, I must not exist.

"Harlan," she said. "I don't even know what Indian is supposed to be. How could you know?"

"Well, that's the thing," he said. "I wrote those poems because I wanted to know. They weren't statements of fact, I guess. They were more like questions."

"But Harlan, that's what poetry is for. It's supposed to be about questions, about the imagination."

"I know, I know. The thing is, I mean, I started reading these poems, asking these questions, around town, you know? At the coffee shops and bookstores and open-mike nights. Late sixties, early seventies, shoot, it was a huge time for poetry. People don't remember it like that, I guess. But poetry was huge. Poets were rock stars. And I was, like, this local rock star, you know? Like a garage-band poet. And people, white people, they really loved my poems, you know? They looked at me onstage, looking as Indian as I do, with my dark skin and long hair and big nose and cheekbones, and they didn't know my poems were just pretend. How could they know? Shoot, half the white people in the crowd thought they were Indian, so why were they going to question me?"

Corliss reached across and took his hand. She hoped he wouldn't interpret it as a sexual gesture. But he didn't seem to notice or acknowledge her touch. He was too involved with his own story. He was confessing; she was his priest.

"Even though my poems were just my imagination," he said, "just my dreams and ideas about what it would've been like to grow up Indian, these white people, they thought my poems were real. They thought I had lived the life I was writing about. They thought I was the Indian I was only pretending to be. After a while, I started believing it, too. How could I not? They wanted me to be a certain kind of Indian, and when I acted like that kind of Indian, like the Indian in my poems, those white people loved me."

July 22, 1973. Seven-twenty-three P.M. Open-mike night at Boo's Books and Coffee on University Way in Seattle. Harlan Atwater walked in with twenty-five copies of In the Reservation of My Mind. He'd printed three hundred copies and planned to sell them for five dollars each, fairly expensive for self-published poetry, but Harlan thought he was worth it. He'd considered bringing all three hundred copies to the open mike, but he didn't want to look arrogant. He figured he'd quickly sell the twenty-five copies he had brought, and it would look better to sell out of his current stock than to have huge piles of unsold books sitting about. He didn't need the money, but he didn't want to give the books away. People didn't respect art when it was free.

He was number twelve on the list of twenty readers for the night. That was good placement. Any earlier and the crowds would be sparse. Any later and the crowds would be anxious to split and might take off while you were trying to orate and berate. There were seven women reading. He'd already slept with three of them, and three others had already rejected him, so that left one stranger with carnal possibilities.

Harlan looked good. "Thin and Indian, thin and Indian, thin and Indian," that was his personal mantra. He wore tight jeans, black cowboy boots, and a white T-shirt. A clean and simple look, overtly masculine. He didn't believe women were truly attracted to that androgynous hippie-boy look. He figured women wanted a warrior-poet.

He impatiently listened to eleven poets read their poems, then he read three of his sonnets, enough to make the crowd happy but not enough to bore them, sold all twenty-five of his books, and then he listened to six other poets read. Normally, he would have eased his way out the door after he'd finished performing, but that stranger girl was reading last, and he wanted to know if he could see more of her.

She was a good poet, funny and rowdy, no earth-loving pieties or shallow radical politics for her. She read poems about a police-chief father who loved his hippie daughter only a little more than he hated her. Okay, so she was no Plath or Sexton, but he wasn't Lowell or O'Hara. And she was cute, wearing rainbow-striped pants and a brown leather shirt. Her hair was long and blond, of course, but she also wore bright red lipstick. Harlan couldn't remember the last time he saw a hippie woman wearing Marilyn Monroe's lips. Shoot, Harlan thought, hippie men were more apt to look like Marilyn Monroe, and that's all right, but it's not always all right.

After she finished reading, Harlan had to hang back as she quickly and politely rejected three other potential suitors, and then he approached her.

"Your poems are good," he said.

"Hey, thanks, man," she said. "You're Harlan Atwater, aren't you?"

She recognized him. That was a good sign.

"Yeah, I'm Harlan. What's your name?"

"I call myself Star Girl," she said. "But you're the real star, man, your poems are good. No, they're the best. You're going to be famous, man."

She was a fan. Things were looking even better for him.

"Hey," he said. "You want to go get a drink or something?"

Two hours later, they were naked in her bed. They hadn't touched or kissed. They'd only read poems to each other. But they were naked. Harlan had played this game before. You took off your clothes to prove how comfortable you were with your body, and how comfortable you were with other people's bodies, and how you didn't think of the body as just a sexual tool. If you could get naked with a woman and not touch her, you were a liberated man unafraid of true intimacy. But shoot, men were simpleminded about female nudity, despite how complicated naked women wanted naked men to be. Throughout human history, Harlan thought, men have been inventing ways to get women naked, and this hippie thing seemed to be the most effective invention of all time. Harlan knew his chances of sex with Star Girl increased with every passing minute of noncontact nudity. And she was so smart, funny, and beautiful—she'd read Rimbaud, Barnes, and Baraka to him!—he'd stay naked and sexless for six weeks.

"Tell me about your pain," she said.

"What about my pain?" he asked.

"You know, being Indian, man. That has to be a tough gig. The way we treated you and stuff. We broke your hearts, man. How do you deal with all that pain?"

"It's hard," he said. He looked down at his hands as he spoke. "I mean, I grew up so poor on the reservation, you know? We call it the rez, you know? And the thing is, Indian poor is the poorest there is. Indian poor is the basement of the skyscraper called poverty."

"That's sad and beautiful," she said. "You're sad and beautiful." She reached over and brushed a stray hair away from his face. Tender gestures.

"I was raised by my grandmother," he said. "My mom and dad, they were killed in a house fire. My two sisters died in the fire, too. I was the only one who lived. I was a baby when the fire happened. Somebody, they don't know whether it was my mom or dad, threw me out a window, and I landed in a tree. At first they thought I'd burned up in the fire with everyone else, but a fireman found me sleeping high up in that tree."

"That's just it, man," she said. "That's how it happens. That's how pain visits, man. You break somebody's heart two hundred years ago, and it's like this chain reaction, man. Hearts keep on getting broken. Oh, Harlan, you're breaking my heart."

She hugged him. She kissed him on the cheek. She kissed him on the mouth. He pushed her down and climbed on top of her. She reached down and helped him put his penis inside her. But he felt passive and removed from the act.

"Put your pain into me," she said. "I can take it. I need it. I deserve it."

He didn't know whether to laugh or cry. He knew some folks got off on being punished, on being degraded during sex. But he'd never made love to a woman who wanted him to take revenge against her for hundreds of years of pain she never caused. Who could make love with that kind of historical and hysterical passion? He laughed.

"What is it?" she asked. "What's so funny?"

"I don't know, I'm scared, I'm scared," he said. It was always good to admit your fear, or to pretend you were afraid. Women loved men who confessed their fears and doubts, however real or imaginary they might be.

"It's okay to be afraid," she said. "Give me everything you are."

He couldn't look at her. He didn't want to see the need in her eyes, and he didn't want her to see the deceit in his eyes. So he flipped her over onto her stomach and pushed into her from behind. She moaned loudly, louder than she had before, reached back and under and played with herself while he pumped in and out, in and out. He looked down at the back of her head, her face buried in the pillow, and he understood she could be any white woman. This wasn't a new and exciting position, a bid for a different kind of intimacy, or carnal experimentation. He wanted her to be faceless and anonymous because he was faceless and anonymous. He didn't know her real name, and she didn't know his.

"Give it to me," she said. "I'm here for you, I'm here for you, I'm here for you."

He felt like a ghost watching a man make love to a woman, and he wondered how a man could completely separate his body from his soul. Can women separate themselves like that? Of course they must be able to. They must have to. Star Girl was not making love to him. She was making love to an imaginary man. His body was inside her body, but who was he inside her mind? Am I her father? Am I her brother, her mother, her sister? Or am I only her Indian?

He flipped her over onto her back and penetrated her again. He pushed and pushed and pushed, and she closed her eyes.

"Look at me," he said.

She opened her eyes and looked at him. She smiled. How could she smile? She was a stranger with strange ideas.

"Say my name," he said.

"Harlan," she said.

She was wrong and didn't know she was wrong.

"Say my name," he said again.

"Harlan," she said. "Harlan Atwater."

He pulled out of her and crawled off the bed. He ignored her as he quickly dressed, and then he ran out the door, away from her. He ran to the house he shared with his white parents, grabbed the box filled with his self-printed poetry books, and ran back out into the world. He ran twenty-two blocks to Big Heart's, the Indian bar on Aurora. He threw open the door and strode into the crowded bar like a warrior chief.

"I am a poet!" he screamed to the assembled Indians.

The drunken Indians, those broken men and women, let Harlan be their poet for the night. They let him perform his poems between juke-box songs. They listened and applauded. They hugged and kissed him. They told him his poems sounded exactly like Indian poems were supposed to sound. They recited their poems to him, and asked if their poems were as good as his poems, and he said they were very good, very good, so keep working on them. They all wanted copies of his books. Harlan was so happy he gave them away for free. He autographed 275 books and gave them to 275 different Indians. They all bought him drinks. He didn't need their charity. He had money. But he wanted to be part of their tribe, their collective, so he drank the free drinks, and he laughed and sang and danced and performed his poems again and again. And yes, he could recite all of them by memory because he loved his poems so much. He asked them if he was Indian, and they said he was the best Indian they'd ever known, and he was happy to hear it, so he drank the free drinks and bought drinks for others, and they all drank together, completely forgetting who had paid for what. He drank more, and the lights and faces blurred, and he could see only one bright red light, and then he could see nothing at all.

Harlan woke the next morning in the alley behind the bar. He staggered to his feet, retched, and emptied his stomach onto a pile of

his poetry books lying on the dirty cement. Dry-heaving, he knelt,
cleaned his vomit off his books, and read the inscriptions inside:

To Junior, my new best friend, Love, Harlan
To Agnes! Indian Power! From Harlan!
To Hank, who fought in the Nam and don't give a damn, Harlan
To Pumpkin, who always remembers the elders, Always, Harlan
To Dee, the rodeo queen, from the rodeo king, Harlan

Carrying the damp books, Harlan staggered down the alley and
onto the street. Sunrise. The street was empty of cars and people, but
Harlan could see a dozen of his books lying abandoned on the street.
He knew hundreds of others were lying on hundreds of other streets.
Harlan dropped the books he carried, let them join the rest of their
tribe, and walked home to his parents.

In the used-book store, Corliss covered her face with her hands. She
couldn't look at the world where such a sad thing could take place.

"Shoot, that's the thing," Harlan said. "That's why I was so surprised to hear one of my books was in the library. In the end, I didn't
write poems. I wrote litter."

He laughed. Corliss wondered how he could laugh. But she laughed
with him and didn't know why. What was so funny about the world?
Everything! Corliss and Harlan laughed until the hearing-impaired
bookstore owner probably felt the floor shake.

"So, what lessons can we learn from this story?" Corliss asked.

"Never autograph books for drunk Indians," he said.

"Never have sex with women named after celestial bodies."

"Never self-publish your poetry."

"Never perform at open-mike nights."

"Never pretend to be an Indian when you're not," he said. He took off his glasses and wiped tears from his eyes. Two Indians crying in the back of a used-book store. Indians are always crying, Corliss thought, but at least we're two Indians crying in an original venue. What kind of ceremony was that? An original ceremony! Every ceremony has to be created somewhere; her Eden was a used-book store. In the beginning, there was the word, and the word was on sale at the local bookstore. That was only natural, she thought, it was apt and justified and ordained. Again, she felt blessed and chosen. She felt young and epic. Can one be young and epic? She didn't know, but she'd gladly be the first such adventurer, or second, or thirty-third, or one millionth. She was Odysseus, and Harlan was Homer. Or vice versa.

"I never wrote another poem after that night," Harlan said. "It seemed indecent."

"I think poetry writing is supposed to feel indecent."

"Well, maybe. You're young. I was young, too. And I made a lot of fuss about some fairly inconsequential poems. It's not like I was famous or rich or talented. I was ordinary, or maybe a little better than ordinary, and I wanted to be more than that, and I couldn't be, and it hurt for a long time. I think writing poems, I think if I would've kept writing them, I would've always been reminded of that, of how ordinary I am."

Corliss wondered what sort of person could continue working jobs that made him feel ordinary. But everybody worked those jobs. Corliss didn't believe there was a huge difference between the average pizza deliveryman's self-esteem and Clint Eastwood's. Or maybe she only wanted to believe there was no real difference. How do small people feel larger? Well, silly, they pretend the large people are smaller. In an ideal world, Corliss thought, everybody weighs 150 pounds!

"Can I ask you a human question?" she asked.

"What's a human question?" he asked.

"A homeless guy taught me the phrase. I think it's a variation on a personal question."

"You're a strange, strange woman," he said.

She couldn't disagree.

"All right," he said. "Go ahead. Ask away."

"What have you been doing all these years?"

"I still drive a forklift down on the waterfront. Nothing spectacular. I'm going to retire at the end of the year. I've got a big pension coming. It's good money, honest work, I guess, as long as I don't think too hard about what's in the boxes, you know?"

Corliss knew about denial.

"And I take care of my folks," he said. "I still live with them in the house. That's why I didn't let you in. They're old and sick. They took care of me then. I take care of them now."

"Were they good parents?" she asked.

"Better than most, I suppose," he said. "But the thing is, shoot, they could have completely ignored me, and it wouldn't have mattered much. Because they saved my life. I mean, I know they're white and I'm Indian, and that's supposed to be such a sad-sack story, but well, they did, they really saved my life."

"What do you mean?" she asked.

"Well, shoot," he said. "I went looking for my real mother once. And it took me a few years, but I found her. She was living alone in Los Angeles. Living in some downtown dive hotel, and she was smoking crack, you know? That's what my real mother was doing the first time I saw her. I was sitting in my car outside that hotel, because it was scary, you know? And I saw this old Indian woman walking down the street, walking with a cane, and her face was all swollen, and her legs were all swollen. And she had all these sores all over her arms and legs and face. And she looked like a zombie, you know? Like Stephen King's nightmare Indian."

"How'd you know it was your mother?" Corliss asked.

"I don't know," he said. "I just knew. I mean, she looked like me. I looked like her. But there was something else, too. I felt connected. And she started coughing. I was parked fifty feet away, but I could hear her coughing so loud. She was retching up stuff and spitting it on the sidewalk. And it was the saddest thing I'd ever seen. And this was my mother. This was the woman who gave birth to me, who'd left me behind. I felt sorry for her and loved her and hated her all at the same time, you know?"

Corliss knew about mothers and their difficult love.

"I opened the door and got out. I was going to walk across the street and stop her and say to her—I'd rehearsed it all—I was going to say, 'Mother, I am your son.' Basic, simple, clean. Nothing dramatic. Still, I thought even that simple statement might kill her. I keep thinking I might shock her into a heart attack, she looked so frail and weak. I'm walking across the street toward her, and she's coughing, and I'm getting closer, and then she reaches into her pocket, pulls out this crack pipe and a lighter, and she lights up right there in the middle of the street. Broad daylight. She lights up and sucks the crap in. And I kept walking right past her, came within a foot of her, you know. I could smell her. She didn't even look at me. She just kept sucking at that pipe. Old Indian woman sucking on a crack pipe. It was sad and ridiculous, but you know the worst part?"

"What?" Corliss asked.

Harlan stood and walked down the aisle away from Corliss. He spoke with his back to her.

"I was happy to see my mother like that," he said. "I was smiling when I walked away from her. I just kept thinking how lucky I was, how blessed, that this woman didn't raise me. I just kept thinking God had chosen me, had chosen these two white people to swoop in and save me. Do you know how terrible it is to feel that way? And how good it feels, too?"

"I don't have any idea how you feel," Corliss said. Her confusion was the best thing she could offer. What could she say to him that would matter? She'd spent her whole life talking. Words had always been her weapon, her offense and defense, and she felt that her silence, her wordlessness, might be the only thing she could give him.

"The thing is," he said, "the two best, the two most honorable and loyal people in my life are my white mother and my white father. So, you tell me, kid, what kind of Indian does that make me?"

Corliss knew only Harlan could answer that question for himself. She knew the name of her tribe, and the name of her archaic clan, and her public Indian name, and her secret Indian name, but everything else she knew about Indians was ambiguous and transitory.

"What's your name?" she asked him. "What's your real name?"

Harlan Atwater faced her. He smiled, turned away, and walked out of the store. She could follow him and ask for more. She could demand to know his real name. She could interrogate him for days and attempt to separate his truth from his lies and his exaggerations from his omissions. But she let him go. She understood she was supposed to let him go. And he was gone. But Corliss sat for hours in the bookstore. She didn't care about time. She was tired and hungry, but she sat and waited. Indians are good at waiting, she thought, especially when we don't know what we're waiting for. But there comes a time when an Indian stops waiting, and when that time came for Corliss, she stood, took Harlan Atwater's book to the poetry section, placed it with its front cover facing outward for all the world to see, and then she left the bookstore and began her small journey back home.

LAWYER'S LEAGUE

My father is an African American giant who played defensive end for the University of Washington Huskies, and my mother is a petite Spokane Indian ballerina who majored in dance at U-Dub, so genetically speaking, I'm a graceful monster. But my father spent more time reading Frantz Fanon and Angela Davis than pumping iron in the weight room, and my mother played supernatural point guard for an all-Native women's barnstorming basketball team, so culturally speaking, I'm a biracial revolutionary leftist magician with a twenty-foot jumper encoded in my DNA.

I grew up in Seattle, played basketball at Ballard High School, and attended North Seattle Community College on a partial athletic scholarship. But I soon grew bored of school and small ball. I played backup power forward—averaging seven points and five rebounds a game—on a crappy team in the middle of a forty-seven-game losing streak, and I'd taken all of the college-prep courses in high school and had earned eighteen college credits through the Advanced Placement tests. I was underqualified for CC basketball and overqualified for CC academics. Don't get me wrong. I think United States community colleges are the most successful models of socialism in the history of the world, but I was already an intellectual gladiator eager to do battle with the capitalistic lions. I quit the basketball team, transferred to the University of Washington, my folks' alma mater, and earned a summa cum laude BA in political science while playing rat ball at the intramural gym five or six days a week. I still loved basketball and was a better hoopster than 99 percent of the dudes I faced, but I had better things to do and be.

During college, I interned for Norm Rice, the first African American mayor of Seattle; after graduation, I went to work for Gary Locke, the first Chinese American governor in United States history. I am currently Locke's executive liaison to Washington State's twenty-nine Indian tribes, which are growing in political power due to casino revenues, and I also manage the Native Voices Now! voter-registration drive. Let me tell you, that is a tough gig. Do you know how difficult it is to get Indians to trust any politician? In the long history of treaty making and treaty breaking, there have been no significant differences between Democrats and Republicans. I hate to say it, but many Native American politicians are as corrupt and self-serving as any white D or R. So Indian voters don't trust Indian politicians any more than the white variety.

In that regard, Governor Locke is an original. No matter how much Indian tribes might agree or disagree with his policies, he can't be judged on a long history of Chinese American oppression of Native Americans. Locke and his staff were smart enough to hire me, the superstar half-Indian boy, to do most of his tribal communication. That hasn't been easy. Let me tell you a dirty secret: Quite a few of the state's most powerful Indian men and women are functionally illiterate. There are tribal councilmen who cannot spell the word "sovereignty." It's true. The best and brightest Indian folks are not often tribal leaders. A genius Indian is a rare and powerful person, wanted by every college and corporation. A genius Indian is the homecoming king or queen of the private-sector prom. But let's tell more of the truth, okay? The best and brightest white men and women don't become our mayors and governors and presidents, either. Otherwise, Bill Gates would be in the Oval Office, and Martha Stewart would be secretary of state. Think about it. The current United States president graduated from Yale with a 77 percent average. If white folks can survive with a C-plus commander in chief, then Indian folks can survive with a GED tribal chief. But here's a personal truth: I am tired of surviving the incompetent, the average, the mean and median. I want excellence. I want to be a good man and a great politician who makes promises and keeps them. I am one of the best and brightest Native Americans and one of the best and brightest African Americans, and I am ambitious, so I plan on becoming the first half-black half-Indian United States senator. After three or four terms in the Senate, I'll go for the White House. That is my general life plan, but general life plans often go awry. After all, in third grade, John F. Kennedy and Lee Harvey Oswald both wanted to be U.S. president, and look what happened to them. It's the details of any life that are most important, right? Let me tell you about one dinner party and one basketball game.

Last February, I received an invitation to a bipartisan lobbyist dinner at Campagne, a wonderful French restaurant down near Pike Place Market in Seattle. I was excited about the food I would be eating and the company I would be keeping. Most outsiders think of lobbyists as politicians in better suits, but that's not the case at all. Lobbyists don't work in public, so they don't have to worry about public opinion. Lobbyists aren't elected; they're self-selected. They aren't crusaders; they're mercenaries. By and large, lobbyists are as wicked, revenge-minded, poetic, intelligent, candid, and hilarious as any stand-up comedian. Former politicians who become lobbyists might miss the power of public office, but they learn to love the power of anonymity.

I was seated at a table with five lawyers who might be described as two married white couples and a single white woman, and who most accurately could be described as two Republicans and three Democrats.

"Hello," I said. "I'm Richard. I work in Governor Locke's office."

"Oh, come on, Richard," said the first Republican husband. "Does anybody actually *work* in Governor Locke's office?"

"Hey, now," I said. "I thought this was a bipartisan dinner."

"It *is* bipartisan," said the second Republican husband. "I used to be with Senator Gorton. Nobody *ever* worked in his office."

Slade Gorton is a famous Indian fighter who wants to abolish all Indian tribes. I helped register ten thousand Indian first-time voters motivated by their hatred and fear of Gorton. Since he lost his re-election bid by a few thousand votes to a nebulous Democrat, I wonder if he lies in bed at night and does the math.

"Ignore my husband," said the Democrat wife. "He's a right-wing maniac."

"And you, my lovely wife, are a knee-jerk liberal."

"You keep talking like that, and it's going to be a long time before you stick your right wing in my knee jerk."

We laughed.

"I guess this dinner is officially off the record," I said.

"Here's to brutal honesty," the single white woman said and raised her glass of red. As she drank, she looked at me. She *regarded* me. In three seconds, she examined me, asked herself questions about me, answered them, and defined me. She smiled. She thought good things.

"And who are you brutally honest for?" I asked her.

"Pro-choice, all day, all the way," she said.

Yet another pretty liberal from Seattle! Her black business suit probably converted into a rainproof tent. She wore eyeliner, lipstick, and three-inch pumps at dinner, but she likely wore stupid T-shirts (*George can't spell W!*), blue jeans, and huge scuffed boots at the office. She'd probably run twenty-three marathons and climbed Mount Rainier sixteen times, and had great calves and extraordinary upper-body strength, and most certainly had scored 1545 on her SATs and earned some highly challenging and profoundly useless degree from an Ivy League chop shop. She probably still had a cassette of the Smiths stuck in her car stereo: *"Meat is murder! Meat is murder! Meat is murder!"* I wanted her to fall in love with me.

"I fight for the Second Amendment on weekdays," said the Republican wife, "and the First Amendment on weekends."

"Boeing and Microsoft," said her Republican husband.

"Boise Cascade," said the other Republican husband.

"Sierra Club," said his Democrat wife.

"Wait, wait," I said. "So one of you fights for trees and the other fights against trees?"

"No, no," he said. "We make the paper she writes on to file lawsuits against the paper we make."

A well-rehearsed joke, but funny nonetheless.

"You know," the single white woman said, "I've never understood politically mixed marriages."

"Oh, Lord," the Republican husband said. "Here we go again."

"No, I've never understood. Tell me about your marriage."

"It's a good marriage," the Democrat wife said. "We fight forty-nine percent of the time and hump-and-bump the other fifty-one."

Funny and crass! How much had she drunk before she came to dinner? How many alcoholic Democratic women can you fit into a lightbulb? I don't know, go ask Teddy Kennedy.

"No, really," said the single white woman. "I mean, don't you ever wonder how a hard-core Republican like Mary Matalin can be successfully married to a hard-core Democrat like James Carville?"

"Oh, don't bring those cannibals up," said the husband. "We always have to talk about those headhunters."

"Aren't you two cute?" said the wife. She mimicked the idiots she'd heard so often before: "'You're, like, the Mary Matalin and James Carville of Seattle! Come on, argue for us, argue for us!'"

"Sometimes it feels more like theater than marriage," said the husband.

"Well, you guys made that choice when you married each other, right?" said the single white woman. "You were Democrat and Republican when you met, right?"

"I didn't mean our marriage was theater."

"All right, but what is your marriage? What does it mean?"

She wasn't going to let it go. She was a storm maker! I wanted her to rain down on me!

"You know what I love about this restaurant," said the other Republican husband, trying to change the subject. "I love that you can smoke. What good is French food without a cigarette?"

"*Oui, oui,*" said his wife. "I've got an unfiltered Camel in one hand and a fork in the other."

"But is it the correct fork?" asked the Democrat wife.

"Let's see, I have my salad fork, first-course fork, second-course fork, dessert fork, and yes, here it is, I have my cancer fork."

They laughed, entertained by their collective wit.

"Hey," I said to the single white woman. "What's your name?"

"Teresa."

"I'm Richard," I said and offered my hand.

"I know," she said and took my hand. "You already said that."

We held hands a moment longer than necessary. It was no longer a polite greeting; it had become a tactile series of questions. *Are we gonna? Do you wanna? Will it be juicy and joyous?* I wanted to impress her: I wanted to be a member of her tribe.

"You know, I agree with Teresa," I said to the others. "I've always suspected that in mixed marriages, one of the partners is lying about his or her politics."

"Are you calling me a liar?" asked the Republican husband. He'd switched on his lobbyist voice, loud, clear, and resonant. I'd bet a million dollars he soaked in his bathtub at night and pretended he was a guest on *Crossfire* or *Hannity & Colmes* or *Meet the Press*. Hey, little Tucker, what do you want to be when you grow up? I want to be a bow-tied talking head.

"I'm not calling anybody a liar, I'm just talking theory here," I said. "Hypothesis. I'm not talking about your marriage in particular. I don't know you folks at all. I'm talking about politically mixed marriages in general."

Jesus, what the hell was I doing? How impolitic could I be? But Teresa seemed to be enjoying it. I wondered how soon I would see her naked.

"The thing is," I said, "maybe both partners in those marriages are lying. When it counts most—at its most intimate, when two lovers are beneath the sheets—I figure Matalin and Carville are moderates who believe in truth, justice, and multiple orgasms."

"Well, hell, yes!" shouted the Democrat wife. "Now, that's a subject we can all agree on!"

Okay, I was clumsy and obvious in introducing sex as a topic of conversation. But Teresa already knew sex was on my mind, and I wanted her to wonder about the quality and quantity of the sex. I looked at her. I *regarded* her. She smiled, and only the poets know what bright shapes a bright container can contain.

"We all want to be special," I said. "We all want to be the last surviving member of our species. A right-wing woman like Matalin is
the only woolly mammoth, and Carville is the most singular white
donkey ever born in the state of Louisiana. So maybe Matalin and
Carville wear public masks over private faces."

"Or maybe they're like house cats," Teresa said.

"What?" I asked, puzzled by her analogy.

"No, really," she said. "We didn't domesticate cats. They domes-
ticated themselves. But not totally, you know? You take a good look
at any house cat, and you can tell there's eventually going to be a
day when it goes back wild, you know? When it reverts to its true
nature. You fall over and die in a house with your dog, and your dog
will lie down beside your dead body, maybe right on top of it, and
starve to death. But a house cat will feast on your eyes as soon as its
stomach starts growling."

"So what are you?" I asked. "A cat or a dog?"

"Depends on the situation," she said.

I stayed too long after dinner because she stayed too long after
dinner. We wanted to be left alone together, but we didn't want to
leave together while everybody was watching. We stood at the bar
and talked for a few hours about the usual things, but she was un-
usually smart and funny and tender. I thought about marriage. God,
I felt like a sixteen-year-old girl eagerly reading *Bride's* magazine.
And then I saw our reflections in the mirror behind the bar. She
was short, blond, blue-eyed, and white-skinned. I was tall, black-
haired, brown-eyed, and brown-skinned, the love child of Crazy
Horse and Josephine Baker, of Sacajawea and Julius Erving, of Zora
Neale Hurston and Geronimo, of Pocahontas and Malcolm X. I
thought about genetics. What kind of kids would Teresa and I produce? What would they look like? I wondered if a black Indian could
stand at the victor's podium and thank his white wife and half-white

children for all of their support during the long and successful campaign. Sadly, I decided no candidate would deliver that speech during my lifetime, and probably not during my future children's lifetime. A simple politico dinner had presented me with a profound moral dilemma. It was a wonderful opportunity for me to self-define. Were my eccentric needs as an individual more important than the country's desperate need for excellent leadership? I knew I would never achieve my full potential as a public servant if I married a white woman. I would lose votes each time I kissed my wife in public, and I would lose thousands of votes if my wise and terrible opponents created campaign ads that featured public displays of affection between my white wife and me. Any such ads would verbally attack my liberal politics, but the visuals would silently condemn miscegenation. You might think I'm overreacting. But I've learned it's never too early to make your first political mistake. Teresa might have been a wonderful life partner, but I knew my country needed me more than any future wife might. Did I make the correct decision? Personally speaking, I was wrong. Politically speaking, I had no choice. But I didn't cause Teresa any significant pain. I could have taken her home that night, slept with her, and abandoned her. But I am not that kind of man. I am not cruel.

Instead I said good night to Teresa, and gave her my card, and promised to call her, but I never did. After that night, I often saw her at meetings, rallies, fund-raisers, and dinners, and we always exchanged pleasantries. The last time I saw her, she told me she had quit her job and was moving to Paris to experience a different part of the world. I warmly congratulated her and wished her well, but I felt abandoned by her. I had no right to feel that way. I barely knew the woman and had spent only a few close hours with her, but she'd become a religious symbol for me. She was my Lent, my forty days of fasting and penitence, and by denying myself her possibilities, I felt like a stronger and more faithful man.

Two weeks after her farewell, I received an invitation to play basketball in a lawyer's league.

"I'm not a lawyer," I said.

"That's okay. Most of us aren't basketball players," Steve said. He worked in the attorney general's office. I didn't know him very well and didn't care for what I knew—he believed in the death penalty—but he fell half in love with me once he heard I'd played a little college ball. He fell completely for me after I drove past him during a pickup game and dunked on his head.

"I don't have time to commit to a league," I said.

"It's not really a league," Steve said. "It's a bunch of guys who get together once a week. Wednesday night. Very informal. Come on. We need new blood."

I'd played a few lunchtime games with Steve and the other jocks who worked in the Capitol Building. I wasn't too crazy about the competition. Most of them played basketball like Ted Bundy, hiding a pathologically violent core beneath a handsome white-collar exterior. They were either former basketball stars angry about their diminishing skills, or ex-wrestlers and ex-linebackers still trying to play their favorite sport.

"I'm not interested in getting beat up," I said.

"No, man, it's a friendly game," Steve said.

"Lawyers are never friendly."

"Come on, we need you, man. I already told them you'd play. I said you were da bomb."

"Steve, I'm only going to play if you promise never to call me da bomb again."

That next Wednesday I found St. Joseph's Elementary School, the small gym the lawyers rented once a week. Seven of the regulars showed, and I made eight, good enough for full-court four-on-four. As we shot for teams, I sized up the competition. I knew Steve was average, and five of the others couldn't hit a jump shot standing by themselves, but one big white guy looked loose and quick.

"What kind of lawyers are these guys?" I asked Steve.

"Mostly public defenders," he said.

"And who's the big guy?"

"That's Big Bill. He's a prosecutor. He can play."

And Big Bill could play. On the first possession, he posted me up on the low box, caught an entry pass, spun to his right, hooked me with his right arm, and dropped in a left-handed scoop shot.

"Nice move," I said as we ran down the court.

"The first of many," Big Bill said. I couldn't believe it. Thirty seconds into the first game, and he was trash-talking. Lawyers! Seeking vengeance, I made meaningful eye contact with Steve, cut back door on Big Bill, took the bounce pass from Steve, and grease-dunked it, meaning I barely slid the ball over the oily rim. My dunk was more than kin and less than kind.

The lawyers went crazy. Gerald Ford was in office the last time any of them had dunked it.

"Hey, Big Bill," I said. "How'd you like that?"

"It doesn't count," he said.

"What doesn't count?"

"There's no dunking."

"What are you talking about?"

"There's no dunking. House rule."

"Can you even touch the rim?"

"Doesn't matter. No basket."

"Come on, man," I said. "Dunking is part of my game."

What a lie! In games with players of equal ability, I dunked probably once every three months.

"Hey, come on, Bill," Steve said. "He's new. He didn't know."

"He knows now. No basket."

Big Bill was a smug bastard, but I wanted to play ball more than I wanted to argue.

"It's all right, Steve," I said. "We'll get it back."

Big Bill tossed the ball to his short point guard and jogged down the court. He posted up me again on the low box, took another entry pass, and spun on me. But I was ready this time and blocked his shot. Steve picked up the loose ball and raced toward our basket. I ran right behind him, calling out my position, and Steve dropped a nifty bounce pass back to me. Angry and righteous, I leaped high for the dunk, higher than I'd been in many years, and rose a good foot above the rim, but dropped the ball down through the net instead of dunking it.

"No basket!" Big Bill screamed.

"What?" I asked.

"There's no dunking!" he screamed at me, face-to-face.

"That wasn't a dunk!" I screamed back and pushed him away. He pushed back. I couldn't believe it. I was ready to fight, though I hadn't been in a fistfight in twenty-six years. Scratch a pacifist and he'll scratch back.

The other lawyers separated us, but Big Bill kept screaming. "There's no dunking! No dunking! No dunking!"

He was irrational, I thought, and I wondered if he'd gone crazy or if maybe a vein in his head had exploded. But then I realized he was afraid of me. In this Wednesday-night wolf pack, he'd probably been the alpha-male hoopster for a decade. I threatened to demote him to the beta position.

"You dunk again, and I'm going to throw you out myself," he said.

On a neutral court, I might have argued more. But this was his court and his friends, Steve included. Looking back, I suppose I should have packed up my stuff and left. But he'd challenged me. I couldn't back down.

"I don't need to dunk," I said. "Your ball."

Angry and stupid, Big Bill decided to dribble the ball downcourt. I let him get to half-court before I stole the ball from him and raced toward the hoop.

"Foul!" he shouted out.

"I didn't touch you," I said.

"It's my call," he said. "Respect the call."

I tossed him back the ball, let him dribble a few times, and I stole the ball once more.

"Foul!" he repeated.

Again I tossed him back the ball, and again I let him dribble a few times, and I stole the ball a third time. He didn't invent a foul that time, knowing he would only embarrass himself, but he chased after me as I drove toward the hoop. Two of his teammates, quicker than I'd thought, converged on me and slowed me down. Big Bill ran a foot behind. It was a one-on-three fast break, but I wanted to score, so I spun left, spun right, went between my legs, and made a left-handed reverse layup that surprised me. That shot was so beautiful, Big Bill's teammates hugged me.

"No basket!" shouted Big Bill. "No basket!"

"What's wrong now?" I asked.

"Let it go, Big Bill," Steve said. The other lawyers also tried to mollify Bill, but he pushed them away.

"That spinning-traveling garbage," he said. "We don't play that kind of ball here."

"What kind of ball are you talking about?" I asked him.

"You know what kind of ball I'm talking about," he said.

"No, you tell me what kind of ball you're talking about."

"I'm talking about your kind of ball."

Big Bill had pulled out his thesaurus to call me a synonym for "nigger," a metaphor for "nigger." Political Correctness has forced racists to become poets.

"Hey, Big Bill," I said, "why don't you call me what you really want to call me?"

He blinked. Maybe he lied well for his clients, but he didn't lie well for himself.

"You know what I'm thinking, Bill," I said. "I'm thinking you have to work for my kind of ballplayer all day. You have to look at those kinds of ballplayers every day of your life. After a long day in court, sitting next to one ballplayer after another, the last thing you want to see is another one of those ballplayers when you come to shoot hoops with your buddies. Am I right, Big Bill? Am I telling the truth, the whole truth, and nothing but the truth?"

He laughed and walked away.

"I think you better go," Steve said to me.

"What? Am I no longer da bomb?" I asked.

"I'm sorry about all this," he said. "It's awful. How about we have lunch tomorrow and talk it through?"

"I want to talk about it now," I said.

"Come on, man, you're all hopped up. Bill is hopped up. I'm hopped up. Nothing constructive can happen tonight. Just go home and I'll call you later. We'll get a beer. Hell, Bill will probably come with us."

"Are you trying to counsel me?" I asked.

Steve shook his head and walked away. The other lawyers stared at me. They *regarded* me. I hated their eyes.

"Hey, Steve, nice bunch of friends you have here," I said. "I'm so happy you racist white boys are looking after justice in our state."

Immediately ashamed of myself and angry at my shame, I walked off the court, grabbed my gym bag, and headed for the door.

"Yeah, that's right, kid," Big Bill said. "Go home."

I turned and walked back toward him. Steve stepped between us, but I pushed him aside.

"What did you say?" I asked Big Bill. He was three inches taller, but I was three inches angrier.

"I said go home, son."

"I'm not your boy," I said and punched Bill in the face. He fell on his ass. His nose was most certainly broken. My thumb and index finger were broken. He wiped his bloody face and stared at his bloody hand. Incredulous, he stared at me. His friends stared at me. Obviously feeling like my accomplice, Steve sat in a corner and covered his face with his hands. I wondered how long it had been since Bill had been punched, and how long it had been since any of them had seen one man punch another man in the face. Bill's eyes watered. I don't know whether he cried from pain or embarrassment or both. And then I realized I had punched a lawyer in front of six other lawyers. What kind of fool was I? I laughed and laughed and laughed and finally left the gym. Driving home, I wondered about lawsuits and assault charges. Bill did sue me, but I settled the civil charges out of court and plea-bargained to a simple criminal misdemeanor. Maybe I should have gone to court on both counts, but I didn't think I was completely innocent, and I didn't trust a judge or jury's ability to separate the connotative and denotative meanings of a basketball game. If you want more details, you can go to the courthouse and look it up. It's all part of my permanent record.

At night, I lie in bed with my ambition, close my eyes, and imagine the inevitable press conference. Barely ahead in the polls, or maybe trailing by a single percentage point, I face the media and answer the terrible questions: Yes, I hit him, it was a terrible misunderstanding. No, I wasn't trying to hide my history, I just didn't think it was relevant. After I hit him, I entered anger-management classes and became a more patient and tolerant person. I was a foolish young man and learned that violence is never the answer. On the night I struck him, I drove to my church, and I knelt and I wept and I prayed for guidance. I had never hurt another person before that night, and I haven't hurt any person since, and I hope people will understand it was a tragic aberration. Of course I have hurt people emotionally. I have, as they say, broken a few hearts, but I suspect that might be a positive quality in a political candidate. Yes, I punched Bill in the face, and I must admit that it felt good and true. Of course I broke his nose. What else was I supposed to do? He was a racist. If you elect me as your next senator from Washington State, I'll punch every racist in the nose. Yes, it's true I'm single. I haven't found the right woman. I'm searching for my Miss Right. What do I want in a woman? Well, intelligence, wit, beauty, faith in God, and goodness. Would I marry another politician? Only if she were a liberal Democrat! I punched Big Bill because he reminded me of my father. No, I punched him because he reminded me of your father. This country would be a better place if every U.S. president had punched racists in the face. That would mean U.S. presidents would have spent a lot of time punching themselves in the face. Okay, okay, yes, it's true I broke Bill's nose, but he was ugly to begin with. Hey, I broke my hand and was never able to use it properly again. My hand aches when it rains, and this is Seattle, so it aches all the time. Yes, I wonder if I'm going to be alone and lonely for the rest of my life. After all, I think we marry our mirrors, if you understand what I'm saying, but I work in rooms where the walls are covered with paintings of great white men. Listen, I hurt myself when I punched Big Bill. His face is fine, but I can barely make a fist, and I can't straighten my fingers anymore. Okay, yes, her name is Teresa, but I never slept with her. I didn't think we had a future. I barely knew her. She was only a strong possibility. Look at my hand. See how much it pains me? Can you see how much it hurts to use it? Do you understand I have a limited range of motion?

CAN I GET A WITNESS?

After eating lunch alone in Good Food, a postcolonial wonder house that served Japanese teriyaki, Polish sausage sandwiches, Italian American pizza, and Mexican and Creole rice and beans, she sipped the last of her coffee and looked for her waiter. He'd taken her credit card over fifteen minutes earlier and had not yet returned. Maybe he's banging a waitress in the pantry, she thought. Let's not be homophobic, he might be banging the handsome Guatemalan busboy. Maybe he's buying Internet porn or remaindered celebrity biographies with my card; maybe he's a bitter and lazy employee; or maybe he's kind and decent and terrible at his job. Or maybe my bank has finally frozen my overextended accounts and the IRS is on the way to arrest me. She wondered if the United States would ever re-establish debtors' prisons. If so, she would probably be sentenced to life without possibility of parole. But prison might not be so bad, she thought, and solitary confinement would be quiet. She was the wife of a big man and the mother of two teenage sons, and she hated their male cacophony. She'd enjoyed more solitude and meditative silence when she was a seven-year-old living in the endless pine forests of the Spokane Indian Reservation than she did now as a fifty-year-old woman trapped in this water-trapped city. She was a prepubescent monk! She was closer to God when her vocabulary was 75 percent smaller. But she'd give away all of her five-, four-, and three-syllable words if God would return to her. She missed God! And she missed her waiter. But maybe her waiter had never existed. Maybe he was a ghost. Maybe I'm delusional, she thought, and I don't even realize it. Do crazy people know they're crazy? Look at me, she thought, the paranoid schizophrenic at lunch. She laughed and wondered how she had become a lonely person who ate alone and laughed loudly in public. I'm a homeless crazy woman who happens to pay rent, she thought. Pretty soon I'll wear shopping bags for dresses, and what would Donna Karan think of that? And where the hell is the waiter? She looked around the restaurant for any proof of his physical existence: a dirty apron, a ballpoint pen, the smell of pheromone-soaked cologne. But the waiter was gone, missing, absent, destroyed.

Good Food was busier than usual because the sun was finally shining in Seattle after 113 consecutive days of gray and rain. In the absence of UV rays, the white folks had turned penal-colony pale, and the black and brown people had faded to concentration-camp beige, but everybody was happy and hungry today. She'd eaten a chicken burrito and a teriyaki-chicken sandwich. She'd ordered only the burrito, but the sandwich had mistakenly arrived with it. Chicken this, chicken that, she'd chanted to herself as she ate both meals and enjoyed them, though the meat in each tasted like it had been sliced from the same bird. She'd never been one to complain about poor service. She searched the restaurant for her imaginary waiter, checked her watch, and wondered if she was going to get fired for being late yet again. She worked as a paralegal at Ruffatto, Runnette & Kurth, a medium-sized firm that focused on civil rights cases. She knew it was good and great work, and it should have inspired the best in her, but she was a distracted and incompetent employee, a para-

paralegal. She always ran late and had been officially reprimanded four times in the past year for tardiness. Civil rights lawyers might have been reluctant to fire poor employees, but they certainly knew how to humiliate them. Her employee file was four inches thick. Ah, the height, width, and length of her inferiority! She was a parawife and a paramother and a parafriend. She checked her watch once more. She was going to be at least twenty-five minutes late. A new office record! She looked around for her waiter, wondering if she should bother to return to work or if she should buy a newspaper and start scanning the want ads. God, she thought, I am so shockingly average. What had happened to her? Didn't she used to be special? Wasn't she supposed to be somebody important? She couldn't remember a time when she still had potential. She was middle-aged (if she lived a century!) and college-educated and made ten dollars an hour. What kind of life had she created for herself? She was a laboratory mouse lost in the capitalistic maze. She was an underpaid cow paying one tenth of the mortgage on a three-bedroom, two-bath abattoir. And where the hell was her waiter? She stood and stretched her neck and scanned the room like the world's tallest prairie dog, hoping to get somebody's attention, and looked at the front door as a small and dark man stepped inside, shouted in a foreign language, and detonated the bomb he had taped to his chest.

Outside the restaurant, three people were killed by the initial explosion, and two others died during ambulance rides to the hospital; another thirty-seven were injured. Inside the restaurant, twenty-three people were killed instantly, and fourteen more would die within the next twenty-four hours. Forty-one people survived the blast, but thirteen of them suffered serious injures that required long hospital stays and intensive rehabilitation. It was a highly effective and economical suicide bombing. The bomber had spent only $436 to make his bomb, so it had cost him a little over ten dollars a head.

He would eventually be identified as a Syrian American born in Seattle and raised in upper-class comfort by his Muslim father and Catholic mother. He'd graduated from Lakeside Upper School and Seattle University, and had been working toward his Ph.D. in economics at the University of Washington. He was engaged to another Ph.D. candidate, a French American woman who sang lead for a local folk band. The FBI and local police would investigate the suicide bomber for a year but would find no evidence that he'd engaged in or espoused terrorist activity or philosophy. They'd find no one who had ever heard the man express an anti-American sentiment. He was a registered and consistent voter who preferred moderate Democrats but whose best friend was a local Republican fund-raiser. Over the last five years, the bomber had made equal monetary contributions to Israeli and Palestinian charities. Exactly equal, right down to the penny. The investigators would conclude the bomber was either the most careful, eccentric, and invisible terrorist of all time, or an unsolvable mystery. The FBI had no ability to deal with the existential, and the American public was notoriously hungry for resolution, so the bomber was finally diagnosed as one more lone nut in the long American history of lonesome killers.

But the bomber hadn't thought of himself as crazy or lonesome as he walked toward Good Food. He'd been listening to the voices in his head and following their orders. Content and proud of his commitment, he'd been smiling when he stepped into the restaurant. Right before he exploded the bomb, she'd seen his smile and thought for a moment that she knew him. Her waiter had disappeared, and her husband and sons were strangers to her, and she'd wondered if this dark-skinned man had come to rescue her. A ridiculous notion, to be sure, but she'd been smiling back at him when he detonated the bomb he had taped to his chest.

She'd been knocked unconscious by the explosion and woke crushed by the terrible weight of dead bodies. Pushing and crawling through anonymous body parts and building debris, she rescued herself. Bloody and bruised but not seriously hurt, not really hurt at all when compared to all of the other survivors, she emerged from the wreckage. People were screaming and dying all around her. They looked up at the skyscrapers and expected them to come crashing down. They expected airplanes to fall out of the sky and catch the city on fire. But this disaster was not that disaster; this explosion was small and real, while that other explosion was larger and distant and existed only on film and video and in memory. Here, in the aftermath, real sirens wailed. Real fire trucks and police cars arrived from all directions. News helicopters filled the sky. Rescuers pulled the bodies of the dead and living from the tangle of cement and metal and wood, from a building reduced to its basic elements. As if she were an innocent bystander, an objective journalist, she watched all of it happen and took mental notes. Six pairs of paramedics performed CPR on two men and four women. A horribly burned man, his skin peeling off his hands and arms in long, bloody strips, wailed for his wife. A little black girl and a little white boy hugged each other in the back of an ambulance. Wearing a soldier's combat bucket hat, a homeless black man pushed his shopping cart in circles and sang "The Star-Spangled Banner." On the ground around her were plates and forks and spoons and bowls and salt and paper shakers and chairs and tables and aprons and napkins and one baked potato half wrapped in aluminum foil. A white man in a tattered gray suit wept over the mutilated body of another white man wearing another tattered gray suit. Somewhere in the distance, she heard a radio playing the Latin Playboys. She didn't know which song, but she recognized the harmonies. Across the street, in a sixth-floor window, a white woman leaned out and filmed it all with a video camera.

"Are you okay?" a man asked her.

She turned to look at him. He was a short forty-something Caucasian in a black leather coat. Handsome, with kind eyes and a stupid mustache, he was maybe twenty pounds overweight and would certainly carry thirty extra pounds in ten more years and forty in twenty and so on and so on. The inevitable obesity of the American male! But for now, he looked like the sexy bass player for a bad garage band. Maybe his belly was soft, but his art was rock-hard! In another place or time, she would have smiled at him, flirted, and possibly thought of him the next time she made love with her awful husband. Why was she thinking about sex at a time like this? Worse, why was she thinking about adulterous sex? The world, or at least a small part of the world, was coming to an end, and she was thinking about another man's naked body. How perverse! Or was it a reflexive and natural reaction? With so much death and pain around her, wouldn't it be good to throw this man down in the middle of the rubble and make love to him? Wouldn't it be good to create life, to conceive it? After all, didn't these self-martyring terrorists believe they would be rewarded with seventy-two virgins in heaven? Political posturing aside, didn't a few thousand stupid men believe terrorism was another way to get laid? What would happen if the United States offered seventy-three virgins to each terrorist if he would abstain from violence? Instead of deploying an army of pissed-off U.S. soldiers to Afghanistan and Iraq, we could send a mercy team of patriotic virgins. Oh, God, what is happening to me, she thought, I'm losing my mind. She was in shock, of course, but she wondered if her brain had been more seriously damaged by the blast than she'd thought. Maybe her skull had been ripped open and her brain was exposed for all to see. Wouldn't that be the most extreme form of public nudity? Wouldn't that be the greatest shame? My brains are leaking out of my head, she thought, and I don't even know it. She touched the top of her head and expected to feel soft tissue but felt only her strong and bony skull. She was going crazy, and she welcomed it. She wanted to be crazy.

"Were you in there?" the chubby bass player asked her and pointed at the destroyed restaurant. He was strangely calm, she thought. What kind of man can calmly point at an exploded building? Maybe he'd gone crazy along with her. Maybe everybody had gone crazy.

"I wasn't in there," she said. She lied, and it felt good to lie. "I saw it. I just saw it."

"What happened?" he asked.

"A bomb guy ran into the restaurant," she said. "With a bomb. He opened up his coat, and there was a bomb, and he screamed something. I don't know what language it was. After he screamed, he blew up the bomb."

"Were you in there?" he asked again. Of course, she thought, of course I was in there, you idiot! How could she know exactly what had happened if she hadn't been inside to witness it? He knew something was wrong with her story but was too confused and frightened to figure it out.

"No, I wasn't in there," she said. "I was standing right here when it happened."

"Are you okay?" he asked. He was close to her. She could smell the cigarettes on his breath. Or maybe everybody smelled of fire and smoke. Maybe everybody would always smell of fire and smoke.

"No," she said. Given the opportunity to tell the truth, she kept lying. "I was just walking by."

"I saw you coming out of there," he said. He was interrogating her. How dare he question her at a time like this?

"I was looking for people," she said. "I was trying to save them, but there's nobody. There's just pieces of people."

She realized she was shouting to be heard over the din.

"Are you hurt?" he shouted back at her. What kind of conversation was this? What kind of madness were they sharing? "Are you hurt?" he asked. He kept asking her the same question. She had to stop him from asking it again.

"No, no," she said. "Just get me out of here. I don't want to be here. Help me get out of here."

He took her hand and led her away from the crime scene. For ten blocks, he pushed through the advancing crowds of would-be rescuers, media saints, journalistic vultures, emergency workers, and the curiously morbid. Everywhere there were still and video cameras. She wondered how many thousands of photographs would be taken, how many films would be made. How many of those photographs and films might include her image? Had somebody captured the very moment when she emerged Jesus-like from her exploded tomb? After all, she thought, Jesus is still here because Jesus was once here and parts of Jesus are still floating in the air. Jesus' DNA is part of the collective DNA. We're all part of Jesus; we're all Jesus in part. If you breathe deep during the storm, you can sometimes taste Jesus in a good hard rain. Maybe pieces of Jesus have burned into skin and bone and cement and wood. Maybe you can see the face of Jesus in every blood-stain. Maybe you can see Jesus in my bloody face, she thought, maybe I look like Jesus. Or maybe I'm not Jesus-like, maybe I'm Jesus himself. Maybe I'm a resurrection of the resurrected.

"Where do you live?" he asked. "Do you want me to take you home?"

"No," she said. "Take me where you live."

He hesitated. He didn't understand what was happening. He wanted to be logical. He wanted to make it make sense. He lived at the end of the next block. It was close and safe, and therefore he decided it was logical to take this stranger, this strange woman, to his apartment. He wondered if they were going to have sex. He knew it happened. He'd read of strangers who fell into each other's arms during earthquakes and tornadoes and hurricanes and wars. His uncle Ernie, a Vietnam War veteran, had rescued a young Vietnamese woman and her infant son in 1967, married her, adopted the kid, and brought them back to Seattle. They were still married, somewhat unhappily, but stayed together. Who can explain these things? Maybe I'm supposed to take this woman home, he thought, maybe we're supposed to fall in love. Okay, maybe it's not logical, maybe it's nonsensical. But what makes any sense in a world where a man can run into a crowded restaurant and explode a bomb? He looked at this woman with her long black hair and brown skin and brown eyes, and wondered if she was Iraqi or Saudi Arabian or Afghani. Maybe she was a Muslim terrorist who'd exploded the restaurant and was using him to make her escape. God, he thought, I've watched too many action movies and too much FOX News, and worse, I'm a racist who has watched too many Stallone flicks and too much Bill O'Reilly.

"I don't know what to do," he said. He was being honest. He wondered if his honesty was real.

"Just take me where you live," she said again. "And then we'll figure it out."

He led her to his apartment building in Pioneer Square and three flights up to his place. He unlocked the door, followed her inside, closed the door behind them, and sat her down on his living room couch.

"Do you want something to drink?" he asked. How basic and inane! Why hadn't he offered her something important, like world peace or spiritual redemption? He couldn't have delivered either of those wonderful abstractions, but his offer would have been solid.

"I'd love some water," she said.

"Water is important," he said. "Whenever I'm depressed or lonely or whatever, I drink a glass of water, and I usually feel better."

What the hell was he talking about? What kind of fool was he? He walked into the kitchen to get the water. He was happy to step away from her. He wondered if his charity was not really charity at all. Perhaps he'd helped her, a smallish act of human goodness, as a way of dealing with a larger fear. What if this one explosion was only the first? How many more terrorists were walking the streets of Seattle? How many more suicide bombers were building bombs? There was no way of knowing. That information would be forever unknowable. He would sooner know if God were real.

While he was gone, she stood and looked around the apartment.

What a strange time for a self-guided tour! The front room was large, with exposed brick walls. Tasteful and anonymous two-sided prints hung suspended from the ceiling. Forming a sort of art curtain, they cut the room in half. Odd and beautiful, she thought. The bedroom was large enough for only an unmade bed and an end table stacked high with books. The bathroom was small as well, with a clean white sink, a toilet, and a shower. She'd never be able to live without a tub. But there were no guitars, no musical instruments of any kind. So maybe this chubby guy wasn't a bass player. She walked into the small kitchen where he stood quietly and stared out the window.

"What's going on?" she asked.

"I can see the smoke," he said.

She heard the sirens and the helicopters and the other human and machine noise. If anything, it was louder than it had been before. Nobody would sleep tonight.

"Here's your water," he said and handed her a full glass.

She drank it all in one swallow.

"You drink water like a man," he said.

"What does that mean?" she asked.

"I don't know," he said and laughed. She laughed with him. They were flirting. How could they flirt at a time like this? She's beautiful, he thought, and then he was ashamed of himself for noticing.

"I'm married," she said.

"Do you want to call him?" he asked, relieved that she'd established her barriers.

"No," she said. "I hate him."

"I'm sorry."

"I have children, too," she said. "Two sons."

Oh, man, he thought, maybe she was covered with her children's blood.

"They weren't in the restaurant with you, were they?" he asked.

"No, they're in school. And I told you, I wasn't in the restaurant when it happened."

"You're lying. I don't know why you're lying. But you are lying."

"If you think I'm a liar, then why did you bring me home?"

"I don't know. I thought you needed help."

"You thought you might help by getting me in bed, right?"

"No."

"Now who's lying?" she asked and walked back into the living room.

He followed her. "Listen," he said. "I think you might have hit your head or something. You're not talking right. I think you need to see a doctor."

"Maybe I talked like this before the bomb," she said. "Maybe I've always talked like this."

"But what about your husband and kids? Won't they be worried about you?"

"I told you, I hate my husband."

"But you can't hate him."

"A wife can't hate her husband? You can't be that naive, can you?"

"No, I was married."

She laughed. "You're funny," she said.

"I'm not trying to be funny," he said.

"Funny people don't have to try."

"Listen, forget all that. What about your kids?"

"They hate me more than I hate them."

"I don't believe that."

"You don't think a mother can hate her kids?"

"No, it's not that. Mothers aren't supposed to hate their kids."

"What kind of jerk are you?"

She threw her empty glass against the brick wall, and this second explosion was stronger for him than the first one. He was afraid of this woman and her possibilities.

"I don't want you to be here anymore," he said.

"I don't want to be anywhere," she said.

"No, really, I want you to leave now. If you don't leave, I'll call the cops."

"Yeah, and I'm sure they'll be here right away. I'm sure you'll be really high on their priority list."

"All right, I'll throw you out myself."

"Oh, aren't you the tough guy? Just like my husband. All you want to do is fight. All right, I fight him, I'll fight you."

She balled her hands into fists, but she stuck her thumbs inside. If she landed a punch, she'd break a thumb. He knew she'd never thrown a real punch in her life. She looked pathetic.

"Why are you smiling?" she asked.

"You're scared," he said. "I'm scared, too. I haven't been in a fight since third grade. And she beat me up. Her name was Susan. She broke my nose with her Snoopy lunch box."

Yes, she thought, this man is funny and smiles like a fragile little boy, as if he's slightly ashamed of his crooked teeth and crooked sense of humor. She dropped her fists and paced around the room. She felt an ineffable anxiety. She knew she needed to make plans, but she couldn't figure out what to do first.

"Listen," she said, "I'm sorry about being such a bitch."

"It's okay," he said. "Considering the circumstances, I think we're probably doing all right."

"Okay, okay, you're a good man. We need more good men in the world. How about we start over? How about we introduce ourselves and pretend like we just met?"

How could she say something so banal? What was wrong with her?

"Look at yourself," he said. "I don't think it's possible to start over."

She was covered with blood and dirt. She was surprised. How had she forgotten that? And why was she worried about this stranger's feelings? Again she wondered if she was crazy, if she was dreaming this whole day, if this man and his apartment were illusions.

"Hey," he said, "I've got a clean robe in the bathroom and clean towels. Why don't you take a shower, wash all that stuff away. How does that sound?"

Now he sounded trivial: Hey, the city is burning, but you'll feel so much better if you floss your teeth.

"You just want to get me naked," she said.

"You're very pretty, and I will admit I thought briefly about sex. But mass murder and suicide bombs sort of shrink the wonder wand, you know?"

She laughed again. She sat on the couch and laughed. She covered her face with a pillow and laughed. She threw the pillow at him and laughed. "You're so funny," she said.

"Come on," he said. "I was not trying to be funny. I was trying to tell you how I feel."

"Maybe everything you feel is funny," she said and wiped tears from her eyes.

"Maybe everything is funny to you," he said. "But you're crazy pussy, and I was married to crazy pussy before, and I have no real interest in getting near it again."

"Crazy pussy!" she shouted and laughed. She rolled off the couch onto the floor and laughed. "Nobody has ever called me crazy pussy!"

She lay facedown on the floor and laughed into the carpet. She cried and wailed and kicked and punched. She convulsed. He rolled her onto her side and held her head while she seized. When it was over, she inhaled deeply and fell asleep. He knew about seizures. When she woke, she'd feel like a buffalo had kicked her in the skull. He sat on the couch and stared down at her. God, he thought, I hope she doesn't die on my carpet. How would I explain that? He picked up the telephone and dialed 911, but all he heard was a busy signal. He tried again and again, ten, eleven, twelve times, but heard only that same awful busy signal each time. After looking up the general numbers for the police and fire departments in the Yellow Pages, he dialed them and heard more busy signals. He called individual precincts and firehouses, but nobody answered. He called hospitals and clinics and churches but couldn't get past the computerized answering machines. God, he thought, what a fragile world I live in. One building explodes, and the whole system falls apart. He was more afraid than he'd been before, but then he dialed another number he knew by rote.

"Domino's Pizza, how can I help you?"

How many times had this young man answered the telephone that way? Did he know how the tone of his voice completely changed the meaning of the words?

"Domino's Pizza, how can I help you?"

If the pizza guy repeated the question enough times, it might become a prayer.

"Domino's Pizza, how can I help you?"

"I can't believe you're open."

"Well, it's just me. Everybody else left. I stayed. I didn't know what else to do."

"You're not really going to deliver pizzas, are you?"

"I don't know. You're the first person to call since it happened."

"Isn't your family worried about you?"

"They know I'm okay. My dad told me to stay here and lock the door. He said I'd be safer here than trying to get home by myself."

"What are you going to do now?"

"I don't know. I'm scared. Do you think this is the start of World War Three?"

The pizza boy sounded like he was eighteen or nineteen years old. How could he know how many teenagers around the world had already survived bombings, and lived with the daily threat of more bombings, and still found courage enough to dance, sing, curse, and make love in the tall grass beside this or that river?

"Are you a cook or a driver?"

"I'm both."

"Well, kid, I've got a great idea. Why don't you start making pizzas? Make as many as you can and stack them high. A whole bunch of hungry people will be wandering the streets. Put a sign in the window that says, 'Free Pizza for Rescue Workers!,' and you'll be a hero."

"I don't think the corporate office will like that."

"Forget the corporate office."

Surely this young man was incapable of socialistic rebellion, no matter how smart or self-contained.

"What did you say?" the pizza boy asked.

"The city's on fire. Make the pizzas. Forget the corporate office."

The young man thought about it.

"Yeah, you're right," he said. "Forget the corporate office."

"I can't hear you."

"Forget the corporate office."

"What did you say?"

"Forget the corporate office."

"That sounds good, but your language, it's not acceptable."

"What do you mean, sir?"

"'Forget' is not a powerful verb."

"I don't know about that, sir. I feel pretty bad when somebody forgets about me."

"You're right. That's a fairly wise thing to say. But there is a more powerful verb, a more powerful F-word."

"Oh, sir," he said, "I can't say that word. That's cursing. And I'm a Christian."

He was a Christian working for an international conglomerate and worried about foul language?

"All right, then, pizza man, you have your mission. Forget the other F-word and forget the corporate office. Make those free pizzas."

"Yes, sir."

He hung up the phone, laughed at the ceiling, then looked down at the crazy woman lying on the floor. She stared back at him.

"What did you just do?" she asked.

"I think I started a pepperoni and double-cheese revolution," he said. She laughed and winced. "Oh, man," she said. "My head hurts."

"You had a seizure," he said.

"I know. I was sort of having it and watching me have it at the same time."

For years, she'd been living a binary life as participant and eye-witness. She'd been so bored and unhappy, and so objective about her boredom and unhappiness, that she'd been conducting social experiments on her family. Last July, she'd served dinner five minutes later than usual, an innocuous change in the family ceremony. But the next evening, she'd served dinner ten minutes later than usual, and then fifteen minutes later than usual the night after that, and so on and so on. By the end of the month, she was serving the meat and potatoes as the eleven o'clock *SportsCenter* was beginning. Her husband and sons had never once uttered a comment or complaint about the gradual and profound change in dinnertime. How could they be so compliant and disinterested? How could they be so dependent on her and so unaware of her blatant manipulations? As they'd eaten and cursed at the football and hockey highlights, she'd studied the man and two boys, her personal space aliens, and couldn't believe all three of them had spent significant time in her womb.

Now she lay on the floor of a stranger's apartment, ambivalent about her life. Maybe she could lie on that floor forever. Maybe she could ossify or fossilize. Maybe she could change into a bizarre coffee table. As a piece of furniture, she might feel valued and useful. She closed her eyes and wondered if the other furniture would come to accept and love her.

"Wake up!" he shouted at her.

"I'm very tired," she said.

"I bet you have a concussion or something," he said. "We should get you to the doctor. But the thing is, I'm going to have to take you there. The phones aren't working. I can order a pizza, but I can't order an ambulance."

"I don't think I'd be able to walk very far. Not for a while. I need to rest first."

"Okay, but if you seize again, I'm going to pick you up and carry you there, okay? It's about a mile up to Harborview. I'll drag you there if I have to."

"I don't think I'm going to seize again."

"You don't know that."

"I'm pretty sure it's not going to happen again."

"You're the one lying on the floor. I don't think that says much for your psychic ability."

"Have you always been funny?" she asked.

"Yes," he said. His sense of humor had destroyed his marriage. With each joke, he'd punched a hole in his ex-wife's heart. But he couldn't help it. His entire family was hilarious and inappropriate. During his wedding, as his soon-to-be wife walked up the aisle toward him, his little brother had loudly told an AIDS joke. How grotesque was that? If his wife had been smarter and less in love, she would have turned around and fled the church. But she'd believed her soon-to-be husband was better than his homophobic and racist and wildly stupid brother, and when her husband proved to be kinder and more progressive but just as wildly stupid, she'd felt cheated.

On the night his wife had signed their divorce papers, she called him up and cursed him. She was drunk and lonely and enraged.

"All right, Mr. Funny!" she had yelled. "Let's see how long you can go without telling a joke! How long! How long, Mr. Funny?"

"About seven seconds," he'd said after seven seconds of silence.

She'd cried and cursed him again and hung up the phone. He'd sat alone in the dark and wondered how he could so easily hurt a woman he loved. Why was it more necessary for him to tell a joke than to acknowledge her pain?

And now, two years after his divorce, he stared down at the strange woman lying on his floor and wondered if she'd been delivered to him as punishment for his sins. Maybe God hated jokesters. Or maybe she was a test. Maybe he could prove his worth by helping her, by saving her. Maybe God was giving him a chance to be serious and reverential.

"My ex-wife used to call me Mr. Funny," he said.

"That's a cute name," she said.

"It wasn't meant as a compliment."

"All right, Mr. Funny, let me rest here for a little while, and then you can take me to the hospital."

"It's a deal. But I'm not going to let you sleep. You're going to stay awake. So you better start talking."

"What should I talk about?"

"Tell me about your husband and kids."

"I hate them."

"You already told me that. Tell me why you hate them."

She didn't talk for a few moments. He nudged her with his foot. "Talk," he said.

"Where were you on September eleventh?" she asked.

"On September eleventh, when I was seventeen, I lost my virginity to a girl named Atlanta."

"Always the wise guy. You know what day I'm talking about."

"On that September eleventh, I was working."

"What do you do?"

"I design computer games."

"If you design computer games, why don't you have a computer in your apartment?"

"What are you, a detective?"

"I'm good with details."

"It's a boundary thing. I want my work life and my home life to be separate."

"How's that going for you?"

"I'm never here."

"That must be fun."

"It was until the eleventh. I was working on the final stages of a terrorist game. A first-person shooter."

"What's a first-person shooter?"

"You see through the eyes of the gunman."

"You get to shoot terrorists? Must have been a big seller."

"In our game, you play a terrorist who shoots civilians. You can attack a shopping mall, an Ivy League college, or the World Trade Center."

"Oh, God, that's disgusting."

"We spent hundreds of thousands of dollars to develop and manufacture it. Even before the eleventh, we figured that kind of game would be controversial. We figured it would get tons of press, and every dumbass rebel teenager would have to own it. We were looking forward to the censorship and the lawsuits. We were manufacturing units based on how much negative publicity we estimated we'd receive."

"How could you live with yourself?"

"We redesigned the game after the eleventh. Now you play a cop who hunts terrorists in a shopping mall or a college. We dropped the World Trade Center completely."

"And that's supposed to make it all better?"

"We've presold ten million copies. I'm going to be very rich."

"It's blood money."

"All money is blood money."

"Is that what you tell yourself so you can sleep at night?"

"For a few days after the eleventh, I thought about suiciding. I thought about going up to the top of the Space Needle and jumping off. I figured it would be appropriate for me to die that way."

"There's a bunch of people who would have helped you jump."

"Yeah, but it was all about self-pity. I mean, I'm alive, right? Think about how many people died in the World Trade Center. It took Giuliani how many hours to read all the names?"

"There were about twenty-five hundred of them."

"Yeah, twenty-five hundred innocent people dead, and me, a living, breathing coward."

"A millionaire coward," she said.

On September 11, she'd been collating files in the law firm's library when the first plane hit the first tower. When the second plane hit the second tower, she'd been watching it on the conference room television along with the entire firm, forty-five white-collar professionals who watched with equal parts revulsion and excitement. She remembered how, when the first tower collapsed, she'd closed her eyes and listened to her colleagues' anguished moans and wondered why they sounded so erotic. We're so used to sex on TV that everything on TV becomes sexy, she thought. Their law offices were on the sixtieth floor of the Columbia Center. From the conference room windows, all of the lawyers and staff had at one point or another looked south and watched airplanes arrive and depart from Boeing Airfield and Sea-Tac Airport. After the tower collapsed, she'd looked out the window after somebody screamed the fearsome question they'd all been asking themselves—*What if they hit us?*—and she'd almost seen a passenger jet cutting through the sky. Everybody else in the conference room must have seen their own illusory jets, because they'd all panicked as a group and run screaming out of the room, down sixty flights of stairs and onto the streets below. She'd stayed in the conference room. She'd walked to the window and waited for her airplane to come. She'd wondered if she would be able to see the pilot's face, and perhaps recognize him, before he destroyed her. And she'd wondered, as she waited to die, if some other unhappy woman or man had stood in a World Trade Center window that morning and committed suicide by inertia.

"You know," she said, "I don't think everybody who died in the towers was innocent."

"Who are you?" he asked. "Osama's press agent?"

"Those towers were filled with bankers and stockbrokers and lawyers. How honest do you think they were?"

"They didn't deserve to die."

"Think about it. Maybe they did deserve to die. Open your mind."

"It's tough to be open-minded about this stuff."

"But you've got to be. You can let any event have one meaning, right? Your games don't have one meaning, do they?"

"No."

"All right, then, maybe September eleventh means things nobody has thought of yet."

"You've thought of other meanings, right?"

"Yes, I have. So listen to this. Let's say twelve hundred men died that day. How many of those guys were cheating on their wives? A few hundred, probably. How many of them were beating their kids? One hundred more, right? Don't you think one of those bastards was raping his kids? Don't you think, somewhere in the towers, there was an evil bastard who sneaked into his daughter's bedroom at night and raped her in the ass?"

He couldn't believe she was doing this math, this moral addition and subtraction, this terrible algebra. He wondered if God would kill thousands of good people in order to destroy one monster. He wondered if he was a monster, making the games he made and earning the money he earned. Ha, ha, he thought, but I'm Mr. Funny. I'm the highlight of every party. I'm the best dinner guest in the history of the world. I can make any woman fall in love with me in under five minutes and alienate her five minutes later.

"I'm not some wimpy liberal or anything," he said. "I believe in capital punishment. I believe in the necessity of war. But I don't think anybody deserves to die."

"You're contradicting yourself."

"Fine, then I'm a contradiction, but at least I admit that. You're talking about these things like you know more than the rest of us. Like you're absolutely right."

"Somebody has to be right," she said and tried to sit up but could only fall back and close her eyes against the nausea.

"Are you okay?" he asked, happy she was quiet for a moment. How could she say the things she was saying? Wasn't she afraid of God?

"I'm just dizzy," she said. "If I keep my eyes open, I'm going to vomit."

"You've got a concussion, I told you. I'm sure of it. We've got to get you to the hospital."

"No, you wanted to talk, and we're going to talk. I'm going to tell you everything, and you're going to listen, and then you're going to take me to the hospital."

"I don't want to hear the things you're saying."

"That's the problem. Nobody wants to hear these things, but I'm thinking them, and I have to say them."

He stood and walked around the room. He wondered if he was supposed to ignore this woman. Maybe that was the lesson he was supposed to learn. Words were dangerous. His nouns and verbs had destroyed his marriage and created a game that mocked the dead. Her story seemed more potentially destructive than any bomb or game he could create or imagine.

"Are you going to listen to me?" she asked.

"Talk," he said.

"All right, all right," she said. "Didn't you get sick of all the news about the Trade Center? Didn't you get exhausted by all the stories and TV shows and sad faces and politicians and memorials and books? It was awful and obscene, all of it, it was grief porn."

"I got so tired of it, I picked up my TV, carried it down the stairs, and threw it in the Dumpster."

"That's exactly what you should have done. I wished I could do it. But my husband and my sons—they're twins, they're both sixteen—watched that garbage every day. My husband put U.S. flags in every window of our house. What kind of Indians put twenty-two flags in their windows?"

Her husband had been a champion powwow fancydancer when she'd met him, a skinny, beautiful, feminine boy who moved in bright-feathered circles, but he'd become a tired grunting old man. And a patriot! He'd already talked the twins into joining the marines when they graduated from high school.

"Hey, Ma," they'd said in their dual grating voices. "The marines will pay for college. Isn't that great?"

Jesus, she was raising two wanna-be marines. How could any Indian put on an U.S. military uniform and not die of toxic irony? Hell, she hadn't let her boys play with toy guns when they were little, and now her husband took them on three hunting trips a year. She lived in a house with deer antlers mounted on the walls. Antlers and flags! Antlers and flags! Antlers and flags! Men have walked on the moon and written *Hamlet* and painted the Sistine Chapel and played the piano like Glenn Gould, she thought, and other men still have the need to hang antlers and flags on their walls. She wondered why anybody was surprised when men crashed jets into buildings.

"Nobody is innocent, right?" she said. "Isn't that what all of the holy books say? We're all sinners? But after the Trade Center, it was all about the innocent victims, all the innocent victims, and I kept thinking—I *knew* one of those guys in the towers was raping his daughter. Raping her. Maybe he was raping his son, too. And beating his wife. I think about that morning, and I wonder if the bastard was smiling when he hopped on a train for work. I think about his daughter and son sitting in some generic and heartless suburban classroom, just sad and broken and dying inside. And his wife sitting at home dying inside. That bastard gets off his train and walks up to his office on the hundred and seventh floor or something, and everybody loves him there. He's a hero at work. And Mr. Hero is sitting at his desk, smiling and being heroic, when that airplane flies straight into his office. Flies right through the window and obliterates him, completely disappears him. And the news travels, right? The wife turns on the television and sees the towers burning, and the teachers wheel televisions into the classrooms, and the son and daughter watch the towers burning. The wife and kids count the floors, right? They count all the way up to the hundred and seventh floor, and they see it burning, and they're happy, right? They're hopeful, right? Aren't they hopeful? Then the first tower comes down. Both towers come down. And the wife is jumping up and down at home. She's celebrating. But the kids have to stay calm, because they're in public, you know, but inside they're jumping up and down like their mom. They run home, and all three of them sit in the living room together and watch the news, and they wait. Yeah, they wait for him to come home. The news is talking about the survivors, right? About the people who made it out. And the wife and kids are praying to God he died. That he burned to death or jumped out a window or was running down the stairs when the tower fell. They sit in the living room for three days, waiting for him to come home, and then they wait for three more days, waiting for him to come home, and on the seventh day, they realize he isn't coming home. He's dead and they're happy. The monster is gone and they're celebrating. They dance around the living room and sing songs and dance dances and they're happy. Don't you think all of this is possible? Don't you think there was at least one man in the towers who deserved to die? Don't you think there's a wife and kids who are happy he died? Don't you think there's some daughter walking around who whispers Osama's name with tenderness and affection? Don't you think there's a wife out there who thanks God or Allah or the devil for Osama's rage?"

She wept. He sat on the floor beside her and held her head in his lap. He stroked her hair until she calmed down.

"We're going to go now," he said. "I'm going to take you to the hospital, okay?"

"Wait, wait," she said. "There's more."

"I don't want to hear it," he said. "I don't want to hear these things. I don't want to think about them. I don't want to remember them."

"Please," she whispered. "Please listen to me."

She was desperate. She needed him. He wanted to be needed. He nodded.

"The thing is," she said, "the biggest thing is, ever since the Trade Center fell down, I've been hoping it would happen to me. I kept hoping I'd be at work or in some shopping mall or theater when it blew up. So when that bomber ran inside the restaurant and shouted at us, I was happy. I knew God had answered my prayers. I knew I was going to survive. I was going to live, and I was going to crawl out of the ruins, and I was going to walk away from my life. I knew they'd never find me and would figure I was dead. They'd mark me down as dead, but I'd be alive. I'd be so alive, and I'd walk away. I'd walk away and start a new life, a better life. I was going to escape."

How could anyone be so unhappy? How could anybody survive so much pain and loneliness? But these questions were inadequate, he knew, and he was inadequate. She needed him to be a good man, and he had never been that, not once in his life. He pushed her away and ran for the bathroom. But he was not fast enough and vomited on the living room carpet.

"It's awful," he said. "It's so awful."

"I'm sorry," she said. "I'm so sorry. I am, I am."

"What am I supposed to do?"

"Take me to the hospital. Make sure I'm safe, and you never have to see me again. Promise you'll take me to the hospital. Promise me I'll be safe."

Stronger than he knew, he picked her up like a child and carried her out the door and down three flights of stairs. Curled in his arms, she cried and prayed. Through the crowded and hectic streets, he carried her. All around them, men and women and children stared up into the skies and waited for death to swoop down and claim them. He looked at those strangers and knew each of them lived with terrible secrets. He knew that man cheated on his wife with her sister and that woman pinched her Alzheimered mother's arms until they bled. And that teenage boy set dogs on fire and that pretty teenage girl once knocked down a fat ugly girl and spit in her mouth. And he knew that father had two sons, one who couldn't read and one who wore dresses, and he made them punch each other because they were stupid and weak. And there was a white grandmother who hated her Mexican grandchildren and a priest who burned himself with cigarettes whenever he dreamed about sex with little boys. And that man had abandoned his wife and children and didn't know they were now living in a car, and that woman hadn't talked to her father in fifteen years and didn't know he was now dying of prostate cancer. And none of these people, not one of them, had loved any of the others well enough. Failures, he thought, we're all failures. Carrying the woman, he walked among these sinners, the obese and the vain, the intolerant and the selfish, the liars and thieves, the wasteful and the avaricious. And wasn't he the greatest sinner? Wasn't he more dangerous to the people who loved him than any terrorist could ever be? Wasn't he the man who failed the woman who'd loved him most? Didn't he explode her life and burn her to the ground? Right now, somewhere in the world, wasn't she still grieving the death of their marriage and the death of some large part of her? Forgive me, God, oh, forgive me, he thought as he carried this other exploded woman. If he could save her, he hoped he might be saved. But she wanted to escape. She pushed and pulled against his grip and he set her down. Everything smelled of smoke and fire. She kissed him hard and touched his face. He wanted to talk, to say the words that would free her. But he was silent and she was silent. And wasn't silence more ambiguous and terrifying than anything else? Loose-limbed, he trembled. He wanted to love her, and he wanted his love to be bittersweet and irrepressible. He wanted his love to be different than everybody else's. He wanted his love to be the only true image of God. He wanted his love to be the tyrant that saved the world no matter if the world desired to be saved. He wanted his love to be the wine and bread, and the blood and flesh. He reached for her, a dangerous stranger in a city of dangerous strangers, but she turned away from him and walked unsteadily through the crowd. How many loveless people walk among the barely loved? She looked back once, and he thought to chase after her, but she shook her head, and again walked away from him. And he watched her until he couldn't see her anymore.

DO NOT GO GENTLE

My wife and I didn't know Mr. Grief in person until our baby boy got his face stuck between his mattress and crib and suffocated himself blue. He died three times that day, Mr. Grief squeezing his lungs tight, but the muscular doctors and nurses battled that suffocating monster man and brought our boy back to life three times. He was our little blue baby Jesus.

I'm lying. Our baby wasn't Jesus. Our baby was alive only a little bit. Mostly he was dead and slept his way through a coma. In Children's Hospital, our baby was hooked up to a million dollars' worth of machines that breathed, pissed, and pooped for him. I bet you could line up all of my wife's and my grandmothers and grandfathers and aunts and uncles and brothers and sisters and mothers and fathers and first, second, and third cousins, and rob their wallets and purses, and maybe you'd collect about $512.

Mr. Grief was a billionaire. He could afford to check on our baby every six hours, but every six hours, my wife and I cussed him out and sent him running. My wife is beautiful and powerful and only twenty-five years old, but she is magic like a grandmother, and Indian grandmothers aren't afraid of a little man like Mr. Grief.

One night, while I guarded over our baby, my wife wrapped her braids in a purple bandana, shoved her hands into thick work clothes, sneaked up on Mr. Grief in the hallway, and beat him severely about the head and shoulders like she was Muhammad Ali.

When you're hurting, it feels good to hurt somebody else. But you have to be careful. If you get addicted to the pain-causing, then you start hurting people who don't need hurting. If you turn into a pain-delivering robot, then you start thinking everybody looks like Mr. Grief and everybody deserves a beating.

One day when my wife was crying, I swear I saw Mr. Grief hiding behind her eyes. So I yelled and screamed at her and called her all of the bad names. But I got really close to her to yell, because it's more effective to yell when you're closer to your enemy, and I smelled her true scent. I knew it was only my wife inside my wife, because she smelled like tenderness, and Mr. Grief smells like a porcupine rotting dead on the side of the road.

My wife and I didn't even name our baby. We were Indians and didn't want to carry around too much hope. Hope eats your flesh like a spider bite. But my wife and I loved our little Baby X and took turns sitting beside his bed and singing to him. The nurses and doctors let us bring in our hand drums, so we sang powwow songs to our baby. I'm a pretty good singer, and my wife is the best there is, and crowds always gathered to listen to us, and that made us feel good.

It was great to feel good about something, because my wife and I were all the way grieving. We took turns singing honor songs and falling asleep. Mr. Grief is a wizard who puts sleep spells on you. My wife spent more time sleeping than I did. I figure she was sadder because she had carried our baby inside her womb and had memorized the way he moved.

One day about a week after our baby fell into his coma, it was me who fell into a waking sleep in a hospital bathroom. Sitting on the bowl, pants wrapped around my ankles, I couldn't move. I was awake and paralyzed by the deadly venom of the grief snake. I wondered if I was going to die right there in that terrible and shameful and hilarious way. I don't want to die like Elvis, I kept saying to myself like it was a prayer.

But right then, when I was ready to roll onto the floor and crawl my way to safety like a grief soldier under grief fire, I heard two other sad men come walking into the bathroom. Those men didn't know I was trapped on the toilet, so they spoke freely and honestly about some sad woman.

"Did you see that woman?" asked man #1.

"You mean the fat one in sweatpants?" asked man #2.

"Yeah, can you believe how terrible she looked? I know our kids are sick, but that doesn't mean we have to let ourselves go like that."

"If you let yourself get ugly on the outside, you're gonna feel even worse on the inside."

"Yeah, what are your kids gonna think when they see you looking so bad?"

"They're gonna be sad."

"And things are sad enough without having to look at your fat mom wearing ugly sweatpants."

"The worst part is, that woman's kid, he isn't even that sick. He isn't terminal. He's only on the third floor."

"Yeah, put her kid on the fourth floor with our kids, and let's see how ugly she gets then."

Listening to their awfulness, I found the strength to stand and walk out of the stall. They were shocked to see me, and they went all quiet and silent and still and frozen. They were ashamed of themselves, I guess, for building a secret clubhouse out of the two-by-four boards and ten-penny nails of their pain. I could be deadly serious and deadly funny at the same time, so I washed my hands really slow, making sure each finger was cleaner than the finger before. I dried them even slower, using one towel for each hand. And then I looked at those two men. I studied the angles and shapes of them like I was taking a geometry test.

I almost yelled at them. I wanted to scream at them for being as shallow and dirty as a dog dish. But hell, their kids were dying. What else were they going to do but punish the world for it? A father with a sick child is an angry god. I know I would have earthquaked Los Angeles, Paris, and Rome, and killed a million innocent people, if it guaranteed my baby boy would rise back to his full life.

But that whole bathroom crazy-scene gave me some energy. I don't know why. I can't explain it. I felt like a good woman and I wanted to be a good mother-man. So I left the hospital and went out shopping for baby toys. The hospital was on Fifteenth and John, and over the past few days, on my journey between home and hospital, I'd been driving past a toy store over on Pike and Seventh. It was called Toys in Babeland, and that was a cute name, so I figured I'd buy some stuffed teddy bears and a rattle and maybe some of those black-and-white toys the experts say are good for babies' eyes. Those seemed like good toy ideas, but I wasn't sure. What kind of toys do you buy, exactly, for a coma baby? I walked over to the store and strolled in, feeling religious about my mission, and shocked myself to discover Toys in Babeland was a sex-toy store.

"Honey," I said to my wife later, "those women were selling vibrators and dildos and edible underwear and butt plugs and lubricants and some stuff I had no idea what the hell you were supposed to do with it. Sweetheart," I said to her, "some of those sex toys looked like a genius and a crazy scientist made them." Now, I was surely embarrassed, but I'm not a prude, so I browsed around, not expecting to buy anything but not wanting to run out of the store like a frightened Christian. Then I turned the corner and saw it, the vibrator they call Chocolate Thunder.

"Darling," I said to my wife later, "I heard that big old music from that *2001: Space Odyssey* movie when I saw that miracle vibrator."

Chocolate Thunder was dark brown and fifteen inches long and needed a nine-volt battery. I like to think my indigenous penis is powerful. But it would take a whole war party of Indian men to equal up to one Chocolate Thunder. I was shy but quick to buy the thing and ran back to the hospital with it. I ran into the fourth-floor ICU, pulled Chocolate Thunder out of its box, held it up in the air like a magic wand, and switched it on.

Of course, all the doctors and nurses and mothers and fathers were half stunned by that vibrator. And it was a strange and difficult thing. It was sex that made our dying babies, and here was a huge old piece of buzzing sex I was trying to cast spells with. I waved it over our baby and ran around the room waving it over the other sick babies. I was laughing and hooting, and other folks were laughing and hooting, and a few others didn't know what the hell to do. But pretty soon everybody was taking their turn casting spells with Chocolate Thunder. Maybe it was blasphemous, and maybe it was stupid and useless, but we all were sick and tired of waiting for our babies to die. We wanted our babies to live, and we were ready to try anything to help them live. Maybe some people can get by with quiet prayers, but I wanted to shout and scream and vibrate. So did plenty of other fathers and mothers in that sickroom.

It was my wife who grabbed Chocolate Thunder and used it like a drumstick to pound her hand drum. She sang a brand-new song that echoed up and down the hallways of Children's Hospital. Every sick and dying and alive and dead kid heard it, and they were happy and good in their hearts. My wife sang the most beautiful song anybody ever heard in that place. She sang like ten thousand Indian grandmothers rolled into one mother. All the while, Chocolate Thunder sang with her and turned the whole thing into a healing duet.

We humans are too simpleminded. We all like to think each person, place, or thing is only itself. A vibrator is a vibrator is a vibrator, right? But that's not true at all. Everything is stuffed to the brim with ideas and love and hope and magic and dreams. I brought Chocolate Thunder back to the hospital, but it was my magical and faithful wife who truly believed it was going to bring our baby back to us. She wanted it to bring every baby back to life. Over the next week, my wife sat beside our baby's bed and held that vibrator in her two hands and sang and prayed along with its buzzing. She used up the energy of two batteries, and maybe our baby would have woken up anyway, and a few other babies never did wake up at all, but my wife still believes our son heard the magic call of Chocolate Thunder and couldn't resist it. Our beautiful, beautiful boy opened his eyes and smiled, even if he was too young to smile, but I think sick kids get old and wise and funny very fast.

And so my wife and I named him Abraham and carried him home and lay him in his crib and hung Chocolate Thunder from the ceiling above him like a crazy mobile and laughed and laughed with the joy of it. We deported Mr. Grief back to his awful country. Our baby boy was going to live a long and good life. We wondered aloud what we would tell our Abraham about the wondrous world when he was old enough to wonder about it.

FLIGHT PATTERNS

At 5:05 A.M., Patsy Cline fell loudly to pieces on William's clock radio. He hit the snooze button, silencing lonesome Patsy, and dozed for fifteen more minutes before Donna Fargo bragged about being the happiest girl in the whole USA. William wondered what had ever happened to Donna Fargo, whose birth name was the infinitely more interesting Yvonne Vaughn, and wondered *why* he knew Donna Fargo's birth name. Ah, he was the bemused and slightly embarrassed owner of a twenty-first-century American mind. His intellect was a big comfy couch stuffed with sacred and profane trivia. He knew the names of all nine of Elizabeth Taylor's husbands and could quote from memory the entire Declaration of Independence. William knew Donna Fargo's birth name because he *wanted* to know her birth name. He wanted to know all of the great big and tiny little American details. He didn't want to choose between Ernie Hemingway and the Spokane tribal elders, between Mia Hamm and Crazy Horse, between *The Heart Is a Lonely Hunter* and Chief Dan George. William wanted all of it. Hunger was his crime. As for dear Miss Fargo, William figured she probably played the Indian casino circuit along with the Righteous Brothers, Smokey Robinson, Eddie Money, Pat Benatar, RATT, REO

Speedwagon, and dozens of other formerly famous rock- and country-music stars. Many of the Indian casino acts were bad, and most of the rest were pure nostalgic entertainment, but a small number made beautiful and timeless music. William knew the genius Merle Haggard played thirty or forty Indian casinos every year, so long live Haggard and long live tribal economic sovereignty. Who cares about fishing and hunting rights? Who cares about uranium mines and nuclear-waste-dump sites on sacred land? Who cares about the recovery of tribal languages? Give me Freddy Fender singing "Before the Next Teardrop Falls" in English and Spanish to 206 Spokane Indians, William thought, and I will be a happy man.

But William wasn't happy this morning. He'd slept poorly—he always slept poorly—and wondered again if his insomnia was a physical or a mental condition. His doctor had offered him sleeping-pill prescriptions, but William declined for philosophical reasons. He was an Indian who didn't smoke or drink or eat processed sugar. He lifted weights three days a week, ran every day, and competed in four triathlons a year. A two-mile swim, a 150-mile bike ride, and a full marathon. A triathlon was a religious quest. If Saint Francis were still around, he'd be a triathlete. Another exaggeration! Theological hyperbole! Rabid self-justification! Diagnostically speaking, William was an obsessive-compulsive workaholic who was afraid of pills. So he suffered sleepless nights and constant daytime fatigue.

This morning, awake and not awake, William turned down the radio, changing Yvonne Vaughn's celebratory anthem into whispered blues, and rolled off the couch onto his hands and knees. His back and legs were sore because he'd slept on the living room couch so the alarm wouldn't disturb his wife and daughter upstairs. Still on his hands and knees, William stretched his spine, using the twelve basic exercises he'd learned from Dr. Adams, that master practitioner of white middle-class chiropractic voodoo. This was all part of William's regular morning ceremony. Other people find God in ornate ritual, but William called out to Geronimo, Jesus Christ, Saint Therese, Buddha, Allah, Billie Holiday, Simon Ortiz, Abe Lincoln, Bessie Smith, Howard Hughes, Leslie Marmon Silko, Joan of Arc and Joan of Collins, John Woo, Wilma Mankiller, and Karl and Groucho Marx while he pumped out fifty push-ups and fifty abdominal crunches. William wasn't particularly religious; he was generally religious. Finished with his morning calisthenics, William showered in the basement, suffering the water that was always too cold down there, and threaded his long black hair into two tight braids— the indigenous businessman's tonsorial special—and dressed in his best travel suit, a navy three-button pinstripe he'd ordered online. He'd worried about the fit, but his tailor was a magician and had only mildly chastised William for such an impulsive purchase. After knotting his blue paisley tie, purchased in person and on sale, William walked upstairs in bare feet and kissed his wife, Marie, good-bye.

"Cancel your flight," she said. "And come back to bed."

"You're supposed to be asleep," he said.

She was a small and dark woman who seemed to be smaller and darker at that time of the morning. Her long black hair had once again defeated its braids, but she didn't care. She sometimes went two or three days without brushing it. William was obsessive about his mane, tying and retying his ponytail, knotting and reknotting his braids, experimenting with this shampoo and that conditioner. He greased down his cowlicks (inherited from a cowlicked father and grandfather) with shiny pomade, but Marie's hair was always unkempt, wild, and renegade. William's hair hung around the fort, but Marie's rode on the warpath! She constantly pulled stray strands out of her mouth. William loved her for it. During sex, they spent as much time readjusting her hair as they did readjusting positions. Such were the erotic dangers of loving a Spokane Indian woman.

"Take off your clothes and get in bed," Marie pleaded now.

"I can't do that," William said. "They're counting on me."

"Oh, the plane will be filled with salesmen. Let some other salesman sell what you're selling."

"Your breath stinks."

"So do my feet, my pits, and my butt, but you still love me. Come back to bed, and I'll make it worth your while."

William kissed Marie, reached beneath her pajama top, and squeezed her breasts. He thought about reaching inside her pajama bottoms. She wrapped her arms and legs around him and tried to wrestle him into bed. Oh, God, he wanted to climb into bed and make love. He wanted to fornicate, to sex, to breed, to screw, to make the beast with two backs. *Oh, sweetheart, be my little synonym!* He wanted her to be both subject and object. Perhaps it was wrong (and unavoidable) to objectify female strangers, but shouldn't every husband seek to objectify his wife at least once a day? William loved and respected his wife, and delighted in her intelligence, humor, and kindness, but he also loved to watch her lovely ass when she walked, and stare down the front of her loose shirts when she leaned over, and grab her breasts at wildly inappropriate times—during dinner parties and piano recitals and uncontrolled intersections, for instance. He constantly made passes at her, not necessarily expecting to be successful, but to remind her he still desired her and was excited by the thought of her. She was his passive and active.

"Come on," she said. "If you stay home, I'll make you Scooby."

He laughed at the inside joke, created one night while he tried to give her sexual directions and was so aroused that he sounded exactly like Scooby-Doo.

"Stay home, stay home, stay home," she chanted and wrapped herself tighter around him. He was supporting all of her weight, holding her two feet off the bed.

"I'm not strong enough to do this," he said.

"Baby, baby, I'll make you strong," she sang, and it sounded like she was writing a Top 40 hit in the Brill Building, circa 1962. How could he leave a woman who sang like that? He hated to leave, but he loved his work. He was a man, and men needed to work. More sexism! More masculine tunnel vision! More need for gender-sensitivity workshops! He pulled away from her, dropping her back onto the bed, and stepped away.

"Willy Loman," she said, "you must pay attention to me."

"I love you," he said, but she'd already fallen back to sleep—a narcoleptic gift William envied—and he wondered if she would dream about a man who never left her, about some unemployed agoraphobic Indian warrior who liked to cook and wash dishes.

William tiptoed into his daughter's bedroom, expecting to hear her light snore, but she was awake and sitting up in bed, and looked so magical and androgynous with her huge brown eyes and crew-cut hair. She'd wanted to completely shave her head: *I don't want long hair, I don't want short hair, I don't want hair at all, and I don't want to be a girl or a boy, I want to be a yellow and orange leaf some little kid picks up and pastes in his scrapbook.*

"Daddy," she said.

"Grace," he said. "You should be asleep. You have school today."

"I know," she said. "But I wanted to see you before you left."

"Okay," said William as he kissed her forehead, nose, and chin. "You've seen me. Now go back to sleep. I love you and I'm going to miss you."

She fiercely hugged him.

"Oh," he said. "You're such a lovely, lovely girl."

Preternaturally serious, she took his face in her eyes and studied his eyes. Morally examined by a kindergartner!

"Daddy," she said. "Go be silly for those people far away."

She cried as William left her room. Already quite sure he was only an adequate husband, he wondered, as he often did, if he was a bad father. During these mornings, he felt generic and violent, like some caveman leaving the fire to hunt animals in the cold and dark. Maybe his hands were smooth and clean, but they felt bloody.

Downstairs, he put on his socks and shoes and overcoat and listened for his daughter's crying, but she was quiet, having inherited her mother's gift for instant sleep. She had probably fallen back into one of her odd little dreams. While he was gone, she often drew pictures of those dreams, coloring the sky green and the grass blue—everything backward and wrong—and had once sketched a man in a suit crashing an airplane into the bright yellow sun. Ah, the rage, fear, and loneliness of a five-year-old, simple and true! She'd been especially afraid since September 11 of the previous year and constantly quizzed William about what he would do if terrorists hijacked his plane.

"I'd tell them I was your father," he'd said to her before he left for his last business trip. "And they'd stop being bad."

"You're lying," she'd said. "I'm not supposed to listen to liars. If you lie to me, I can't love you."

He couldn't argue with her logic. Maybe she was the most logical person on the planet. Maybe she should be illegally elected president of the United States.

William understood her fear of flying and of his flight. He was afraid of flying, too, but not of terrorists. After the horrible violence of September 11, he figured hijacking was no longer a useful weapon in the terrorist arsenal. These days, a terrorist armed with a box cutter would be torn to pieces by all of the coach-class passengers and fed to the first-class upgrades. However, no matter how much he tried to laugh his fear away, William always scanned the airports and airplanes for little brown guys who reeked of fundamentalism. That meant William was equally afraid of Osama bin Laden and Jerry Falwell wearing the last vestiges of a summer tan. William himself was a little brown guy, so the other travelers were always sniffing around him, but he smelled only of Dove soap, Mennen deodorant, and sarcasm. Still, he understood why people were afraid of him, a brown-skinned man with dark hair and eyes. If Norwegian terrorists had exploded the World Trade Center, then blue-eyed blondes would be viewed with more suspicion. Or so he hoped.

Locking the front door behind him, William stepped away from his house, carried his garment bag and briefcase onto the front porch, and waited for his taxi to arrive. It was a cold and foggy October morning. William could smell the saltwater of Elliott Bay and the freshwater of Lake Washington. Surrounded by gray water and gray fog and gray skies and gray mountains and a gray sun, he'd lived with his family in Seattle for three years and loved it. He couldn't imagine living anywhere else, with any other wife or child, in any other time.

William was tired and happy and romantic and exaggerating the size of his familial devotion so he could justify his departure, so he could survive his departure. He did sometimes think about other women and other possible lives with them. He wondered how his life would have been different if he'd married a white woman and fathered half-white children who grew up to complain and brag about their biracial identities: *Oh, the only box they have for me is Other! I'm not going to check any box! I'm not the Other! I am Tiger Woods!* But William most often fantasized about being single and free to travel as often as he wished—maybe two million miles a year—and how much he'd enjoy the benefits of being a platinum frequent flier. Maybe he'd have one-night stands with a long series of traveling saleswomen, all of them thousands of miles away from husbands and children who kept looking up "feminism" in the dictionary. William knew that was yet another sexist thought. In this capitalistic and democratic culture, talented women should also enjoy the freedom to emotionally and physically abandon their families. After all, talented and educated men have been doing it for generations. Let freedom ring!

Marie had left her job as a corporate accountant to be a full-time mother to Grace. William loved his wife for making the decision, and he tried to do his share of the housework, but he suspected he was an old-fashioned bastard who wanted his wife to stay at home and wait, wait, wait for him.

Marie was always waiting for William to call, to come home, to leave messages saying he was getting on the plane, getting off the plane, checking in to the hotel, going to sleep, waking up, heading for the meeting, catching an earlier or later flight home. He spent one third of his life trying to sleep in uncomfortable beds and one third of his life trying to stay awake in airports. He traveled with thousands of other capitalistic foot soldiers, mostly men but increasing numbers of women, and stayed in the same Ramadas, Holiday Inns, and Radissons. He ate the same room-service meals and ran the same exercise-room treadmills and watched the same pay-per-view porn and stared out the windows at the same strange and lonely cityscapes. Sure, he was an enrolled member of the Spokane Indian tribe, but he was also a fully recognized member of the notebook-computer tribe and the security-checkpoint tribe and the rental-car tribe and the hotel-shuttle-bus tribe and the cell-phone-roaming-charge tribe.

William traveled so often, the Seattle-based flight attendants knew him by first name.

At five minutes to six, the Orange Top taxi pulled into the driveway. The driver, a short and thin black man, stepped out of the cab and waved. William rushed down the stairs and across the pavement. He wanted to get away from the house before he changed his mind about leaving.

"Is that everything, sir?" asked the taxi driver, his accent a colonial cocktail of American English, formal British, and French sibilants added to a base of what must have been North African.

"Yes, it is, sir," said William, self-consciously trying to erase any class differences between them. In Spain the previous summer, an elderly porter had cursed at William when he insisted on carrying his own bags into the hotel. "Perhaps there is something wrong with the caste system, sir," the hotel concierge had explained to William. "But all of us, we want to do our jobs, and we want to do them well."

William didn't want to insult anybody; he wanted the world to be a fair and decent place. At least that was what he wanted to want. More than anything, he wanted to stay home with his fair and decent family. He supposed he wanted the world to be fairer and more decent to his family. We are special, he thought, though he suspected they were just one more family on this block of neighbors, in this city of neighbors, in this country of neighbors, in a world of neighbors. He looked back at his house, at the windows behind which slept his beloved wife and daughter. When he traveled, he had nightmares about strangers breaking into the house and killing and raping Marie and Grace. In other nightmares, he arrived home in time to save his family by beating the intruders and chasing them away. During longer business trips, William's nightmares became more violent as the days and nights passed. If he was gone over a week, he dreamed about mutilating the rapists and eating them alive while his wife and daughter cheered for him.

"Let me take your bags, sir," said the taxi driver.

"What?" asked William, momentarily confused.

"Your bags, sir."

William handed him the briefcase but held on to the heavier garment bag. A stupid compromise, thought William, but it's too late to change it now. God, I'm supposed to be some electric aboriginal warrior, but I'm really a wimpy liberal pacifist. *Dear Lord, how much longer should I mourn the death of Jerry Garcia?*

The taxi driver tried to take the garment bag from William.

"I've got this one," said William, then added, "I've got it, sir."

The taxi driver hesitated, shrugged, opened the trunk, and set the briefcase inside. William laid the garment bag next to his briefcase. The taxi driver shut the trunk and walked around to open William's door.

"No, sir," said William as he awkwardly stepped in front of the taxi driver, opened the door, and took a seat. "I've got it."

"I'm sorry, sir," said the taxi driver and hurried around to the driver's seat. This strange American was making him uncomfortable, and he wanted to get behind the wheel and drive. Driving comforted him.

"To the airport, sir?" asked the taxi driver as he started the meter.

"Yes," said William. "United Airlines."

"Very good, sir."

In silence, they drove along Martin Luther King Jr. Way, the bisector of an African American neighborhood that was rapidly gentrifying. William and his family were Native American gentry! They were the very first Indian family to ever move into a neighborhood and bring up the property values! That was one of William's favorite jokes, self-deprecating and politely racist. White folks could laugh at a joke like that and not feel guilty. But how guilty could white people feel in Seattle? Seattle might be the only city in the country where white people lived comfortably on a street named after Martin Luther King, Jr.

No matter where he lived, William always felt uncomfortable, so he enjoyed other people's discomfort. These days, in the airports, he loved to watch white people enduring random security checks. It was a perverse thrill, to be sure, but William couldn't help himself. He knew those white folks wanted to scream and rage: *Do I look like a terrorist?* And he knew the security officers, most often low-paid brown folks, wanted to scream back: *Define terror, you Anglo bastard!* William figured he'd been pulled over for pat-down searches about 75 percent of the time. Random, my ass! But that was okay! William might have wanted to irritate other people, but he didn't want to scare them. He wanted his fellow travelers to know exactly who and what he was: *I am a Native American and therefore have ten thousand more reasons to terrorize the U.S. than any of those Taliban jerk-offs, but I have chosen instead to become a civic American citizen, so all of you white folks should be celebrating my kindness and moral decency and awesome ability to forgive!* Maybe William should have worn beaded vests when he traveled. Maybe he should have brought a hand drum and sang "Way, ya, way, ya, hey." Maybe he should have thrown casino chips into the crowd.

The taxi driver turned west on Cherry, drove twenty blocks into downtown, took the entrance ramp onto I-5, and headed south for the airport. The freeway was moderately busy for that time of morning.

"Where are you going, sir?" asked the taxi driver.

"I've got business in Chicago," William said. He didn't really want to talk. He needed to meditate in silence. He needed to put his fear of flying inside an imaginary safe deposit box and lock it away. We all have our ceremonies, thought William, our personal narratives. He'd always needed to meditate in the taxi on the way to the airport. Immediately upon arrival at the departure gate, he'd listen to a tape he'd made of rock stars who died in plane crashes. Buddy Holly, Otis Redding, Stevie Ray, "Oh Donna," "Chantilly Lace," "(Sittin' on) The Dock of the Bay." William figured God would never kill a man who listened to such a morbid collection of music. Too easy a target, and plus, God could never justify killing a planeful of innocents to punish one minor sinner.

"What do you do, sir?" asked the taxi driver.

"You know, I'm not sure," said William and laughed. It was true. He worked for a think tank and sold ideas about how to improve other ideas. Two years ago, his company had made a few hundred thousand dollars by designing and selling the idea of a better shopping cart. The CGI prototype was amazing. It looked like a mobile walk-in closet. But it had yet to be manufactured and probably never would be.

"You wear a good suit," said the taxi driver, not sure why William was laughing. "You must be a businessman, no? You must make lots of money."

"I do okay."

"Your house is big and beautiful."

"Yes, I suppose it is."

"You are a family man, yes?"

"I have a wife and daughter."

"Are they beautiful?"

William was pleasantly surprised to be asked such a question. "Yes," he said. "Their names are Marie and Grace. They're very beautiful. I love them very much."

"You must miss them when you travel."

"I miss them so much I go crazy," said William. "I start thinking I'm going to disappear, you know, just vanish, if I'm not home. Sometimes I worry their love is the only thing that makes me human, you know? I think if they stopped loving me, I might burn up, spontaneously combust, and turn into little pieces of oxygen and hydrogen and carbon. Do you know what I'm saying?"

"Yes sir, I understand love can be so large."

William wondered why he was being honest and poetic with a taxi driver. There is emotional safety in anonymity, he thought.

"I have a wife and three sons," said the driver. "But they live in Ethiopia with my mother and father. I have not seen any of them for many years."

For the first time, William looked closely at the driver. He was clear-eyed and handsome, strong of shoulder and arm, maybe fifty years old, maybe older. A thick scar ran from his right ear down his neck and beneath his collar. A black man with a violent history, William thought and immediately reprimanded himself for racially profiling the driver: *Excuse me, sir, but I pulled you over because your scar doesn't belong in this neighborhood.*

"I still think of my children as children," the driver said. "But they are men now. Taller and stronger than me. They are older now than I was when I last saw them."

William did the math and wondered how this driver could function with such fatherly pain. "I bet you can't wait to go home and see them again," he said, following the official handbook of the frightened American male: *When confronted with the mysterious, you can defend yourself by speaking in obvious generalities.*

"I cannot go home," said the taxi driver, "and I fear I will never see them again."

William didn't want to be having this conversation. He wondered if his silence would silence the taxi driver. But it was too late for that.

"What are you?" the driver asked.

"What do you mean?"

"I mean, you are not white, your skin, it is dark like mine."

"Not as dark as yours."

"No," said the driver and laughed. "Not so dark, but too dark to be white. What are you? Are you Jewish?"

Because they were so often Muslim, taxi drivers all over the world had often asked William if he was Jewish. William was always being confused for something else. He was ambiguously ethnic, living somewhere in the darker section of the Great American Crayola Box, but he was more beige than brown, more mauve than sienna.

"Why do you want to know if I'm Jewish?" William asked.

"Oh, I'm sorry, sir, if I offended you. I am not anti-Semitic. I love all of my brothers and sisters. Jews, Catholics, Buddhists, even the atheists, I love them all. Like you Americans sing, 'Joy to the world and Jeremiah Bullfrog!'"

The taxi driver laughed again, and William laughed with him.

"I'm Indian," William said.

"From India?"

"No, not jewel-on-the-forehead Indian," said William. "I'm a bows-and-arrows Indian."

"Oh, you mean ten little, nine little, eight little Indians?"

"Yeah, sort of," said William. "I'm that kind of Indian, but much smarter. I'm a Spokane Indian. We're salmon people."

"In England, they call you Red Indians."

"You've been to England?"

"Yes, I studied physics at Oxford."

"Wow," said William, wondering if this man was a liar.

"You are surprised by this, I imagine. Perhaps you think I'm a liar?"

William covered his mouth with one hand. He smiled this way when he was embarrassed.

"Aha, you do think I'm lying. You ask yourself questions about me. How could a physicist drive a taxi? Well, in the United States, I am a cabdriver, but in Ethiopia, I was a jet-fighter pilot."

By coincidence or magic, or as a coincidence that could willfully be interpreted as magic, they drove past Boeing Field at that exact moment.

"Ah, you see," said the taxi driver, "I can fly any of those planes. The prop planes, the jet planes, even the very large passenger planes. I can also fly the experimental ones that don't fly. But I could make them fly because I am the best pilot in the world. Do you believe me?"

"I don't know," said William, very doubtful of this man but fascinated as well. If he was a liar, then he was a magnificent liar.

On both sides of the freeway, blue-collared men and women drove trucks and forklifts, unloaded trains, trucks, and ships, built computers, televisions, and airplanes. Seattle was a city of industry, of hard work, of calluses on the palms of hands. So many men and women working so hard. William worried that his job—his selling of the purely theoretical—wasn't a real job at all. He didn't build anything. He couldn't walk into department and grocery stores and buy what he'd created, manufactured, and shipped. William's life was measured by imaginary numbers: the binary code of computer languages, the amount of money in his bank accounts, the interest rate on his mortgage, and the rise and fall of the stock market. He invested much of his money in socially responsible funds. Imagine that! Imagine choosing to trust your money with companies that supposedly made their millions through ethical means. Imagine the breathtaking privilege of such a choice. All right, so maybe this was an old story for white men. For most of American history, who else but a white man could endure the existential crisis of economic success? But this story was original and aboriginal for William. For thousands of years, Spokane Indians had lived subsistence lives, using every last part of the salmon and deer because they'd die without every last part, but William only ordered salmon from menus and saw deer on television. Maybe he romanticized the primal—for thousands of years, Indians also died of ear infections—but William wanted his comfortable and safe life to contain more *wilderness*.

"Sir, forgive me for saying this," the taxi driver said, "but you do not look like the Red Indians I have seen before."

"I know," William said. "People usually think I'm a longhaired Mexican."

"What do you say to them when they think such a thing?"

"*No habla español. Indio de Norteamericanos.*"

"People think I'm black American. They always want to hip-hop rap to me. 'Are you East Coast or West Coast?' they ask me, and I tell them I am Ivory Coast."

"How have things been since September eleventh?"

"Ah, a good question, sir. It's been interesting. Because people think I'm black, they don't see me as a terrorist, only as a crackhead addict on welfare. So I am a victim of only one misguided idea about who I am."

"We're all trapped by other people's ideas, aren't we?"

"I suppose that is true, sir. How has it been for you?"

"It's all backward," William said. "A few days after it happened, I was walking out of my gym downtown, and this big phallic pickup pulled up in front of me in the crosswalk. Yeah, this big truck with big phallic tires and a big phallic flagpole and a big phallic flag flying, and the big phallic symbol inside leaned out of his window and yelled at me, 'Go back to your own country!'"

"Oh, that is sad and funny," the taxi driver said.

"Yeah," William said. "And it wasn't so much a hate crime as it was a crime of irony, right? And I was laughing so hard, the truck was halfway down the block before I could get breath enough to yell back, 'You first!'"

William and the taxi driver laughed and laughed together. Two dark men laughing at dark jokes.

"I had to fly on the first day you could fly," William said. "And I was flying into Baltimore, you know, and D.C. and Baltimore are pretty much the same damn town, so it was like flying into Ground Zero, you know?"

"It must have been terrifying."

"It was, it was. I was sitting in the plane here in Seattle, getting ready to take off, and I started looking around for suspicious brown guys. I was scared of little brown guys. So was everybody else. We were all afraid of the same things. I started looking around for big white guys because I figured they'd be undercover cops, right?"

"Imagine wanting to be surrounded by white cops!"

"Exactly! I didn't want to see some pacifist, vegan, whole-wheat, free-range, organic, progressive, gray-ponytail, communist, liberal, draft-dodging, NPR-listening wimp! What are they going to do if somebody tries to hijack the plane? Throw a Birkenstock at him? Offer him some pot?"

"Marijuana might actually stop the violence everywhere in the world," the taxi driver said.

"You're right," William said. "But on that plane, I was hoping for about twenty-five NRA-loving, gun-nut, serial-killing, psychopathic, Ollie North, Norman Schwarzkopf, right-wing, Agent Orange, post-traumatic-stress-disorder, CIA, FBI, automatic-weapon, smart-bomb, laser-sighting bastards!"

"You wouldn't want to invite them for dinner," the taxi driver said. "But you want them to protect your children, am I correct?"

"Yes, but it doesn't make sense. None of it makes sense. It's all contradictions."

"The contradictions are the story, yes?"

"Yes."

"I have a story about contradictions," said the taxi driver. "Because you are a Red Indian, I think you will understand my pain."

"*Su-num-twee*," said William.

"What is that? What did you say?"

"*Su-num-twee*. It's Spokane. My language."

"What does it mean?"

"Listen to me."

"Ah, yes, that's good. *Su-num-twee, su-num-twee*. So, what is your name?"

"William."

The taxi driver sat high and straight in his seat, like he was going to say something important. "William, my name is Fekadu. I am Oromo and Muslim, and I come from Addis Ababa in Ethiopia, and I want you to *su-num-twee*."

There was nothing more important than a person's name and the names of his clan, tribe, city, religion, and country. By the social rules of his tribe, William should have reciprocated and officially identified himself. He should have been polite and generous. He was expected to live by so many rules, he sometimes felt like he was living inside an indigenous version of an Edith Wharton novel.

"Mr. William," asked Fekadu, "do you want to hear my story? Do you want to *su-num-twee?*"

"Yes, I do, sure, yes, please," said William. He was lying. He was twenty minutes away from the airport and so close to departure.

"I was not born into an important family," said Fekadu. "But my father worked for an important family. And this important family worked for the family of Emperor Haile Selassie. He was a great and good and kind and terrible man, and he loved his country and killed many of his people. Have you heard of him?"

"No, I'm sorry, I haven't."

"He was magical. Ruled our country for forty-three years. Imagine that! We Ethiopians are strong. White people have never conquered us. We won every war we fought against white people. For all of our history, our emperors have been strong, and Selassie was the strongest. There has never been a man capable of such love and destruction."

"You fought against him?"

Fekadu breathed in so deeply that William recognized it as a religious moment, as the first act of a ceremony, and with the second act, an exhalation, the ceremony truly began.

"No," Fekadu said. "I was a smart child. A genius. A prodigy. It was Selassie who sent me to Oxford. And there I studied physics and learned the math and art of flight. I came back home and flew jets for Selassie's army."

"Did you fly in wars?" William asked.

"Ask me what you really want to ask me, William. You want to know if I was a killer, no?"

William had a vision of his wife and daughter huddling terrified in their Seattle basement while military jets screamed overhead. It happened every August when the U.S. Navy Blue Angels came to entertain the masses with their aerial acrobatics.

"Do you want to know if I was a killer?" asked Fekadu. "Ask me if I was a killer."

William wanted to know the terrible answer without asking the terrible question.

"Will you not ask me what I am?" asked Fekadu.

"I can't."

"I dropped bombs on my own people."

In the sky above them, William counted four, five, six jets flying in holding patterns while awaiting permission to land.

"For three years, I killed my own people," said Fekadu. "And then, on the third of June in 1974, I could not do it anymore. I kissed my wife and sons good-bye that morning, and I kissed my mother and father, and I lied to them and told them I would be back that evening. They had no idea where I was going. But I went to the base, got into my plane, and flew away."

"You defected?" William asked. How could a man steal a fighter plane? Was that possible? And if possible, how much courage would it take to commit such a crime? William was quite sure he could never be that courageous.

"Yes, I defected," said Fekadu. "I flew my plane to France and was almost shot down when I violated their airspace, but they let me land, and they arrested me, and soon enough, they gave me asylum. I came to Seattle five years ago, and I think I will live here the rest of my days."

Fekadu took the next exit. They were two minutes away from the airport. William was surprised to discover that he didn't want this journey to end so soon. He wondered if he should invite Fekadu for coffee and a sandwich, for a slice of pie, for brotherhood. William wanted to hear more of this man's stories and learn from them, whether they were true or not. Perhaps it didn't matter if any one man's stories were true. Fekadu's autobiography might have been completely fabricated, but William was convinced that somewhere in the world, somewhere in Africa or the United States, a man, a jet pilot, wanted to fly away from the war he was supposed to fight. There must be hundreds, maybe thousands, of such men, and how many were courageous enough to fly away? If Fekadu wasn't describing his own true pain and loneliness, then he might have been accidentally describing the pain of a real and lonely man.

"What about your family?" asked William, because he didn't know what else to ask and because he was thinking of his wife and daughter. "Weren't they in danger? Wouldn't Selassie want to hurt them?"

"I could only pray Selassie would leave them be. He had always been good to me, but he saw me as impulsive, so I hoped he would know my family had nothing to do with my flight. I was a coward for staying and a coward for leaving. But none of it mattered, because Selassie was overthrown a few weeks after I defected."

"A coup?"

"Yes, the Derg deposed him, and they slaughtered all of their enemies and their enemies' families. They suffocated Selassie with a

pillow the next year. And now I could never return to Ethiopia because Selassie's people would always want to kill me for my betrayal,
and the Derg would always want to kill me for being Selassie's soldier. Every night and day, I worry that any of them might harm my
family. I want to go there and defend them. I want to bring them
here. They can sleep on my floor! But even now, after democracy
has almost come to Ethiopia, I cannot go back. There is too much
history and pain, and I am too afraid."

"How long has it been since you've talked to your family?"

"We write letters to each other, and sometimes we receive them.
They sent me photos once, but they never arrived for me to see. And
for two days, I waited by the telephone because they were going to
call, but it never rang."

Fekadu pulled the taxi to a slow stop at the airport curb. "We are
here, sir," he said. "United Airlines."

William didn't know how this ceremony was supposed to end. He
felt small and powerless against the collected history. "What am I
supposed to do now?" he asked.

"Sir, you must pay me thirty-eight dollars for this ride," said Fekadu
and laughed. "Plus a very good tip."

"How much is good?"

"You see, sometimes I send cash to my family. I wrap it up and try
to hide it inside the envelope. I know it gets stolen, but I hope some
of it gets through to my family. I hope they buy themselves gifts from
me. I hope."

"You pray for this?"

"Yes, William, I pray for this. And I pray for your safety on your trip,
and I pray for the safety of your wife and daughter while you are gone."

"Pop the trunk, I'll get my own bags," said William as he gave sixty
dollars to Fekadu, exited the taxi, took his luggage out of the trunk,
and slammed it shut. Then William walked over to the passenger-

side window, leaned in, and studied Fekadu's face and the terrible scar on his neck.

"Where did you get that?" William asked.

Fekadu ran a finger along the old wound. "Ah," he said. "You must think I got this flying in a war. But no, I got this in a taxicab wreck. William, I am a much better jet pilot than a car driver."

Fekadu laughed loudly and joyously. William wondered how this poor man could be capable of such happiness, however temporary it was.

"Your stories," said William. "I want to believe you."

"Then believe me," said Fekadu.

Unsure, afraid, William stepped back.

"Good-bye, William American," Fekadu said and drove away.

Standing at curbside, William couldn't breathe well. He wondered if he was dying. Of course he was dying, a flawed mortal dying day by day, but he felt like he might fall over from a heart attack or stroke right there on the sidewalk. He left his bags and ran inside the terminal. Let a luggage porter think his bags were dangerous! Let a security guard x-ray the bags and find mysterious shapes! Let a bomb-squad cowboy explode the bags as precaution! Let an airport manager shut down the airport and search every possible traveler! Let the FAA president order every airplane to land! Let the American skies be empty of everything with wings! Let the birds stop flying! Let the very air go still and cold! William didn't care. He ran through the terminal, searching for an available pay phone, a landline, something true and connected to the ground, and he finally found one and dropped two quarters into the slot and dialed his home number, and it rang and rang and rang and rang, and William worried that his wife and daughter were harmed, were lying dead on the floor, but then Marie answered.

"Hello, William," she said.

"I'm here," he said.

THE LIFE AND TIMES OF ESTELLE WALKS ABOVE

During the summer of 1976, the city of Seattle was beginning to change from the barbarous seaport of loggers, sailors, and Indians it had always been into the progressive, computerized, and sanitized capital of all things Caucasian it would become. I was thirteen and pretty-skinny-beautiful, with eyelashes so black, long, and curly that grown women lost their minds and manners over me:

1. "Oh, why do boys always get the gorgeous eyelashes?"
2. "I'll give you a million dollars for those eyelashes!"
3. "Hey, Sexy Eyes, why don't you give me a call when you get legal."
4. "Hello, Benjamin, my name is Mrs. Robinson."
5. "Hey, let's play Tonto and the Lone Ranger."

My crazy aunt Bettina thought all of the female attention was going to make me gay, and though I loved a homoerotic circle jerk as much as the next curious teenage boy, I dreamed almost exclusively about girls and women.

Rules for Homoerotic Circle Jerks

1. Keep your hands to yourself.
2. You must open your eyes at least every thirty seconds, and you must keep them open at least thirty seconds at a time.
3. No making fun of larger or smaller penises.
4. Bring your own tissues for cleanup.
5. If you bring pornography, then you must share it.
6. You cannot fantasize about the girlfriends of the boys standing next to you, but you can fantasize about the girlfriends of every other boy in the circle.
7. You can fantasize about any of the boys in the circle jerk, but not if they are standing next to you.
8. An official circle jerk contains seven boys.
9. If fewer than seven boys want to jerk off together, they must stand in single file, and it shall be known as a firing line.
10. If more than seven boys want to jerk off together, it shall be called a Joint Session of Congress.

My head was filled with a disassociated and constantly running montage of vaginas and breasts; I was the Andy Warhol of self-imagined adolescent porn. And yes, even at thirteen years of age, I knew about Andy Warhol's work and found it so completely of its time that I guessed his deconstructive painting of Campbell's soup cans would eventually be used as a paid advertisement for Campbell's soup.

NOTICE OF HISTORICAL REVISION: It was my mother who first advanced that particular anti-Warholian theory, and she might have read it first somewhere else. But she is a powerful Indian who reads art-theory books, so I listen to her, and I often agree with her criticism.

My mother was super smart, and I was smart by osmosis. But she was born smart on the Spokane Indian Reservation and studied her way into the University of Washington during a time when she was pretty much the only Indian on campus, aside from two Snohomish janitors and a Yakama cook at one of the dorms. It's tough to be a smart girl anywhere, but it's way tough on the rez.

Q: What's the difference between an Indian reservation and a racist, sexist, homophobic, white-trash logging town populated entirely with the mutated children of married second cousins?
A: The Indians have braids.

If you think about it, my mother was as heroic as Thor Heyerdahl, Sir Edmund Hillary, John Glenn, or any of those white-boy explorers. My mother broke speed limits, climbed mountains, and sailed oceans nobody else had dreamed up. And she did it all by herself, with one hand holding a textbook and the other hand holding a squealing baby (*me!*) to her breast. Maybe I'm smart because my mother's breast milk had little pieces of Albert Einstein and Madame Curie floating around in it. As for my father, he was so long gone that my mother and I called him Long Gone and told each other bedtime stories that always ended with him getting eaten by wild dogs.

NOTICE OF HISTORICAL REVISION: I greatly missed my father and only pretended to hate him as much as my mother did.

My mother and I lived in a two-bedroom rental house in Ballard, the Scandinavian neighborhood of Seattle. We were poor, but anybody can afford fruits and vegetables, and that's what we ate. I wasn't a vegetarian by choice; I was a vegetarian by economic circumstance. On July 5 (I remember the exact day because I remember the acrid smell of leftover fireworks smoke), my mother and I were shopping in the local free-range, whole-wheat, lactose-intolerant co-op when she picked up a hand-stapled magazine and self-administered a parenting quiz:

1. Do you know the names of all of your child's friends?
2. Do you give your child gender-neutral gifts?
3. When your child cries, what color are you thinking of?
4. Are you fully clothed, partially clothed, or nude when you breast-feed your baby?
5. What are you teaching your child about peace and justice?
6. Have you taught your child to play a musical instrument?
7. Do you heart-listen to your child?

Despite her roving and restless intelligence, my mother was the kind of person who believed the garbage she read in magazines. We all have our blind spots, I suppose. She was distrustful enough to write a master's thesis titled "John F. Kennedy's Murder: How Rich Men Tell One Lie for Each Dollar They're Worth," but she still believed in astrology. She was genuinely shocked and hurt when she caught another human being lying to her, which meant she lived in a constant state of painful surprise, but oh, she would violently punish those liars by screaming surrealistic curses:

1. "Your great-grandfather starred in silent porno movies!"
2. "Gravity was invented to keep you from realizing your dreams!"
3. "Every time you masturbate, you give birth to ten thousand mosquitoes!"
4. "I hope Hitler eats your dog in hell!"

So my mother was naive and vengeful, just like Napoleon, Alexander the Great, Joan of Arc, and about 99 percent of all the other famous world leaders you ever heard about. But she wasn't famous; she was only my mother, and she so miserably failed the parenting quiz that she decided to become my best friend. She never asked my opinion of her parenting skills, but I would have told her this: "Dear Ma; you forgot my ninth birthday, and still to this day have not remembered you forgot it. I'll probably be presented with a ninth-birthday card on my elderly and senile deathbed. But you're also the woman who drove me to school during my entire scholastic career, all the way from White Rabbit's Wonderful Preschool until I graduated from Garfield High School, because it's pretty darn cute to ride the bus when you're six years old, but you're on the Loser Cruiser once you enter the teen years. As a mother, you suffered from a soap-opera style of amnesia (*Let's deal with stressful events by pretending they never happened!*) but were critically aware of the Jane Austen-Dinner-Party-meets-Cannibal-Zombies-on-the-Moon social structures of public schools. I truly hated the goofy clothes you wore, which were all sorts of white-hippie-chick-porn-star-Jane-Fonda-in-*The Electric Horseman* trendy, but you did frame three of my baby outfits and hang them in the front hallway. So I guess you were hopelessly romantic and easily distracted, a B-plus mother, certainly good enough to get into Matriarchal State University but not quite good enough for St. Mary's College of the Blessed Womb Warriors."

But my mother never asked me what I thought of her, and she went crazy after she failed that parenting quiz, and attempted to spend every moment of her waking life with me. She took me to seven baseball games and fourteen poetry readings, and I found both pastimes remarkably similar:

1. Am I supposed to clap now?
2. Was that a strike?
3. Why is he scratching his nuts?

She took me to folk-music concerts and ballets. Once, during *Swan Lake*, a secondary ballerina took a wrong turn onstage and smashed into the prima ballerina, sending them both sprawling to the ground. Undaunted, the women jumped back up and resumed dancing, eliciting tremendous applause from the previously sedate crowd (as if they'd only then realized these women were serious athletes and had made a highlight-worthy recovery), but my mother wept.

"What's wrong, Ma?" I asked.

"That poor woman," she said. "Her career is over."

"No, they're okay, they're both okay, look at them dance."

"But the young one," said my mother, weeping so profusely that people around us were getting uncomfortable. "She will never get to dance with the prima again. They'll punish her. I know it. They'll make fun of her. They'll fire her, and she'll quit dancing and regret it for the rest of her life."

"I think you're overreacting, Ma."

"No, no," she said, so loudly I'm sure the ballerinas heard her. "Don't you see? Your whole life can be determined by one moment. You make one choice, one mistake, and that's it. You've made the map you've got to follow for the rest of your life."

"Ma, you're making a scene."

She was always making scenes. She yelled at mothers and fathers who publicly spanked their children (Hey, *Mussolini, how would you like me to do that to you?*), and commented loudly at any display of public rudeness:

1. "Oh, look at Prince Pushy of Monaco, cutting in line. Hey, Prince, do you keep your crown in your ass?"
2. "Oh, excuse me, excuse me, Ms. Moneybags, but I see that your party of eight left only a dollar tip for the waitress. I assume that was an honest mistake."

3. "Okay, okay, everybody, listen up, we're all waiting in line to get our driver's licenses, but this man here, he's cursing a lot, so he obviously needs his license more than anybody else in the history of the world. Can somebody please get him a special driver's license, please, hurry."

If she'd been a man and talked like that to strangers, she would have been punched four times a week. How does a self-proclaimed pacifist get herself into so many confrontations? I don't know; I don't understand her, not then or now. She's a contradiction. She has always contained multitudes. But no matter how unpredictable she can be, she fought plenty of justified battles as well. When my elementary school principal, a ROTC pack leader named Wolff (not his real name!), wanted to control my exuberant nature by shoving sedatives down my throat on a highly regular basis, my mother stormed into his office with a bottle of lithium. She poured the pills onto Wolff's desk, swallowed one dry, and then told Wolff it was his turn.

"I figure if we're going to give my kid a narcotic," she said, "then we both should know how it will make him feel."

The Wolff-Man never mentioned pills again. And my mother never told anybody (not even me) her lithium pills were only aspirin. I discovered it only when I took one of the pills and expected to see a life-altering vision but felt nothing except pain relief.

That was my mother: fierce and protective, open and permissive (*No, don't call it your wang-doodle, it's your penis*), and a total embarrassment.

"Ma," I yelled at her. "Why can't you ignore me sometimes, like all of the other moms and dads? Why can't you just give me a pair of scissors and tell me to run, boy, run?"

She sat me down once a week and gave me sex advice:

1. "Condoms make you less sensitive, and you'll last much longer, thereby giving your partner a much more pleasurable experience."
2. "If you spend an hour kissing every part of your lover's body while purposefully ignoring her orifices, then she will feel more like a holy woman and less like a pincushion."
3. "Make her laugh while making love, and she will love you forever."

Yes, I admit my mother's sexual advice was outstanding, but what son wants to hear these things from his mother?

"Ma, you're going to kill me," I shouted.

"I understand your anger," she said.

She "understood" everything because she bought self-help books that taught her how to understand the teenage male ego. She understood my rage, my volcanic need to kick holes in every interior door of the house.

"I understand your need to physically express yourself," she said, "so I won't fix these doors until you find an alternative means of communicating."

Man oh man, she talked exactly like that. She negotiated with me as if I were holding twelve hostages at gunpoint.

But she really started to fall apart when she decided to become a "progressive and whole woman." I have nothing against progressive and whole women—

Q: What kinds of men could resent those kinds of women?
A: Almost all of them.

—but I was a reflexive and cracked teenage boy. If Estelle had pursued her wholeness by herself, I would have supported her gladly: "Go get whole, Ma, rah, rah, rah, sis, boom, bah, go get whole, Ma!" But since she was my new best friend, I was forced to attend every single one of her wholeness seminars, consciousness-raising workshops, and spiritual discussion groups. Don't misunderstand me. Even at thirteen years of age, I knew I was a liberal with socialistic leanings and would vote for socialistic liberals my entire adult life (my spouse, Mary, is the information officer for the local chapter of the Green Party), but there's no boy or man alive who could have survived that summer without serious emotional repercussions.

At first, the women who pursued wholeness alongside my mother would be uncomfortable with my maleness, even though I was only a boy (nits make lice). But eventually they would forget I was there. My penis and scrotum would become irrelevant (a redundancy?), and I'd listen to women tell their stories for hours; I'd hear their secrets. I was afraid of female secrets then, and I'm even more afraid of them now.

"Ma, those woman secrets are killing me," I said.

"You're a good listener," she said, a compliment meant to distract me from the real issue; my mother was a politician; politicians love secrets!

"But Ma, listen to me," I said. "I heard this woman today, the one with the bad perm, she said she thinks about sex as often as any guy does."

"That was a very honest thing for Betty to say. The whole woman embraces and celebrates her sexuality."

"But Ma, what am I supposed to do with that information? If Betty thinks about sex that much, and you think about sex that much, and all women think about sex that much, then girls my age must think about sex a whole bunch, right?"

"I certainly did when I was your age."

"Okay, I'm going to be walking around school looking at all these girls, and I'm going to be thinking about having sex with them. And trust me, Ma, I think about sex all the time. I'm always beating off; I'm like the Denny's of masturbation, Ma. I'm open twenty-four hours a day, and I can get the Grand Slam special anytime I want. I got bruises on it; I got calluses. And now, when I'm thinking about sex with those girls, when I'm running off to the bathroom to do my business, you're telling me they're all thinking about sex with me?"

"Well, not all of them, son. You're not that cute. But I would imagine a very healthy percentage of your female peers think about sex with you."

"Ma, I'm not supposed to know that! Do you have any idea how dangerous that is to know right now? When I'm thirty years old, I'm supposed to look back at the teen years and say, 'Man, if I only knew then what I know now.' Ma, because of you, I know all of it now, so what am I supposed to do with the rest of my life?"

NOTICE OF HISTORICAL REVISION: My early sexual education did not turn me into a sexually precocious teen or promiscuous man. I have slept with seven women, a shockingly average number of lovers.

Now, I'm no Oedipus, at least not Oedipal enough to warrant an epic poem, but I have to admit that my mother was pretty dang sexy herself (so maybe I could write an Oedipal haiku). She was Spokane Indian and looked the part: cheekbones stretching from there to here, big black hair hanging halfway down her back, a big brown face with spelunkable eyes, a big bosom, wide hips, and a flat ass. I looked exactly like her, except for the big bosom. If we lived on the reservation, we'd be only two more Indians. But we lived in the city, so naturally, we had a lot of white friends. Most of our friends were white, in fact, but it wasn't like I spent much time worrying about it. Who cares, right? But my mother started hanging around these white women who were so white I could see through them. They weren't literally translucent, but they engaged in activities that were so damn foreign to me (so dang Caucasian) that it made me feel lonely as hell. The Title IX legislation was beginning to gain real momentum, and these women knew it, so they were voracious, ambitious, and ready to beat the crap out of the patriarchy. They were in training for the upcoming war! Good for them! I love and respect women! Given the chance, I'll vote for the Equal Rights Amendment! I'll be in the Gentlemen's Auxiliary! If asked, I'll donate 30 percent of my income to NOW to make up for the 30 percent difference in salary between men and women working the same jobs:

1. Community-college history teacher's salary = $32,525
2. $32,525 \times 30\% = \$9{,}757.50$
3. Amount of charitable contribution to NOW = $9,758

My mother's friends were religious fundamentalists that summer. As women, they'd been "saved" by other women, and now they were preaching and witnessing: "Hear me roar, I am woman!"

To this day, I rarely look in the mirror and think, I'm an Indian. I don't necessarily know what an Indian is supposed to be. After all, I don't speak my tribal language, and I'm allergic to the earth. If it grows, it makes me sneeze. In Salish, "Spokane" means "Children of the Sun," but I'm slightly allergic to the sun. If I spend too much time outside, I get a nasty rash. I doubt Crazy Horse needed talcum powder to get through a hot summer day. Can you imagine Sacajawea sniffling her way across the Continental Divide? I'm hardly the poster boy for aboriginal pride. I don't even think about my tribal heritage until some white person reminds me of it:

Q: Hey, man, you're an Indian, right?
A: Uh, yeah.

Don't get me wrong; I like being Indian. I love the way Indian men often wear their hair long, cry too easily, wear florid clothes—all reds and pinks and lavenders and turquoises—and sing and dance most every day of their lives. If you think about it, Indian men are probably the most feminized males on the planet (and I mean that as a compliment), despite how ridiculously macho we pretend to be: "I am an Indian man, with your prior approval, hear me roar!"

Yes, I'm an Indian man trying to hold on to the best of Indian:

1. The cheerful acceptance of eccentricity
2. The loving embrace of artistic expression
3. The communistic sense of community

I'm also an Indian man trying to let go of the worst of Indian:

1. Low self-esteem
2. Alcoholism
3. Misogyny
4. Lateral violence

So, okay, in the end, maybe I am proud to be an Indian. But I don't want to wear a T-shirt with my tribal enrollment number printed on the front and a photograph of Sitting Bull ironed on the back. On the long list of things that I am, I'd put Indian at number three, behind "bitterly funny" at number two and "horny bastard" at number one for the last twenty-seven years running.

But oh, my mother's whole white friends loved how Indian we were, and my mother became more Indian in their presence. My mother's *name* became more Indian.

"Oh, Estelle Walks Above," said Ginger, the militant vegan. "That's such a beautiful Indian name. What does it mean?"

"Oh, well," my mother said, "I guess it means I walk above . . . *stuff*."

She didn't have the guts to tell her that Walks Above wasn't her real name. Her real last name was Miller, but that wasn't so romantic.

"Oh, Estelle Miller, that's such a beautiful Indian name. What does it mean?"

"Oh, well, I guess it means I mill . . . *stuff*."

Growing up on the reservation, my mother was cousin to Indians who had authentic Indian names, like Builds-the-Fire, FallsApart, Morning Owl, and Black Bird. She was jealous of those poetic names and felt shortchanged by her own colonized moniker, so she simply changed her name when she left the reservation. Like many of the other immigrants into the United States (and leaving the rez for Seattle is immigration), my mother reinvented herself when she landed on these democratic shores.

On the rez, she was that smart and strange girl who was always preparing to leave, and was loved by many and respected by most (and hated by a few), but she became a wise woman in the presence of her white friends. They asked her for advice about their love lives, spiritual directions, political positions, and fashion styles. Her white friends wanted to be my mother, so they started to dress and talk like her. Imagine a dozen white women running around Seattle, speaking with singsong reservation accents. How confusing! Homeless Indians had no idea what to make of these blondes who sounded like they'd just gotten off a bus from Crow Agency, Montana.

"Are you Indian?" asked the homeless men.

"No," said my mother's disciples. "But we know an amazing Indian woman named Estelle. Do you know her?"

"Where I come from, every Indian woman is named Estelle."

Ha, ha! How can Indians laugh so much? How can they make so many jokes? I don't know. Ask my mother!

My mother both loved and resented the attention she received from her white-women friends.

"How can these women become whole if they're trying so hard to be wholly like me?" she asked me.

"I don't know, Ma, I'm just a manual laborer."

All that summer, I worked for my mother in the basements of Unitarian churches:

1. I folded and unfolded chairs and arranged them in sacred circles.
2. I brewed and poured coffee.
3. I lit cigarettes and dumped ashtrays.
4. I ran to the store for sandwiches and drinks.
5. I swept and mopped the floors.

I worked for free, but I worked for women who at first tolerated and then loved me. I was the son of their saint! In their lives away from my mother, these women were lawyers, doctors, teachers, parole officers, chefs, and social workers, but they turned into children in her presence. I resented their immaturity; I was supposed to be the immature one; I was the child!

Those women surrounded my mother and pushed me into the corners of the meeting rooms. These women competed with me for my mother's attention, and they often won.

"What should I do, Estelle, what should I do?"

"I don't know, Erin, what do you think you should do?"

Like any good shaman, professional baseball player, or politician, my mother always answered questions with questions.

"It makes me sound Zen," she had said to me on the bus ride home after one of those meetings.

"How do you do it, Ma?" I asked. "These women are killing me. They want you to do everything for them."

"No, they don't. They just want somebody to listen."

"Ma, they think you're magic."

"Don't you think I'm magic?" she asked and laughed. Of course she wasn't a magician. She was a mess! She failed parenting quizzes! She'd raised a son who would grow up to break the hearts of 67 percent of the women who'd loved him! How could a powerful woman raise a fragile man like that?

Q: How do you find out the true nature and character of a hero?
A: Ask his or her children.

Ask me about my mother's relationship with her women's group, and I'll tell you my version of the truth. I was thirteen and should have been running the streets with other thirteen-year-old boys, not making sure there was one pitcher of ice water for Lucy and one pitcher of lukewarm water for Abigail. I was supposed to be engaged in rough play with a father. He was supposed to grab me by the hands and spin me around the room! He was supposed to be my helicopter, my dump truck, my race car, my dragon and my dragon killer! Where was my father, the bastard, and where was the good man who should have been vainly attempting to take my father's place in my life? I was always hungry for paternity, but during the summer of 1976, a matriarchal woman starved me. With difficulty, I still loved my mother, but she found blind acceptance from her white friends.

NOTICE OF HISTORICAL REVISION: During that particular time period, I probably hated my mother more often than I loved her.

What is it about Indians that turns otherwise intelligent, interesting, and capable people into blithering idiots? I don't think every white person I meet has the spiritual talents and service commitment of a Jesuit priest, but white folks often think we Indians are shamanic geniuses. Most Indians are only poor folks worried about paying the rent and the light bill, and they usually pray to win the damn lottery.

"White people!" my mother cursed on a daily basis, though her paternal grandfather was half white and her maternal grandmother was mostly white.

My mother went to college on scholarships funded by white people; she was a teaching assistant to a white professor; she borrowed money from white people who didn't have much money to lend; our white landlord let us pay half rent for a whole year and never asked for the rest; my favorite baby-sitter was a white woman with red hair.

"White people!" My mother should have sung their praises; I should sing their praises! But we didn't sing for them. Indians are not supposed to sing for white people. Does the antelope sing honor songs for the lion?

My mother the friend, benefactor, and beneficiary of white liberal women said these things about white liberals:

1. "Your average white liberal would die before she sat down to a raccoon and squirrel dinner with some illiterate shotgun-shack Arkansas white folks who believe the Good Lord is their one and only savior. But that same white liberal will happily eat fried SPAM and white bread with a Lakota Sioux shaman who never graduated high school, and give him a highly transcendent blow job after dinner."

2. "White pacifist liberals in favor of gun control will race from their latest antiwar demonstration to rally for the American Indian

Movement, a radical Indian organization that accomplished
much of its mission through gunfire and threat of gunfire."

3. "I'm not scared of the Jerry Falwells and Pat Robertsons of the
   world. Jerry and Pat aren't the ones crawling in and out of
   sweathouses and pontificating about how much they admire
   Indian culture. I'm scared of the white liberals who love Indians. I figure about 75 percent of white liberals who hang around
   Indians will eventually start believing they're Indians, then
   start telling us Indians how to be Indian."

4. "If you put an Indian on the poster, white liberals will flock to
   the meeting. For instance, I happen to believe that Leonard
   Peltier is a political prisoner. Leonard is in jail for a crime he
   didn't commit. He didn't shoot and kill those two FBI agents
   back in Pine Ridge in '75, but some Indian did. Think about
   it. Some Indian, or Indians, walked up to two men, two human
   beings, lying defenseless on the ground, already shot and
   wounded numerous times during a gunfight they might have
   started, but still, two human beings lying on the ground, critically wounded, unable to defend themselves. And some Indian
   who was not Leonard Peltier but was with Leonard Peltier stood
   over those two FBI men lying on the ground and shot them in
   their faces. Leonard is in prison for a crime he didn't commit,
   but I happen to believe his imprisonment is the natural result
   of picking up a gun in the first place. Those white liberals should
   change the name of the Leonard Peltier Defense Committee
   to the Free Leonard by Finding the Indigenous Bastards Who
   Did It Committee."

Despite my mother's sarcasm and racism, most of her friends are
liberal white women! And most of my friends are liberal white men!
My mother and I are the hostages of colonial contradictions:

1. "Liberal white man, you can steal my land as long as you plant organic peas and carrots in the kidnapped soil!"
2. "Liberal white woman, you can practice my religion as long as you teach third grade at the co-op tribal school!"

I was engaged to a liberal white woman named Cynthia when I met and began the affair with the Crow Indian woman who would eventually marry me and mother our twin daughters, Charlotte and Emily (I'm a pretentious Indian who married a pretentious Indian!). How could I cheat on a woman I'd loved for years with another woman I'd fallen in love with during the course of one brief conversation? I don't know. I made the choice to betray my girlfriend, and it turned out well (all three of us live better lives than we lived before), but I know it could have been otherwise. In our rage and pain, any one or combination of the three of us could have thrown a punch or grabbed a knife or pulled a trigger. Instead, after I'd separately cried to each woman about how much I loved the other, Cynthia and Mary went to lunch together and listened to each other's stories. Over sandwiches and coffee, the betrayed and betrayer confessed their sins and forgave each other, or perhaps they only promised to try and forgive, and isn't that the best we can do? But did they forgive me? I don't know! They never told me! I never asked! How could they, the North and South Korea of my heart, conduct such a delicate negotiation without me? How could two women sign a peace treaty without me, the one-man army? I didn't even matter; I wasn't invited. I needed answers, so I ran to my mother.

"What am I supposed to do?" I asked her. "I don't understand how they can do such a thing. How can they eat together?"

"Well, it's obvious, isn't it?" she said. "You're my son, and I love you. But those women are much more ambitious than you are. You've always been happy with your unhappiness. But those women want their lives to be better. Frankly, I wish they'd fall in love with each other."

My mother, my wife, and my former girlfriend have always searched for something better. Good for them, good for them! Estelle left her reservation because she wanted to live near a great library; Mary left Montana because she wanted to work for Ralph Nader; Cynthia left me because she wanted a tacit life. A defense attorney for the city, she met and married a carpenter who doesn't believe in metaphors. They moved to "the country," whatever that is, and they send us Christmas cards. So maybe all is forgiven, or maybe Cynthia wants to teach me something; she was always teaching me something.

"All those books in your house, and all those books in your head," Cynthia had said to me when she left me for good. "And you don't know a damn thing about a damn thing!"

Oh, she was right then, and she's right now. Smart women surround me and lovingly tolerate my stupidity. My wife and daughters believe me to be a Holy Fool, a builder of nothing and a fixer of less. But damn, I make them laugh, and I do my share of the household chores!

"Son," my mother said to me on the night of my high school graduation, "if you want your future wife to lust after you for the rest of your days, then all you have to do is complete this to-do list:

1. "Wash the dishes on a regular basis."
2. "If you're feeling lonely and you want her to suck on your toes or any of your other projectiles, do the laundry."
3. "Do you want to keep love alive? All you have to do is vacuum. Oh, my son, vacuum in the middle of the night, and your future wife will rise naked from her bed and make love with you at three in the morning!"
4. "Reverse the stereotypical gender roles, my dear, dear boy, and you shall be redeemed!"

But it was my mother who first gave up on love, who, since my childhood, has lived what I assume to be a chaste life. She could not love a man who did not respect her; she could not sleep with a man who made her feel dirty. So as far as I can tell, and I believe she would tell me otherwise, she has simply gone without. She is a secular nun! My crazy aunt Bettina thinks all that whole-woman talk turned my mother into a lesbian (and what better way for a woman to show her love for women than by romantically loving women?), but I think my mother has decided that she'd rather spend more time with open books than with closed men. My mother refuses to lower her standards! She'll read any book once but will toss it aside if it doesn't hold up to a second reading. As for me, as crazy as it sounds, I want to become the kind of man my mother would sleep with. Ha, ha, ha, ha! I don't want to sleep with my mother, but I want to sleep with women my mother loves. Ha, ha, ha, ha! I don't want to be cherished by my mother (and I am beloved) as much as I want to be respected by her.

Estelle and I both grew up to be white-collar community-college teachers. At North Seattle Community College, I teach three classes of American history (imagine that: An Indian teaches white kids about Benjamin Franklin and Susan B. Anthony, isn't that joyous!), while Estelle teaches two art-appreciation classes and one in women's studies at Seattle Central Community College. My mother has become a respected and well-loved academic bureaucrat (Teacher of the Year for seven years running!), but that's hardly the stuff of New Age fantasies. This is what my mother teaches now:

1. A thousand years from now, the Egyptian pyramids and middle-class white American all-you-can-buffet restaurants will be viewed with equivalent awe at their majesty and disgust at their excess.

2. President William Jefferson Clinton is the epitome, perhaps the evolutionary apex, of white male behavior, and that's why most white people, liberal and conservative, hate him so vehemently.

3. Twenty-seven-year-old white men look exactly the same as three-month-old white babies of either gender.

4. White men are endlessly creative because they're so damn bored. Shakespeare and golf were invented for the same reason. Hitler and Pee-wee Herman were motivated by the same existential dread and masculine insecurity. Hugh Hefner and Napoleon should be flavors of ice cream. World domination and the complete line of Sears power tools are equally important goals.

5. White men are terrified of being better and kinder and more intelligent men than their fathers; therefore, they invented nostalgia and have canonized slave owners like Thomas Jefferson and George Washington.

6. The average white male working the graveyard shift at a 7-Eleven in the year 2003 is a more educated and advanced and decent human being than the average white male attending an opera in New York City in 1876.

7. If you want to make a white man cry, despite the amount of time it's been since he last wept aloud, then all you have to do is employ "baseball" and "father" in three consecutive sentences.

My mother is no longer on a wholehearted journey to claim her female wholeness. I don't ask her about it, but I'm sure she loves her life and considers it complete, as filled as it is with her students, colleagues, books, grandchildren, and the mountains that surround Seattle on all sides. Call her answering machine (she rarely picks up the phone even when she's home), and you'll hear: "Hi, this is Estelle, and I'm not here, so I'm probably climbing a dormant volcano. Leave me a message, and I'll give you a call when I come back down."

I don't know if my mother keeps in contact with those needy white women from the summer of 1976. I read about them in the newspapers; I see them on television. Some of them have become locally famous, and one is famous everywhere. A former lawyer, she recently won an Emmy for her role as a lawyer in a TV movie.

My mother invited me over to watch the movie with her. It was bad.

"I remember when she couldn't orgasm," my mother said of the woman. "I wonder if she can orgasm now."

I learned about female orgasms at a very young age. I never once in my life believed in the vaginal orgasm. I learned I'd find Jimmy Hoffa and Amelia Earhart before I found a vaginal orgasm.

My mother made me read the feminist bible titled *Our Bodies, Ourselves*. I read it once and gave it back to my mother and never said another word about it. But I came home early from school one afternoon and found my mother and twelve white women studying their vaginas with handheld mirrors.

"Ma!" I shouted after the women had pulled up their pants and fled into the kitchen. "I'm not supposed to see things like that! Well, maybe I'm supposed to see things like that, but only one at a time!"

"The vagina is a beautiful flower," said my mother.

"I know it's a beautiful flower," I said. "I'm drowning in the garden!"

All of those flowery women now sit on the Seattle city council, anchor the local news, sell mattresses, sing in pubs, manage the money of rich men, and design computer programs. They all wanted to become better women, and they have indeed become better at what they do; I have no idea whether they're happy. I wouldn't know how to ask that question, and I doubt they'd know how to answer it. I don't know if I'm happy; I know only that I'm going to work tomorrow, come home and spend the evening with my wife and daughters, and sleep well for approximately eight hours before I do it all over again.

It seems to be a good enough life. But could it be better? Am I the best man I can possibly be (a slightly depressing thought, considering the extensive list of my flaws), or have I simply settled into a routine, a comfortable and lifelong ceremony that allows me to live a full live but not an expansive one?

Near the end of the summer of 1976, a few days before I went back to school, my mother decided to spend one last day with me.

"Special you-and-me time," she said. "Before my best friend leaves me for the young women of Garfield High School."

We woke early, ate banana and pecan pancakes at a dive on the waterfront, and shopped for new school clothes. I wanted tight jeans and T-shirts with TV stars printed on them; she bought me cords and white dress shirts.

"I'm going to get beat up," I said.

"And all those boys who beat you up," she said, "will be working for you when you grow up."

She was wrong, of course; those tough boys run the trade unions and own the golf courses.

After shopping, we ate greasy hamburgers and french fries for lunch, told each other dirty jokes, and looked for the car. My mother and I have always been cursed with poor short-term memories, so we never remember where we park the car. I've been forced to ride the bus home from teaching because I can't remember on which street I parked my car. I'm ashamed of my poor memory, but my mother was always amused by her eccentricities.

"I'm a kook, huh?" she said over and over while we searched for the car.

"Yes, you're a kook, and I'm a kook," I said.

"We're a kooky couple," she said. "We could start a cuckoo-clock company because we're such a completely kooky couple."

Oh, sometimes I felt like her son, and other times I felt like her boyfriend, and most times I felt like her willing audience, laughing when she wanted me to laugh.

A few minutes after five, right when the city was its busiest with rush-hour traffic and people, when so many commuters were so happy to be done with work, we found our car hidden between two delivery trucks. We'd walked past it ten or twelve times before finally spotting it. Even then, the car was wedged in too tightly to open the doors, so my mother had to climb through the open sunroof, then back the car out so I could get in.

"It's a good thing your mother is a world-class gymnast," she said.

"Mothers aren't supposed to climb through sunroofs," I said.

"Sexist fantasy," she said and laughed and laughed.

The streets were packed with people. Five thousand, ten thousand people, more. Downtown Seattle was alive with color and noise. My mother drove the streets like she was the grand marshal of a parade. She waved and smiled. At stoplights, she poked her head out of the sunroof and praised the blue skies and the golden sun. She sang along with the radio and warbled so loudly and badly that pedestrians heard her and laughed or sang along with her for a few bars. My mother's joy was infectious. She smiled and caused others to smile. Strangers smiling at strangers! It was no longer a city but a tribe!

And then I saw a woman cross against the light on Pike and Seventh. She wore a white dress.

She was beautiful and strong, with long blond hair hanging down past muscled and taut shoulders. A runner, maybe, a marathoner, a lovely kickboxer, I thought. She was a reader, too, swinging a book bag stuffed with paperbacks. I couldn't see the titles, but I hoped she read an equal mixture of formal poetry and comic books. She was tall, almost six feet, I guessed, but was unashamed of her stature and walked with a graceful and perfect posture. She wore heels! *I am tall with a decent and easy happiness*, she seemed to say with her step, *and I am getting taller and happier!* Best of all, she wore that luminous white dress, lacy and conservative for the times, with the hem falling a few inches below her knees. I was in love, in love, in love, and then I saw the menstrual blood that stained the back of her dress, a line of dried blood that ran from her upper thigh down to the hem of the dress.

"Mom," I said, but she'd already seen the blood, and we both saw the hundreds of people walking with and against this woman, and how many other hundreds of people had already walked with and against this woman and her blood?

"Mom," I said, already crying, wanting to save this woman but unable to think how.

"I know, I know," my mother said, but she was frozen. She slowed the car and drove close to the sidewalk, keeping pace with the woman, but that's all she could do.

"Mom!"

"I know, I know!"

Of course other people noticed the blood. Some of the men and boys laughed and pointed. Some of the women gasped in horror and embarrassment and ran for shelter. Most people remained silent and kept walking, more interested in their own lives than in helping this woman with menstrual blood running down the back of her dress.

Oh God, I wondered if she was still bleeding and had left a trail of fresh blood behind her. Would she arrive at work in the morning and find the janitors scrubbing clean the carpet of her office? Would she have nightmares about birds swooping down to sip her blood from the sidewalk? Would she dream about hungry rats? And how long had she been bleeding? Did she start bleeding and staining her dress on her way to work? Had she been bleeding and staining her dress all day? Had she gone to lunch with her lover and stained the restaurant chair? Had she left evidence all over the city? How could she trust her friends and coworkers ever again? How could she walk through a city with so much blood staining her white dress and not be stopped by another human being? Would she lose her faith in people, in God, in goodness?

"Mom!" I cried and cried. "Mom! Mom!"

"I know! I know!" my mother screamed at me. She stopped the car but still could not find strength enough to open the door, run for the woman, and save her dignity.

"Mom!"

"I know!"

At that moment, an older woman ran a red light, steered her car across three lanes of traffic, and braked to a stop halfway onto the sidewalk. She exploded out of her car with a coat in her hands, wrapped it around the waist of the woman in the white dress, and rushed back to her car. The older woman ran another red light and drove away from the scene.

"Mom!" I shouted. I grabbed her arm, leaving a bruise that took two weeks to heal, and pulled her toward me. "Do something!" I shouted at her.

"I know!" my mother screamed and slapped me. "I know!" she screamed and slapped me once more and cut my face with her ring. She slapped me a third time, cutting me again, and she hugged me close and wept. I wept with her. We wept together while the city moved all around us, while one woman led another woman to safety.

My mother and I have loved and failed each other, and we keep on loving and failing each other, and one of us will eventually bury the other, and the survivor will burn down the church with grief's hungry fire.

DO YOU KNOW WHERE I AM?

Sharon and I were college sweethearts at St. Jerome the Second University in Seattle, or, as it is affectionately known, St. Junior's. We met at the first mixer dance of our freshman year and soon discovered we were the only confirmed Native American Roman Catholics within a three-mile radius of campus, so we slept together that inaugural night, in open defiance of Pope Whomever, and kept sleeping together for the next three years. It was primary love: red girl and red boy on white sheets.

Sharon was Apache, and I was Spokane, but we practiced our tribal religions like we practiced Catholicism: We loved all of the ceremonies but thought they were pitiful cries to a disinterested god.

My white mother, Mary, bless her soul, raised me all by herself in Seattle because my Indian daddy, Marvin, died of stomach cancer when I was a baby. I never knew him, but I spent half of every summer on the Spokane Reservation with his mother and father, my grandparents. My mother wanted me to keep in touch with my tribal heritage, but mostly, I read spy novels to my grandfather and shopped garage sales and secondhand stores with my grandmother. I suppose, for many Indians, garage sales and trashy novels are highly traditional and sacred. We all make up our ceremonies as we go along, right? I thought the reservation was ordinary and magical, like a sedate version of Disneyland. All told, I loved to visit but loved my home much more. In Seattle, my mother was a corporate lawyer for old-money companies and sent me to Lakeside Upper School, where I was a schoolmate of Bill Gates and Paul Allen, who have become the new-money kings of the world.

Sharon went to St. Therese's School for Girls. Her parents, Wilson and Pauline, were both architects; they helped build three of the tallest skyscrapers in downtown Seattle. If Zeus ate a few million pounds of glass, steel, and concrete, his offal would look something like those buildings. However fecal, those monstrosities won awards and made Wilson and Pauline very popular and wealthy. They lived in a self-designed home on Lake Washington that was lovely and tasteful in all ways except for its ridiculously turquoise exterior. I don't know whether they painted the house turquoise to honor the sacred stone of the Southwest or if they were being ironic: *Ha! We're Apache Indians from the desert, and this is our big blue house on the water! Deal with it!*

Sharon and I were Native American royalty, the aboriginal prince and princess of western Washington. Sure, we'd been thoroughly defeated by white culture, but dang it, we were conquered and assimilated National Merit Scholars in St. Junior's English honors department.

Sharon and I were in love and happy and young and skinny and beautiful and hyperliterate. We recited Shakespeare monologues as foreplay: *To be or not to be, take off your panties, oh, Horatio, I knew him well, a fellow of infinite jest, I'm going to wear your panties now.* All over campus, we were known as Sharon-and-David-the-Bohemian-Indians. We were inseparable. We ate our meals together and fed each other. Risking expulsion for moral violations, we sneaked into each other's dorm rooms at night and made love while our respective roommates covered their heads with pillows. Sharon and I always tried to take the same classes and mourned the other's absence whenever we couldn't. We read the same books and discussed them while we were naked and intertwined. Oh Lord, we were twins conjoined at the brain, heart, and crotch.

I proposed to Sharon on the first day of our senior year, and she accepted, and we planned to secretly elope on the day after our graduation.

In June, the day before graduation, Sharon and I were taking one last walk along the path beside the anonymous creek that ran through the middle of campus. We were saying good-bye to a good place. Overgrown with fern and blackberry thickets, the creek had been left wild and wet.

"'Whose woods these are I think I know'," I said.

"Robert Frost wrote the poem," said Sharon. We were playing Name the Poet, a game of our own invention.

"'Know' and 'poem,'" I said. "A clumsy rhyme, don't you think?"

"You stink," she said and laughed too loudly. Her joy was always rowdy, rude, and pervasive. I laughed with her and pulled her close to me and pressed my face into her hair and breathed in her scent. After the first time we'd made love, she'd said, *Now I know what you smell like, and no matter what else happens to us, I'm always going to know what you smell like.*

"Hey," I said as we walked the creek. "How about we climb into the bushes and I get you a little wild and wet?"

We kissed and kissed until she pulled away.

"Do you hear that?" she said.

"What?"

"I think it's a cat. Can you hear it meowing?"

I listened and heard nothing.

"You're imagining things," I said.

"No, it's a cat. I can hear it. It sounds pitiful."

"There must be a hundred cats around here. City cats. They're tough."

"No, it sounds hurt. Listen."

I listened and finally heard the faint feline cry.

"It's down there in the creek somewhere," she said.

We peered over the edge and could barely see the water through the thick and thorny overgrowth.

"I'm sure it's hunting rats or something," I said. "It's okay."

"No, listen to it. It's crying. I think it's stuck."

"What do you want me to do? It's just a dumb-ass cat."

"Can you go find it?"

I looked again at the jungle between that cat and me.

"I'd need a machete to get through there," I said.

"Please," said Sharon.

"I'm going to get all cut up."

"'All in green went my love riding,'" she whispered in that special way, "'on a great horse of gold into the silver dawn.'"

"Cummings wrote the poem, and I'm in love and gone," I said and made my slow way down the creek side. I didn't want to save the cat; I wanted to preserve Sharon's high opinion of me. If she hadn't been there to push me down the slope, I never would have gone after that cat. As it was, I cursed the world as I tripped over ferns and pushed blackberry branches out of the way. I was cut and scraped and threatened by spiders and wasps, all for a dumb cat.

"It's like *Wild Kingdom* down here," I said.

"Do you see him?" she said, more worried about the cat. I could hear the love in her voice. I was jealous of that damn cat!

I stopped and listened. I heard the cry from somewhere close.

"He's right around here," I said.

"Find him," she said, her voice choking with fierce tears.

I leaned over, pushed aside one last fern, and saw him, a black cat trapped in blackberry branches. He was starved, too skinny to be alive, I thought, but his eyes were bright with fear and pain.

"Man," I said. "I think he's been caught in here for a long time."

"Save him, save him."

I reached in, expecting the cat to bite or claw me, but he remained gratefully passive as I tore away the branches and freed him. I lifted and carried him back up the bank. He was dirty and smelly, and I wanted all of this to be over.

"Oh my God," said Sharon as she took him from me. "Oh, he's so sad, so sad." She hugged him, and he accepted it without protest.

"What are we going to do with him?" I asked.

"I don't know."

"We can't keep him," I said. "Let's let him go here. He's free now. He'll be okay."

"What if he gets stuck again?"

"Then it'll be natural selection. Come on, he doesn't have a tag or anything. He's just a stray cat."

"No, he's tame, he's got a home somewhere." She stared the cat in the eyes as if he could tell us his phone number and address.

"Oh, wait, wait," she said. "I remember, in the newspaper, last week or something, there was a lost-cat ad. It said he was black with white heart-shaped fur on his belly."

Sharon had a supernatural memory; she could meet a few dozen new people at a party and rattle off their names two days later. During an English-department party our sophomore year, she recited by memory seventy-three Shakespeare sonnets in a row. It was the most voluminous display of erudition any of us had ever witnessed. Tenured English professors wept. But I was the one who enjoyed the honor and privilege of taking her home that night and making her grunt in repetitive monosyllables.

Beside the creek, Sharon gently turned the cat over, and we both saw the white heart. Without another word, Sharon ran back to her dorm room, and I followed her. She searched for the newspaper in her desk but couldn't find it, and none of her floormates had a copy of the old paper, either, so she ran into the basement and climbed into the Dumpster. I held the cat while she burrowed into the fetid pile of garbage.

"Come on," I said. "You're never going to find it. Maybe you imagined the whole thing. Let's take him to the shelter. They can take care of him."

She ignored me and kept searching. I felt like throwing the cat into the wall.

"This is it," she said and pulled a greasy newspaper out of the mess. She flipped to the classifieds, found the lost-cat ad, and shouted out the phone number. She jumped out of the Dumpster, grabbed the cat, ran back to her room, and quickly dialed.

"Hello," said Sharon over the telephone. "We have your cat. Yes, yes, yes. We found him by the creek. At St. Junior's. We'll bring him right over. What's your address? Oh God, that's really close."

Sharon ran out of the dorm; I ran after her.

"Slow down," I called after her, but she ignored me. Maybe Sharon wasn't a good Apache or Catholic, but she was religious when she found the proper mission.

We sprinted through a residential neighborhood, which may or may not have been a good idea for two brown kids, no matter how high our grade-point averages. But it felt good to run fast, and I dreamed about being a superhero. Fifteen minutes later and out of breath, Sharon knocked on the front door of a small house. An old couple opened the door.

"Lester," shouted the old man and took the cat from Sharon. The old woman hugged the man and the cat. All three cried to one another.

"How'd you find him?" asked the old man, weeping hard now, barely able to talk, but unashamed of his tears. "He's been gone for a month."

"I heard him crying," I said (I lied) and stepped into the doorway. Sharon stood behind me and peered over my shoulder.

"Oh, thank you, bless you," said the old woman.

"I pulled him out of some blackberry thorns," I said. "And then I remembered your ad in the newspaper, and I found the paper in the garbage, and I called you, and here I am."

The old man and woman hugged me, holding the cat between us, all of us celebrating the reunion, while Sharon stood silently by. I think I lied because I wanted to be briefly adored by strangers, to be remembered as a handsome and kind man, a better man, more complete, even saintly. But it was Orwell who wrote that "saints should be always judged guilty until they are proved innocent."

All during this time, Sharon never spoke. I can only guess at her emotions, but I imagine she was shocked and hurt by my disloyalty. Standing in the presence of such obvious commitment between two people and their damn cat, she must have lost faith in me and, more importantly, in herself.

"How can we ever repay you?" asked the old woman.

"Nothing," I said. "We need nothing."

"Here, here," said the old man as he opened his wallet and offered me a twenty.

"No, no," I said. "I don't need that. I just wanted to be good, you know?"

He forced the money into my hand; I accepted it.

"You're a good man," said the old woman.

I shook my head, took Sharon's hand, and walked away, leaving those grateful strangers to their beloved pet.

"Why did you do that?" Sharon asked as we walked.

"I needed to," I said. That was the best answer I could give her. It wasn't enough.

"You lied to me, you lied to them, and you took their money," she said. "How could you do that?"

"I don't know," I said.

Sharon broke away from me and ran.

I didn't see her that night as I got ready for graduation, and I didn't see her the next morning.

"Where's Sharon?" asked my mother as she adjusted my cap and gown.

"She's with her parents," I said, which was a true statement, I suppose, but hardly close to the truth.

I went through the ceremony alone; Sharon went through the ceremony alone; we sat ten chairs apart.

The day after graduation, Sharon was still missing. I didn't know where she was. When my mother asked me about her absence, I said she was on a spiritual retreat.

"One month of silence," I said, lying to my mother, to another woman who loved me. "After a big event, like a graduation or birth, the Apaches leave for a month. It's an Apache thing."

"I wish I could do that," she said. "I think everybody should do that. Make it a law. Once a year, everybody has to be silent for a month. We'd all rotate, you know? You have to be quiet during your birth month."

"It's a good idea, Mom, I'm sure it would go over well."

"Sarcasm is a sin, honey."

After another day of unceremonial silence, I assumed Sharon had
left me forever, and I finally confessed my fears to my mother.

"Mom," I said. "I love Sharon and I destroyed her."

Was I overreacting to Sharon's overreaction? I'd told such a small
lie, had taken credit and reward for such a small act of heroism. But
then I wondered if Sharon had always had her doubts about my character, and perhaps had always considered me an undependable brag-
gart. What if she'd been gathering evidence against me all along, and
I'd finally committed the last unpardonable crime?

"You have to go find her," my mother said.

"I can't," I said, and it was true and cowardly.

My mother turned away from me and cried while she fixed dinner. Later that night, while she washed dishes and I dried, my mother
told me how much she still missed my father.

"He's been gone twenty-two years," she said. "But I can still feel him
right here in the room with us. I can still smell him, his hair, his skin."

My mother didn't call my father by name because she wanted the
dead to stay dead; I wanted to learn magic and open a twenty-four-
hour supermarket that sold resurrection and redemption.

The next morning, Sharon came to see me. I was so grateful for
her presence that I leaned against the wall to keep from falling down.
My mother hugged Sharon until they both cried. Then Sharon asked
my mother to give us some privacy. After my mother left, Sharon
took my face in her hands.

"You're a liar," Sharon said. "I'm going to marry a liar."

I didn't want to ask her why she came back. We were so fragile, I
worried that one wrong word could completely break us.

For the next twenty-nine years, we lived as wife and husband, as
the mother and father of four kids (Sarah, Rachael, Francis, and Joshua)
who suddenly grew into adults and became wives and husbands and
mothers and fathers. During our long marriage, Sharon and I buried

her mother and father and my mother, all of our grandparents, and many of our aunts, uncles, and cousins. I covered high school sports and reviewed movies for the local alternative weekly; an odd pair of beats, I suppose, but I enjoyed the appearance of being odd while living a sedate life. Sharon ran her own coffee shop and wrote lyric odes she never published. We paid our taxes, owned a modest home, and made love an average of three times a week. We didn't have nearly as much money as our parents, and that could be viewed as our failure, but we felt successful. We weren't triumphant, by any means, but we lived a good and simple life, and I often wondered if I deserved it.

All during those years, at every house party, group dinner, family gathering, and company picnic, Sharon told the story of the lost cat.

"My husband, the liar," she always called me. At first, she told the story to hurt me, then she told it out of habit, and then she told it because she'd turned it into a wildly funny and exaggerated adventure: *And then he fell in the creek!* She loved to make people laugh, and so they laughed at my small sins. I wanted the laughter to absolve me, but I'm not sure if that was its purpose. I never asked to be forgiven, and Sharon never offered her forgiveness. We never talked about the lost cat in private; it was our most public secret.

But there were other secrets, of course. Sharon kept most of hers, and I kept most of mine. Those kept secrets were small and ordinary, having to do with broken diets and hidden pornography, and they were of little consequence, but one evening, a decade into our marriage, Sharon confessed to an extramarital affair.

"I don't love him," she said. "It's over now. I only slept with him three times. To be fair, you can ask me three questions about it, and I'll answer them as honestly as possible, and then I don't ever want to talk about it again."

I was hurt by the frankness of her words, by her deal-making, but she cried, and her voice trembled as she spoke, and she'd never been one to feign emotion or cry for dramatic purposes, so I was lost in her contradictions.

"How could you do that to me?" I asked.

"Is that a real question?" she asked. "Or is it rhetorical?"

I panicked. I didn't want to waste my three questions. I wanted to know details, the facts and figures, and not emotional states. But which particular details did I want to know? And which questions would elicit the most information? I needed to be a brutally efficient interrogator. I couldn't believe I was participating in this horrible transaction.

"Listen," I said, "this is ridiculous. Let's talk this out like normal people."

"That's the problem," she said. "Everything is so normal. You didn't used to be normal. I didn't marry normal."

She was a thirty-two-year-old woman with four young kids, and she owned and managed a small business. So she was one of those notorious superwomen. I knew she was always exhausted, but what could I do to help her? I could never tell her she worked too hard, and I certainly couldn't tell her she should spend more time with the kids. I couldn't ask her to choose between her work life and her home life. As a man, I would never be asked to make a similar choice. I spent most Friday and Saturday nights watching other people's children play football, basketball, and volleyball. What kind of father was I? I could best be described as cordially absent on weekends and lovingly distracted on weekdays. What kind of husband was I? Apparently, I was the kind of husband whose wife needed to sleep with at least one other man and an untold number of others who might be waiting in line. There are millions of those clueless husbands, aren't there? Wasn't I yet another cuckolded husband, slightly distinguished by knowing how to self-define with an Old English word? I was eight hundred years old. I was historic, predictable, and planned. I was normal.

"Who is he?" I asked.

"His name is Michael Joyce," she said. "He's a regular at the shop. I've asked him to never come back. He agreed. He's a good man."

I was surprised to discover I wanted to hit my wife. I wanted to punch her in the stomach and make her fall to the floor. I wanted to see her gasping with physical pain. I would never hurt her that way— I hadn't struck another human being since the third grade—but the violent impulse was there, and I was frightened and exhilarated by it. My wife had no idea how dangerous I could be. I felt better knowing I could hurt her far more than she'd hurt me. And then I was revolted. How could I love a person and want to hurt her so much? How could I look at my wife, the mother of my children, and feel only the need for revenge? I paced around the room, ran my fingers roughly through my hair, because I needed to move. I needed to find another space in which to exist. I studied the details of the living room: the antique lamps purchased for full price and the end tables rescued from garage sales and refurbished; the brown leather couch and black leather recliner; the Monet and Kahlo prints on the walls; the bookshelves stuffed with novels and sports histories; and the coffee tables adorned with art books. All of it was tasteful and beautiful and appropriate and hard-earned and useless.

Sharon wore a red blouse and blue jeans. Her feet were bare and needed a pedicure. Once a month, her feet were scrubbed clean and polished by a Vietnamese woman whose name and exact place of business I would never know. Sharon wore a fake pearl necklace her mother had given her for some birthday, and real pearl earrings I'd given her on our fifth anniversary. The fake pearls were prettier than the real ones. I don't know why I noticed her physical details, but it seemed important to take note of all I could. I felt the insistent need to be exact. Since it was laundry day, I knew she'd be wearing her oldest brassiere, and would never initiate lovemaking while wearing it, but would gladly receive my advances after first dashing into the

bathroom to quickly remove the tattered bra. How many times had
she emerged topless from the bathroom and run laughing toward me?
Who keeps accurate count of such wonderful moments? Wouldn't a
better husband know that number by heart?

"I'm a bad husband," I said. Why was I apologizing?

She turned away and sat on the couch as far away from me as possible. I kept pacing around the room.

"He's white," she said, volunteering the information, and I was
strangely relieved. My emotions were changing and shifting ran-
domly. If I'd been an actor in a musical, I would have broken into
song for no apparent reason. I would have tap-danced to the primal
4/4 beat of betrayal. I would have leaped over the couch where she
was sitting and rewon her heart with my grace and strength. What a
dream life I have, and how instantly I can immerse myself in it! Can
you believe I was happy to hear she'd slept with only a white man? I
would have been tortured to hear she'd slept with another Indian
man. Considering her beauty, ambition, and intelligence, I could
conceive of an amazing white man or black man who might love her
and be loved in return, but I doubted another Indian man of my particular talents existed out there in the world. Call it a potent mix of
arrogance and self-hatred, but I was certain I was the one Indian man
who was good enough for my Indian wife.

I believed I was being rational, but who can be rational in such a
painful situation? Wouldn't my wife and I hold entirely different standards for what made a man good or great? What if she'd slept with a
plumber or a construction worker? What if she'd slept with a supermarket graveyard-shift worker or a high school dropout? I couldn't stand
the thought of my wife sleeping with a blue-collar man who'd read fewer
books than I had. I wanted to believe my wife slept with another man
because she needed to be loved in a new way, a more educated and
intellectual way, and not because she wanted to hurt me. I didn't under-

stand what I was feeling, and I didn't know what to do, and I couldn't ask her to help me, because that might qualify as my second question and would leave me with only one.

"Don't look at me that way," she said.

"What way?" I asked.

"Like this is inconceivable. Like I'm the Loch Ness Monster."

"I don't know what I'm thinking, feeling, or seeing."

"That's the problem. You've been blind for years."

I sat on the couch beside her. I tried to take her hand, but she pulled it away.

"No," she said. "You don't get to comfort me. And I don't get to comfort you. You have two questions. Ask them."

I was struck with the terrible fear that she'd had sex with Michael Joyce in our house, in our bed.

"Where did it happen?" I asked.

"The first time was in a hotel," she said. "The Westin downtown. A suite. Early. Eight in the morning. I got the kids off to school, opened up the shop. Jody ran the register and Rick made the coffee and Christy waited tables. I told them I had a dentist appointment."

"You told me you had a dentist appointment," I said.

"Yes," she said. "I lied to you directly. I never wanted to do that. I knew I was lying to you indirectly, but I hated to look you in the eyes and lie to you. I hated it."

"The Westin is a decent hotel," I said. Jesus, I sounded like a travel agent.

"The second time was in his car. We parked down on Lake Washington. You were down in Tacoma, covering the football championships."

"I called home that night," I said. "Sara was watching the kids. She said you had an emergency at the shop. The espresso maker was overheating."

"She didn't know I was lying. She thought I was at the shop."

Once or twice a month, I ran the path alongside Lake Washington. I knew I would never run it again. How can I survive this? I thought. How many more of my routines will I have to change? Again I tried to take my wife's hand. This time she let me. We interlaced our fingers. A small moment of intimacy, but enough to keep me from running out of the room and house and fleeing down the street.

"The third time was in his apartment," she said. "In his bed. Lunchtime. I fell asleep with him. I hated that. That's why I ended it. Falling asleep with him felt like the worst thing I could do. I never felt evil until I fell asleep with him."

She leaned over and kissed my forehead. I felt her heat. I didn't want to feel her heat. I didn't want to smell her scent. I didn't want to taste her. And it felt like time squared and cubed and then exploded exponentially. Days and months and years passed before I would find enough stupid courage to ask my third question.

"What did you do with him?"

"What do you mean?" she asked.

"I mean, into which parts of you did he put it?"

She flinched so painfully that I might as well have punched her in her chest. I was briefly happy about that.

"Do you really want to know that?" she asked.

"Yes."

She stood and walked away from me. I assume she was afraid I might really punch her.

"We," she said. "He—I mean, we—did everything."

"Say it exactly."

"I don't want to."

"You have to. It's part of the deal."

"I can't. It hurts too much."

"You don't get to feel as much pain as me. Now say it. Tell me exactly."

She closed her eyes and moaned like some tortured animal, like she was the first animal feeling the first pain. I heard that sound again when she buried her mother and, thirteen months later, her father.

"Tell me," I said. "Exactly."

She couldn't speak. Instead, she pointed at her mouth, her vagina, and her ass. She looked like a pornographic mime. I started laughing. I lay down on the couch and laughed. I couldn't stop laughing. She stared at me like I was crazy. Then she started laughing with me. Softly at first, but soon she had to sit down laughing on the floor so she wouldn't fall down laughing on the floor. She crawled across the floor and climbed onto the couch with me. We held each other and laughed. Then, as suddenly as it started, it stopped. We held each other in the silence.

"If you still love me," she said, "please, please, build me a time machine."

She sounded like a little girl talking to her father. I didn't know what to say. But we lay there together for hours until the kids came home from school and surprised us.

"Mommy and Daddy were doing it!" the four of them chanted and danced around the living room. "Mommy and Daddy were doing it!"

Sharon and I danced with our children. We danced the family dance, three quick spins, two hops, and a scream at the ceiling, and then Sharon and I made dinner, and we ate with our kids and gossiped about their school days and played *Chutes and Ladders* and watched *The Lion King* and made them brush their teeth and wash their faces and forced them into their pajamas and pushed them down the hallways into their beds and read them *Curious George* and *Go, Dog, Go!* and turned off the lights and told them good night and gave them our love, and we sat in the kitchen across from each other and drank coffee and added up our wins and our losses and decided to stay married.

It was Emily Dickinson who wrote, "After great pain, a formal feeling comes." So Sharon and I formally rebuilt our marriage. And it was blue-collar work, exhausting and painful. We didn't argue more often than before, but we did live with longer and greater silences. There were times when both of us wanted to quit, but we always found the strength to get up in the morning and go back to the job. And then, one winter night two years after her confession, after eating a lovely dinner at a waterfront restaurant and slow-dancing in the parking lot while a small group of tourists cheered for us, she read a book in bed while I stood at our bedroom window and stared out into the dark. We were comfortable in the silence. A day or week or month or year before, I would have felt the need to end such a wonderful evening by making love to her, by proving I could share our bed and her body with ghosts. But I felt no such need that night, and I realized we'd completed the rebuilding project, we'd constructed a brand-new marriage, a new home, that sat next to the old marriage and its dusty and shuttered house. Standing at the window, I could almost see our old house out there in the dark, and I missed it. I often thought of it as we continued with our lives.

Suddenly, Sharon and I were forty. For my birthday that year, she and the kids all pitched in together and gave me a T-shirt that read LOST CAT on the front and DO YOU KNOW WHERE I AM? on the back.

I laughed and wore that shirt as pajamas. For two years, Sharon fell asleep next to me wearing that shirt.

"Oh, Lord," I said to Sharon on the day I finally tossed the ragged T-shirt into the trash. "With every new day comes a new monument to our love and pain."

"Who wrote that?" she asked.

"I did."

"It's free verse," she said. "I hate free verse."

We laughed and kissed and made love and read books in bed. We read through years of books, decades of books. There were never enough books for us. Read, partially read, and unread, our books filled the house, stacked on shelves and counters, piled into corners and closets. Our marriage became an eccentric and disorganized library. Whitman in the pantry! The Brontë sisters in the television room! Hardy on the front porch! Dickinson in the laundry room! We kept a battered copy of *Native Son* in the downstairs bathroom so our guests would have something valuable to read!

How do you measure a marriage? Three of our children still lived in Seattle and taught high school English, history, and Spanish respectively, while the fourth managed a homeless shelter in Portland, Oregon. Maybe Sharon and I had never loved each other well enough, but our kids were smart and talented and sober. They made less money than we did, as we made less than our parents did. We were going the wrong way on the social-class map! How glorious!

Every Sunday night, we all gathered for dinner (Joshua drove up from Portland with his partner, Aaron, and their son) and told one another the best stories of our weeks. We needed those small ceremonies. Our contentment was always running only slightly ahead of our dissatisfaction.

Was it enough? I don't know. But we knew enough not to ask ourselves too often. We knew to ask ourselves such questions during daylight hours. We fought hard for our happiness, and sometimes we won. Over the years, we won often enough to develop a strong taste for winning.

And then suddenly and mortally, Sharon and I were sixty-six years old.

On her birthday that year, surrounded by her husband, daughters, sons, and six grandkids, Sharon blew out the candles on her cake, closed her eyes, and made some secret wish.

One year later, after chemotherapy, radiation, organic food, acupuncture, and tribal shaman, Sharon lay on her deathbed in Sacred Hope Hospital. Our children had left their children to gather around Sharon, and it was good-bye Rachael! Good-bye Sarah! Good-bye Francis! Good-bye Joshua! She asked our children to give us some privacy. They cried and hugged her and left us alone.

"I'm going to die soon," Sharon said.

"I know," I said.

"I'm okay with it."

"I'm not. Because I love you so much," I said, "I would fistfight Time to win back your youth."

"You're a liar," she said and smiled, too tired to laugh.

"I lied to you once," I said. "But I haven't lied to you since."

"Is that the truth?"

"Yes," I said.

WHAT YOU PAWN
I WILL REDEEM

Noon

One day you have a home and the next you don't, but I'm not going
to tell you my particular reasons for being homeless, because it's my
secret story, and Indians have to work hard to keep secrets from hungry white folks.

I'm a Spokane Indian boy, an Interior Salish, and my people have
lived within a one-hundred-mile radius of Spokane, Washington, for
at least ten thousand years. I grew up in Spokane, moved to Seattle
twenty-three years ago for college, flunked out within two semesters,
worked various blue- and bluer-collar jobs for many years, married two
or three times, fathered two or three kids, and then went crazy. Of
course, "crazy" is not the official definition of my mental problem,
but I don't think "asocial disorder" fits it, either, because that makes
me sound like I'm a serial killer or something. I've never hurt another human being, or at least not physically. I've broken a few hearts
in my time, but we've all done that, so I'm nothing special in that
regard. I'm a boring heartbreaker, at that, because I've never abandoned one woman for another. I never dated or married more than
one woman at a time. I didn't break hearts into pieces overnight. I

broke them slowly and carefully. I didn't set any land-speed records running out the door. Piece by piece, I disappeared. And I've been disappearing ever since. But I'm not going to tell you any more about my brain or my soul.

I've been homeless for six years. If there's such a thing as being an effective homeless man, I suppose I'm effective. Being homeless is probably the only thing I've ever been good at. I know where to get the best free food. I've made friends with restaurant and convenience-store managers who let me use their bathrooms. I don't mean the public bathrooms, either. I mean the employees' bathrooms, the clean ones hidden in the back of the kitchen or the pantry or the cooler. I know it sounds strange to be proud of, but it means a lot to me, being truthworthy enough to piss in somebody else's clean bathroom. Maybe you don't understand the value of a clean bathroom, but I do.

Probably none of this interests you. I probably don't interest you much. Homeless Indians are everywhere in Seattle. We're common and boring, and you walk right on by us, with maybe a look of anger or disgust or even sadness at the terrible fate of the noble savage. But we have dreams and families. I'm friends with a homeless Plains Indian man whose son is the editor of a big-time newspaper back east. That's his story, but we Indians are great storytellers and liars and mythmakers, so maybe that Plains Indian hobo is a plain old everyday Indian. I'm kind of suspicious of him, because he describes himself only as Plains Indian, a generic term, and not by a specific tribe. When I asked him why he wouldn't tell me exactly what he is, he said, "Do any of us know exactly what we are?" Yeah, great, a philosophizing Indian. "Hey," I said, "you got to have a home to be that homely." He laughed and flipped me the eagle and walked away. But you probably want to know more about the story I'm really trying to tell you.

I wander the streets with a regular crew, my teammates, my defenders, and my posse. It's Rose of Sharon, Junior, and me. We matter to

one another if we don't matter to anybody else. Rose of Sharon is a big
woman, about seven feet tall if you're measuring overall effect, and
about five feet tall if you're talking about the physical. She's a Yakama
Indian of the Wishram variety. Junior is a Colville, but there are about
199 tribes that make up the Colville, so he could be anything. He's
good-looking, though, like he just stepped out of some "Don't Litter
the Earth" public-service advertisement. He's got those great big cheekbones that are like planets, you know, with little moons orbiting around
them. He gets me jealous, jealous, and jealous. If you put Junior and
me next to each other, he's the Before Columbus Arrived Indian, and
I'm the After Columbus Arrived Indian. I am living proof of the horrible damage that colonialism has done to us Skins. But I'm not going
to let you know how scared I sometimes get of history and its ways.
I'm a strong man, and I know that silence is the best way of dealing
with white folks.

This whole story started at lunchtime, when Rose of Sharon, Junior, and I were panning the handle down at Pike Place Market.
After about two hours of negotiating, we earned five dollars, good
enough for a bottle of fortified courage from the most beautiful 7–
Eleven in the world. So we headed over that way, feeling like warrior drunks, and we walked past this pawnshop I'd never noticed
before. And that was strange, because we Indians have built-in pawnshop radar. But the strangest thing was the old powwow-dance regalia I saw hanging in the window.

"That's my grandmother's regalia," I said to Rose of Sharon and
Junior.

"How do you know for sure?" Junior asked.

I didn't know for sure, because I hadn't seen that regalia in person ever. I'd seen only photographs of my grandmother dancing in
it. And that was before somebody stole it from her fifty years ago.
But it sure looked like my memory of it, and it had all the same

colors of feathers and beads that my family always sewed into their powwow regalia.

"There's only one way to know for sure," I said.

So Rose of Sharon, Junior, and I walked into the pawnshop and greeted the old white man working behind the counter.

"How can I help you?" he asked.

"That's my grandmother's powwow regalia in your window," I said. "Somebody stole it from her fifty years ago, and my family has been looking for it ever since."

The pawnbroker looked at me like I was a liar. I understood. Pawnshops are filled with liars.

"I'm not lying," I said. "Ask my friends here. They'll tell you."

"He's the most honest Indian I know," Rose of Sharon said.

"All right, honest Indian," the pawnbroker said. "I'll give you the benefit of the doubt. Can you prove it's your grandmother's regalia?"

Because they don't want to be perfect, because only God is perfect, Indian people sew flaws into their powwow regalia. My family always sewed one yellow bead somewhere on their regalia. But we always hid it where you had to search hard to find it.

"If it really is my grandmother's," I said, "there will be one yellow bead hidden somewhere on it."

"All right, then," the pawnbroker said. "Let's take a look."

He pulled the regalia out of the window, laid it down on his glass counter, and we searched for that yellow bead and found it hidden beneath the armpit.

"There it is," the pawnbroker said. He didn't sound surprised. "You were right. This is your grandmother's regalia."

"It's been missing for fifty years," Junior said.

"Hey, Junior," I said. "It's my family's story. Let me tell it."

"All right," he said. "I apologize. You go ahead."

"It's been missing for fifty years," I said.

"That's his family's sad story," Rose of Sharon said. "Are you going to give it back to him?"

"That would be the right thing to do," the pawnbroker said. "But I can't afford to do the right thing. I paid a thousand dollars for this. I can't give away a thousand dollars."

"We could go to the cops and tell them it was stolen," Rose of Sharon said.

"Hey," I said to her, "don't go threatening people."

The pawnbroker sighed. He was thinking hard about the possibilities.

"Well, I suppose you could go to the cops," he said. "But I don't think they'd believe a word you said."

He sounded sad about that. Like he was sorry for taking advantage of our disadvantages.

"What's your name?" the pawnbroker asked me.

"Jackson," I said.

"Is that first or last?" he asked.

"Both."

"Are you serious?"

"Yes, it's true. My mother and father named me Jackson Jackson. My family nickname is Jackson Squared. My family is funny."

"All right, Jackson Jackson," the pawnbroker said. "You wouldn't happen to have a thousand dollars, would you?"

"We've got five dollars total," I said.

"That's too bad," he said and thought hard about the possibilities. "I'd sell it to you for a thousand dollars if you had it. Heck, to make it fair, I'd sell it to you for nine hundred and ninety-nine dollars. I'd lose a dollar. It would be the moral thing to do in this case. To lose a dollar would be the right thing."

"We've got five dollars total," I said again.

"That's too bad," he said again and thought harder about the possibilities. "How about this? I'll give you twenty-four hours to come up with nine hundred and ninety-nine dollars. You come back here at lunchtime tomorrow with the money, and I'll sell it back to you. How does that sound?"

"It sounds good," I said.

"All right, then," he said. "We have a deal. And I'll get you started. Here's twenty bucks to get you started."

He opened up his wallet and pulled out a crisp twenty-dollar bill and gave it to me. Rose of Sharon, Junior, and I walked out into the daylight to search for nine hundred and seventy-four more dollars.

1:00 P.M.

Rose of Sharon, Junior, and I carried our twenty-dollar bill and our five dollars in loose change over to the 7–Eleven and spent it to buy three bottles of imagination. We needed to figure out how to raise all that money in one day. Thinking hard, we huddled in an alley beneath the Alaska Way Viaduct and finished off those bottles one, two, and three.

2:00 P.M.

Rose of Sharon was gone when I woke. I heard later she had hitchhiked back to Toppenish and was living with her sister on the reservation.

Junior was passed out beside me, covered in his own vomit, or maybe somebody else's vomit, and my head hurt from thinking, so I left him alone and walked down to the water. I loved the smell of ocean water. Salt always smells like memory.

When I got to the wharf, I ran into three Aleut cousins who sat on a wooden bench and stared out at the bay and cried. Most of the homeless Indians in Seattle come from Alaska. One by one, each of them hopped a big working boat in Anchorage or Barrow or Juneau, fished his way south to Seattle, jumped off the boat with a pocketful of cash to party hard at one of the highly sacred and traditional Indian bars, went broke and broker, and has been trying to find his way back to the boat and the frozen north ever since.

These Aleuts smelled like salmon, I thought, and they told me they were going to sit on that wooden bench until their boat came back.

"How long has your boat been gone?" I asked.

"Eleven years," the elder Aleut said.

I cried with them for a while.

"Hey," I said. "Do you guys have any money I can borrow?"

They didn't.

3:00 P.M.

I walked back to Junior. He was still passed out. I put my face down near his mouth to make sure he was breathing. He was alive, so I dug around in his blue-jean pockets and found half a cigarette. I smoked it all the way down and thought about my grandmother.

Her name was Agnes, and she died of breast cancer when I was fourteen. My father thought Agnes caught her tumors from the uranium mine on the reservation. But my mother said the disease started when Agnes was walking back from the powwow one night and got run over by a motorcycle. She broke three ribs, and my mother said those ribs never healed right, and tumors always take over when you don't heal right.

Sitting beside Junior, smelling the smoke and salt and vomit, I wondered if my grandmother's cancer had started when somebody stole her powwow regalia. Maybe the cancer started in her broken heart and then leaked out into her breasts. I know it's crazy, but I wondered if I could bring my grandmother back to life if I bought back her regalia.

I needed money, big money, so I left Junior and walked over to the Real Change office.

4:00 P.M.

"Real Change is a multifaceted organization that publishes a newspaper, supports cultural projects that empower the poor and homeless, and mobilizes the public around poverty issues. Real Change's mission is to organize, educate, and build alliances to create solutions to homelessness and poverty. They exist to provide a voice to poor people in our community."

I memorized Real Change's mission statement because I sometimes sell the newspaper on the streets. But you have to stay sober to sell it, and I'm not always good at staying sober. Anybody can sell the newspaper. You buy each copy for thirty cents and sell it for a dollar and keep the net profit.

"I need one thousand four hundred and thirty papers," I said to the Big Boss.

"That's a strange number," he said. "And that's a lot of papers."

"I need them."

The Big Boss pulled out the calculator and did the math. "It will cost you four hundred and twenty-nine dollars for that many," he said.

"If I had that kind of money, I wouldn't need to sell the papers."

"What's going on, Jackson-to-the-Second-Power?" he asked. He is the only one who calls me that. He is a funny and kind man.

I told him about my grandmother's powwow regalia and how much money I needed to buy it back.

"We should call the police," he said.

"I don't want to do that," I said. "It's a quest now. I need to win it back by myself."

"I understand," he said. "And to be honest, I'd give you the papers to sell if I thought it would work. But the record for most papers sold in a day by one vendor is only three hundred and two."

"That would net me about two hundred bucks," I said.

The Big Boss used his calculator. "Two hundred and eleven dollars and forty cents," he said.

"That's not enough," I said.

"The most money anybody has made in one day is five hundred and twenty-five. And that's because somebody gave Old Blue five hundred-dollar bills for some dang reason. The average daily net is about thirty dollars."

"This isn't going to work."

"No."

"Can you lend me some money?"

"I can't do that," he said. "If I lend you money, I have to lend money to everybody."

"What can you do?"

"I'll give you fifty papers for free. But don't tell anybody I did it."

"Okay," I said.

He gathered up the newspapers and handed them to me. I held them to my chest. He hugged me. I carried the newspapers back toward the water.

5:00 P.M.

Back on the wharf, I stood near the Bainbridge Island Terminal and tried to sell papers to business commuters walking onto the ferry.

I sold five in one hour, dumped the other forty-five into a garbage can, and walked into the McDonald's, ordered four cheeseburgers for a dollar each, and slowly ate them.

After eating, I walked outside and vomited on the sidewalk. I hated to lose my food so soon after eating it. As an alcoholic Indian with a busted stomach, I always hope I can keep enough food in my stomach to stay alive.

6:00 P.M.

With one dollar in my pocket, I walked back to Junior. He was still passed out, so I put my ear to his chest and listened for his heartbeat. He was alive, so I took off his shoes and socks and found one dollar in his left sock and fifty cents in his right sock. With two dollars and fifty cents in my hand, I sat beside Junior and thought about my grandmother and her stories.

When I was sixteen, my grandmother told me a story about World War II. She was a nurse at a military hospital in Sydney, Australia. Over the course of two years, she comforted and healed U.S. and Australian soldiers.

One day, she tended to a wounded Maori soldier. He was very dark-skinned. His hair was black and curly, and his eyes were black and warm. His face with covered with bright tattoos.

"Are you Maori?" he asked my grandmother.

"No," she said. "I'm Spokane Indian. From the United States."

"Ah, yes," he said. "I have heard of your tribes. But you are the first American Indian I have ever met."

"There's a lot of Indian soldiers fighting for the United States," she said. "I have a brother still fighting in Germany, and I lost another brother on Okinawa."

"I am sorry," he said. "I was on Okinawa as well. It was terrible." He had lost his legs to an artillery attack.

"I am sorry about your legs," my grandmother said.

"It's funny, isn't it?" he asked.

"What's funny?"

"How we brown people are killing other brown people so white people will remain free."

"I hadn't thought of it that way."

"Well, sometimes I think of it that way. And other times, I think of it the way they want me to think of it. I get confused."

She fed him morphine.

"Do you believe in heaven?" he asked.

"Which heaven?" she asked.

"I'm talking about the heaven where my legs are waiting for me."

They laughed.

"Of course," he said, "my legs will probably run away from me when I get to heaven. And how will I ever catch them?"

"You have to get your arms strong," my grandmother said. "So you can run on your hands."

They laughed again.

Sitting beside Junior, I laughed with the memory of my grand-mother's story. I put my hand close to Junior's mouth to make sure he was still breathing. Yes, Junior was alive, so I took his two dol-lars and fifty cents and walked to the Korean grocery store over in Pioneer Square.

7:00 P.M.

In the Korean grocery store, I bought a fifty-cent cigar and two scratch lottery tickets for a dollar each. The maximum cash prize was five hundred dollars a ticket. If I won both, I would have enough money to buy back the regalia.

I loved Kay, the young Korean woman who worked the register. She was the daughter of the owners and sang all day.

"I love you," I said when I handed her the money.

"You always say you love me," she said.

"That's because I will always love you."

"You are a sentimental fool."

"I'm a romantic old man."

"Too old for me."

"I know I'm too old for you, but I can dream."

"Okay," she said. "I agree to be a part of your dreams, but I will only hold your hand in your dreams. No kissing and no sex. Not even in your dreams."

"Okay," I said. "No sex. Just romance."

"Good-bye, Jackson Jackson, my love, I will see you soon."

I left the store, walked over to Occidental Park, sat on a bench, and smoked my cigar all the way down.

Ten minutes after I finished the cigar, I scratched my first lottery ticket and won nothing. So I could win only five hundred dollars now, and that would be just half of what I needed.

Ten minutes later, I scratched my other lottery ticket and won a free ticket, a small consolation and one more chance to win money.

I walked back to Kay.

"Jackson Jackson," she said. "Have you come back to claim my heart?"

"I won a free ticket," I said.

"Just like a man," she said. "You love money and power more than you love me."

"It's true," I said. "And I'm sorry it's true."

She gave me another scratch ticket, and I carried it outside. I liked to scratch my tickets in private. Hopeful and sad, I scratched that third ticket and won real money. I carried it back inside to Kay.

"I won a hundred dollars," I said.

She examined the ticket and laughed. "That's a fortune," she said and counted out five twenties. Our fingertips touched as she handed me the money. I felt electric and constant.

"Thank you," I said and gave her one of the bills.

"I can't take that," she said. "It's your money."

"No, it's tribal. It's an Indian thing. When you win, you're supposed to share with your family."

"I'm not your family."

"Yes, you are."

She smiled. She kept the money. With eighty dollars in my pocket, I said good-bye to my dear Kay and walked out into the cold night air.

8:00 P.M.

I wanted to share the good news with Junior. I walked back to him, but he was gone. I later heard he had hitchhiked down to Portland, Oregon, and died of exposure in an alley behind the Hilton Hotel.

9:00 P.M.

Lonely for Indians, I carried my eighty dollars over to Big Heart's in South Downtown. Big Heart's is an all-Indian bar. Nobody knows how or why Indians migrate to one bar and turn it into an official Indian bar. But Big Heart's has been an Indian bar for twenty-three years. It used to be way up on Aurora Avenue, but a crazy Lummi

Indian burned that one down, and the owners moved to the new location, a few blocks south of Safeco Field.

I walked inside Big Heart's and counted fifteen Indians, eight men and seven women. I didn't know any of them, but Indians like to belong, so we all pretended to be cousins.

"How much for whiskey shots?" I asked the bartender, a fat white guy.

"You want the bad stuff or the badder stuff?"

"As bad as you got."

"One dollar a shot."

I laid my eighty dollars on the bar top.

"All right," I said. "Me and all my cousins here are going to be drinking eighty shots. How many is that apiece?"

"Counting you," a woman shouted from behind me, "that's five shots for everybody."

I turned to look at her. She was a chubby and pale Indian sitting with a tall and skinny Indian man.

"All right, math genius," I said to her and then shouted for the whole bar to hear. "Five drinks for everybody!"

All of the other Indians rushed the bar, but I sat with the mathematician and her skinny friend. We took our time with our whiskey shots.

"What's your tribe?" I asked them.

"I'm Duwamish," she said. "And he's Crow."

"You're a long way from Montana," I said to him.

"I'm Crow," he said. "I flew here."

"What's your name?" I asked them.

"I'm Irene Muse," she said. "And this is Honey Boy."

She shook my hand hard, but he offered his hand like I was supposed to kiss it. So I kissed it. He giggled and blushed as well as a dark-skinned Crow can blush.

"You're one of them two-spirits, aren't you?" I asked him.

"I love women," he said. "And I love men."

"Sometimes both at the same time," Irene said.

We laughed.

"Man," I said to Honey Boy. "So you must have about eight or nine spirits going on inside of you, enit?"

"Sweetie," he said, "I'll be whatever you want me to be."

"Oh, no," Irene said. "Honey Boy is falling in love."

"It has nothing to do with love," he said.

We laughed.

"Wow," I said. "I'm flattered, Honey Boy, but I don't play on your team."

"Never say never," he said.

"You better be careful," Irene said. "Honey Boy knows all sorts of magic. He always makes straight boys fall for him."

"Honey Boy," I said, "you can try to seduce me. And Irene, you can try with him. But my heart belongs to a woman named Kay."

"Is your Kay a virgin?" Honey Boy asked.

We laughed.

We drank our whiskey shots until they were gone. But the other Indians bought me more whiskey shots because I'd been so generous with my money. Honey Boy pulled out his credit card, and I drank and sailed on that plastic boat.

After a dozen shots, I asked Irene to dance. And she refused. But Honey Boy shuffled over to the jukebox, dropped in a quarter, and selected Willie Nelson's "Help Me Make It Through the Night." As Irene and I sat at the table and laughed and drank more whiskey, Honey Boy danced a slow circle around us and sang along with Willie.

"Are you serenading me?" I asked him.

He kept singing and dancing.

"Are you serenading me?" I asked him again.

"He's going to put a spell on you," Irene said.

I leaned over the table, spilling a few drinks, and kissed Irene hard. She kissed me back.

10:00 P.M.

Irene pushed me into the women's bathroom, into a stall, shut the door behind us, and shoved her hand down my pants. She was short, so I had to lean over to kiss her. I grabbed and squeezed her everywhere I could reach, and she was wonderfully fat, and every part of her body felt like a large, warm, and soft breast.

Midnight

Nearly blind with alcohol, I stood alone at the bar and swore I'd been standing in the bathroom with Irene only a minute ago.

"One more shot!" I yelled at the bartender.

"You've got no more money!" he yelled.

"Somebody buy me a drink!" I shouted.

"They've got no more money!"

"Where's Irene and Honey Boy?"

"Long gone!"

2:00 A.M.

"Closing time!" the bartender shouted at the three or four Indians still drinking hard after a long hard day of drinking. Indian alcoholics are either sprinters or marathon runners.

"Where's Irene and Honey Bear?" I asked.

"They've been gone for hours," the bartender said.

"Where'd they go?"

"I told you a hundred times, I don't know."

"What am I supposed to do?"

"It's closing time. I don't care where you go, but you're not stay-ing here."

"You are an ungrateful bastard. I've been good to you."

"You don't leave right now, I'm going to kick your ass."

"Come on, I know how to fight."

He came for me. I don't remember what happened after that.

4:00 A.M.

I emerged from the blackness and discovered myself walking be-hind a big warehouse. I didn't know where I was. My face hurt. I touched my nose and decided it might be broken. Exhausted and cold, I pulled a plastic tarp from a truck bed, wrapped it around me like a faithful lover, and fell asleep in the dirt.

6:00 A.M.

Somebody kicked me in the ribs. I opened my eyes and looked up at a white cop.

"Jackson," said the cop. "Is that you?"

"Officer Williams," I said. He was a good cop with a sweet tooth. He'd given me hundreds of candy bars over the years. I wonder if he knew I was diabetic.

"What the hell are you doing here?" he asked.

"I was cold and sleepy," I said. "So I laid down."

"You dumb-ass, you passed out on the railroad tracks."

I sat up and looked around. I was lying on the railroad tracks. Dockworkers stared at me. I should have been a railroad-track pizza, a double Indian pepperoni with extra cheese. Sick and scared, I leaned over and puked whiskey.

"What the hell's wrong with you?" Officer Williams asked. "You've never been this stupid."

"It's my grandmother," I said. "She died."

"I'm sorry, man. When did she die?"

"1972."

"And you're killing yourself now?"

"I've been killing myself ever since she died."

He shook his head. He was sad for me. Like I said, he was a good cop.

"And somebody beat the hell out of you," he said. "You remember who?"

"Mr. Grief and I went a few rounds."

"It looks like Mr. Grief knocked you out."

"Mr. Grief always wins."

"Come on," he said, "let's get you out of here."

He helped me stand and led me over to his squad car. He put me in the back. "You throw up in there," he said, "and you're cleaning it up."

"That's fair," I said.

He walked around the car and sat in the driver's seat. "I'm taking you over to detox," he said.

"No, man, that place is awful," I said. "It's full of drunk Indians."

We laughed. He drove away from the docks.

"I don't know how you guys do it," he said.

"What guys?" I asked.

"You Indians. How the hell do you laugh so much? I just picked your ass off the railroad tracks, and you're making jokes. Why the hell do you do that?"

"The two funniest tribes I've ever been around are Indians and Jews, so I guess that says something about the inherent humor of genocide."

We laughed.

"Listen to you, Jackson. You're so smart. Why the hell are you on the streets?"

"Give me a thousand dollars, and I'll tell you."

"You bet I'd give you a thousand dollars if I knew you'd straighten up your life."

He meant it. He was the second-best cop I'd ever known.

"You're a good cop," I said.

"Come on, Jackson," he said. "Don't blow smoke up my ass."

"No, really, you remind me of my grandfather."

"Yeah, that's what you Indians always tell me."

"No, man, my grandfather was a tribal cop. He was a good cop. He never arrested people. He took care of them. Just like you."

"I've arrested hundreds of scumbags, Jackson. And I've shot a couple in the ass."

"It don't matter. You're not a killer."

"I didn't kill them. I killed their asses. I'm an ass-killer."

We drove through downtown. The missions and shelters had already released their overnighters. Sleepy homeless men and women stood on corners and stared up at the gray sky. It was the morning after the night of the living dead.

"Did you ever get scared?" I asked Officer Williams.

"What do you mean?"

"I mean, being a cop, is it scary?"

He thought about that for a while. He contemplated it. I liked that about him.

"I guess I try not to think too much about being afraid," he said. "If you think about fear, then you'll be afraid. The job is boring most of the time. Just driving and looking into dark corners, you know,

and seeing nothing. But then things get heavy. You're chasing somebody or fighting them or walking around a dark house and you just
know some crazy guy is hiding around a corner, and hell yes, it's scary."

"My grandfather was killed in the line of duty," I said.

"I'm sorry. How'd it happen?"

I knew he'd listen closely to my story.

"He worked on the reservation. Everybody knew everybody. It was
safe. We aren't like those crazy Sioux or Apache or any of those other
warrior tribes. There's only been three murders on my reservation in
the last hundred years."

"That is safe."

"Yeah, we Spokane, we're passive, you know? We're mean with
words. And we'll cuss out anybody. But we don't shoot people. Or
stab them. Not much, anyway."

"So what happened to your grandfather?"

"This man and his girlfriend were fighting down by Little Falls."

"Domestic dispute. Those are the worst."

"Yeah, but this guy was my grandfather's brother. My great-uncle."

"Oh, no."

"Yeah, it was awful. My grandfather just strolled into the house.
He'd been there a thousand times. And his brother and his girlfriend
were all drunk and beating on each other. And my grandfather
stepped between them just like he'd done a hundred times before.
And the girlfriend tripped or something. She fell down and hit her
head and started crying. And my grandfather knelt down beside her
to make sure she was all right. And for some reason, my great-uncle
reached down, pulled my grandfather's pistol out of the holster, and
shot him in the head."

"That's terrible. I'm sorry."

"Yeah, my great-uncle could never figure out why he did it. He
went to prison forever, you know, and he always wrote these long

letters. Like fifty pages of tiny little handwriting. And he was always trying to figure out why he did it. He'd write and write and write and try to figure it out. He never did. It's a great big mystery."

"Do you remember your grandfather?"

"A little bit. I remember the funeral. My grandmother wouldn't let them bury him. My father had to drag her away from the grave."

"I don't know what to say."

"I don't, either."

We stopped in front of the detox center.

"We're here," Officer Williams said.

"I can't go in there," I said.

"You have to."

"Please, no. They'll keep me for twenty-four hours. And then it will be too late."

"Too late for what?"

I told him about my grandmother's regalia and the deadline for buying it back.

"If it was stolen," he said, "then you need to file reports. I'll investigate it myself. If that thing is really your grandmother's, I'll get it back for you. Legally."

"No," I said. "That's not fair. The pawnbroker didn't know it was stolen. And besides, I'm on a mission here. I want to be a hero, you know? I want to win it back like a knight."

"That's romantic crap."

"It might be. But I care about it. It's been a long time since I really cared about something."

Officer Williams turned around in his seat and stared at me. He studied me.

"I'll give you some money," he said. "I don't have much. Only thirty bucks. I'm short until payday. And it's not enough to get back the regalia. But it's something."

"I'll take it," I said.

"I'm giving it to you because I believe in what you believe. I'm
hoping, and I don't know why I'm hoping it, but I hope you can turn
thirty bucks into a thousand somehow."

"I believe in magic."

"I believe you'll take my money and get drunk on it."

"Then why are you giving it to me?"

"There ain't no such thing as an atheist cop."

"Sure there is."

"Yeah, well, I'm not an atheist cop."

He let me out of the car, handed me two fives and a twenty, and
shook my hand. "Take care of yourself, Jackson," he said. "Stay off
the railroad tracks."

"I'll try," I said.

He drove away. Carrying my money, I headed back toward the water.

8:00 A.M.

On the wharf, those three Aleut men still waited on the wooden
bench.

"Have you seen your ship?" I asked.

"Seen a lot of ships," the elder Aleut said. "But not our ship."

I sat on the bench with them. We sat in silence for a long time. I
wondered whether we would fossilize if we sat there long enough.

I thought about my grandmother. I'd never seen her dance in her
regalia. More than anything, I wished I'd seen her dance at a powwow.

"Do you guys know any songs?" I asked the Aleuts.

"I know all of Hank Williams," the elder Aleut said.

"How about Indian songs?"

"Hank Williams is Indian."

"How about sacred songs?"

"Hank Williams is sacred."

"I'm talking about ceremonial songs, you know, religious ones. The songs you sing back home when you're wishing and hoping."

"What are you wishing and hoping for?"

"I'm wishing my grandmother was still alive."

"Every song I know is about that."

"Well, sing me as many as you can."

The Aleuts sang their strange and beautiful songs. I listened. They sang about my grandmother and their grandmothers. They were lonely for the cold and snow. I was lonely for everybody.

10:00 A.M.

After the Aleuts finished their last song, we sat in silence. Indians are good at silence.

"Was that the last song?" I asked.

"We sang all the ones we could," the elder Aleut said. "All the others are just for our people."

I understood. We Indians have to keep our secrets. And these Aleuts were so secretive that they didn't refer to themselves as Indians.

"Are you guys hungry?" I asked.

They looked at one another and communicated without talking.

"We could eat," the elder Aleut said.

11:00 A.M.

The Aleuts and I walked over to Mother's Kitchen, a greasy diner in the International District. I knew they served homeless Indians who'd lucked in to money.

"Four for breakfast?" the waitress asked when we stepped inside.

"Yes, we're very hungry," the elder Aleut said.

She sat us in a booth near the kitchen. I could smell the food cooking. My stomach growled.

"You guys want separate checks?" the waitress asked.

"No, I'm paying for it," I said.

"Aren't you the generous one," she said.

"Don't do that," I said.

"Do what?" she asked.

"Don't ask me rhetorical questions. They scare me."

She looked puzzled, and then she laughed.

"Okay, Professor," she said. "I'll only ask you real questions from now on."

"Thank you."

"What do you guys want to eat?"

"That's the best question anybody can ask anybody," I said.

"How much money you got?" she asked.

"Another good question," I said. "I've got twenty-five dollars I can spend. Bring us all the breakfast you can, plus your tip."

She knew the math.

"All right, that's four specials and four coffees and fifteen percent for me."

The Aleuts and I waited in silence. Soon enough, the waitress returned and poured us four coffees, and we sipped at them until she returned again with four plates of food. Eggs, bacon, toast, hash-brown potatoes. It is amazing how much food you can buy for so little money.

Grateful, we feasted.

Noon

I said farewell to the Aleuts and walked toward the pawnshop. I later heard the Aleuts had waded into the saltwater near Dock 47 and disappeared. Some Indians said the Aleuts walked on the water and headed north. Other Indians saw the Aleuts drown. I don't know what happened to them.

I looked for the pawnshop and couldn't find it. I swear it wasn't located in the place where it had been before. I walked twenty or thirty blocks looking for the pawnshop, turned corners and bisected inter-sections, looked up its name in the phone books, and asked people walking past me if they'd ever heard of it. But that pawnshop seemed to have sailed away from me like a ghost ship. I wanted to cry. Right when I'd given up, when I turned one last corner and thought I might die if I didn't find that pawnshop, there it was, located in a space I swore it hadn't been filling up a few minutes before.

I walked inside and greeted the pawnbroker, who looked a little younger than he had before.

"It's you," he said.

"Yes, it's me," I said.

"Jackson Jackson."

"That is my name."

"Where are your friends?"

"They went traveling. But it's okay. Indians are everywhere."

"Do you have my money?"

"How much do you need again?" I asked and hoped the price had changed.

"Nine hundred and ninety-nine dollars."

It was still the same price. Of course it was the same price. Why would it change?

"I don't have that," I said.

"What do you have?"

"Five dollars."

I set the crumpled Lincoln on the countertop. The pawnbroker studied it.

"Is that the same five dollars from yesterday?"

"No, it's different."

He thought about the possibilities.

"Did you work hard for this money?" he asked.

"Yes," I said.

He closed his eyes and thought harder about the possibilities. Then he stepped into his back room and returned with my grandmother's regalia.

"Take it," he said and held it out to me.

"I don't have the money."

"I don't want your money."

"But I wanted to win it."

"You did win it. Now, take it before I change my mind."

Do you know how many good men live in this world? Too many to count!

I took my grandmother's regalia and walked outside. I knew that solitary yellow bead was part of me. I knew I was that yellow bead in part. Outside, I wrapped myself in my grandmother's regalia and breathed her in. I stepped off the sidewalk and into the intersection. Pedestrians stopped. Cars stopped. The city stopped. They all watched me dance with my grandmother. I was my grandmother, dancing.

WHAT EVER HAPPENED TO FRANK SNAKE CHURCH?

Frank's heart fibrillated as he walked along a tree-line trail on the northern slope of Mount Rainier. He staggered, leaned against a small pine tree for balance, but tumbled over it instead, rolled for twenty or thirty yards down the slope, and fell over a small cliff onto the scree below. A moment later, Frank's arrhythmic heart corrected itself and resumed beating normally, but he wondered if he was going to die on the mountain. He was only thirty-nine years old and weighed only eleven more pounds than he had when he graduated from high school, but he'd been smoking too many unfiltered Camels, and his cholesterol level was a dangerous 344, exactly the same as Ted Williams's career batting average. But damn it, Frank thought, he was a Spokane Indian, and Indians are supposed to die young. Thirty-nine years is old for a Spokane. Old enough to join the American Association of Retired Indians. Frank laughed. Bloody and hurt on this mountain, his heart maybe scarred and twisted beyond repair, and he was still making jokes. How indigenous, Frank thought, how wonderfully aboriginal, applause, applause, applause,

applause for me and my people. Still laughing, Frank pushed himself to his hands and knees and sat on a flat rock. His heart beat slow and steady. He breathed easily. He felt no tingling pain in his chest, arms, or legs. He wasn't lightheaded or nauseated. He seemed to be fine. Maybe his heart was okay; maybe it had missed only one dance step in a lifetime of otherwise lovely coronary waltzes. He was cut and scraped, a nasty gash on his arm would probably need stitches, but none of his wounds seemed to be too serious. He didn't have any broken bones or sprains. So there was the diagnosis: His heart had played a practical joke on him—how terribly amusing, ha, ha, ha, ha, ha, ha, ha, ha—and he was bruised and battered and had one hell of a headache, but he'd live.

Carefully, painfully, Frank crawled back up the slope to the trail. Once there, while still on his hands and knees, he took a few deep breaths and promised himself that he'd visit a superhero cardiologist as soon as he got off the mountain. He'd promise to see an organic nutritionist, aromatherapist, deep-tissue masseuse, feng shui consultant, yoga master, and Mormon stand-up comedian if those promises would help him get off this mountain. Frank stood, tested his balance, and found it to be true enough, so he resumed his rough trek along the trail. He felt stronger with each step. He was now convinced he was going to be okay. Yes, he was going to be fine. But after a few more steps, an electrical charge jolted him. Damn, Frank thought, I have a heart attack, fall down a damn mountain, and then I crawl back only to get struck by lightning. Frank imagined the newspaper headline: HEART-DISEASED FOREST RANGER STRUCK BY LIGHTNING. Frank was imagining the idiot readers laughing at the idiot park ranger when another electrical bolt knocked him back ten feet and dropped him to the ground, where a third lightning strike shocked him again. Damn, Frank thought, this lightning has a personal vendetta against me. He felt a fourth electrical charge shoot up his spine and into his brain. He convulsed and vomited. He kicked and punched at the air, and then he couldn't move at all. As he lay paralyzed on the trail, Frank thought: This is it, now I'm really dead, and I have crapped my pants; I'm going to die with half-digested pieces of mushroom and sausage pizza stuck to my ass; humiliation, degradation, sin, and mortal shame. But Frank didn't die. Instead, as the electricity fired inside his brain, Frank saw an image of his father, Harrison Snake Church, as the old man lay faceup on the floor of his kitchen in Seattle. Harrison's eyes were open, but there was no light behind them; blood dripped from his nose and ears. In great pain, Frank understood that he hadn't suffered a heart attack or been struck by lightning. No, he'd been gifted and cursed with the first real vision of his life, and though Frank was one of the very few Indian agnostics in the world, he accepted this vision as a simple and secular truth: His father was dead.

How much can one son love one father? Frank loved his father enough to stand and stagger five miles to the logging road where he'd parked his truck. He knew he should get on the radio and call for help. He was exhausted and in no safe shape to drive. But he also knew that his father was lying dead on the kitchen floor. Covered with blood and food, half naked in a ratty bathrobe that his father called a valuable antique, Jerry Springer or Dr. Phil lecturing on the television. Frank needed to be the first on the scene. He needed to restore his father's dignity before the proper authorities were called. Perhaps his father's spirit was waiting for him. But Frank didn't believe in spirits, in souls, in the afterlife. Why was he thinking about his father's soul? Mr. Death, Frank thought, you have entered my house and rearranged the furniture. But it didn't matter what Frank believed. With or without soul and spirit, Harrison was lying dead on the kitchen floor and should be lifted, cleaned, and covered with old quilts. Frank needed to perform burial ceremonies. Harrison needed to have his honor restored, and Frank was the only one who could, or should, do the restoration.

So Frank drove his truck dangerously fast along fifteen miles of logging and undeveloped roads. He didn't need a map; he'd been a forest ranger at Mount Rainier for ten years and had driven thousands of miles on these roads. As he drove, Frank thought of his father and wondered how the old man should be remembered. As he traveled toward his father's dead body, Frank composed the eulogy: "Thank you all for coming here today to say good-bye to my father. For those of you who know me, you know I'm not a man of words. But I do have a few things I'd like to say about my father. Harrison was a beloved man. Beloved. I guess you're supposed to use words like that at a funeral. Fancy words. But I guess I should just say it simple. Most people liked my dad, and quite a few loved him. He was an active member of St. Therese Church. He was always a good Catholic, maybe the only Indian of his generation who went to Catholic boarding school on purpose. That was a joke. I don't know if it was funny or not. But I'm an Indian, and Indians are supposed to be funny at funerals. At least that's what it says in the *Indian Funeral Handbook*. That was another joke.

"Here at St. Therese, my dad volunteered for the youth programs, and he was one of the most dependable readers and Eucharistic ministers. He read the gospels with more passion and pride than the Jesuits. Ay, jokes. Sorry about that, Father Terry, but you know it's true. Ay, jokes.

"My dad, Harry, he was fond of telling people how he would've become a priest if he hadn't loved the ladies so much. And there were always a few ladies who would have loved him back, and you know who you are. You're the ones crying the most. Ay, jokes. But of course my loyal dad has been chaste since his wife, my mother, Helen, died of brain cancer twenty-one years ago. So maybe my dad was like a Jesuit, except he didn't have sex, unlike most of the Jesuits. Ay, jokes.

"My mom died only three days after I graduated from high school. It was a terrible, ugly death. And my dad was never really happy again and never looked to be loved again by another woman, but he stayed active like a shark: *Don't stop moving or you die*. Ha, he was the Great Red Whale, my dad. Ay, jokes. Maybe my dad and I were the Great Red Whale together. We were always together. I've lived in the same house with him all of my life. I guess, in some real way, my father became my mother. Harrison was Helen. He adopted some of her mannerisms, you know, like he scratches his head whenever he's frustrated, just like she does.

"Listen to me. I keep talking about them in the present tense. And then I talk about them in the past tense. And I was never any good at English grammar anyway. So you can blame my high school English teacher for that. Sorry about that, Ms. Balum. Ay, jokes.

"After he got old, my dad was the crossing guard at Thirty-fourth and Union and knew the names of all of his kids. Since they were all Catholic kids, they only had twelve names. Or maybe eleven, since nobody has named their kid Judas since Judas was named Judas by his folks. Ay, jokes.

"My old man was strong for an old man, you know, and he could still hit ten or twelve of those long-range set shots in a row. Basketball was always my dad's passion. He was Idaho State High School Basketball Player of the Year in 1952. He loved the Lakers when they played in Minneapolis, and he loved them more after they moved to Los Angeles. Elgin Baylor. Gail Goodrich. Jerry West. Wilt Chamberlain. Happy Hairston. Those guys won thirty-three in a row in 1973.

"After my mother died, my dad and I watched thousands of basketball games on television and in person. Sometimes, on cold Saturday nights, he and I would drive for hours to watch small-town high school teams, not because we knew any of the players but because they were playing a small-town version of basketball, and it was ragged and beautiful and passionate and clumsy and perfect. Davenport Gorillas. Darrington Loggers. Selkirk Rangers. Neah Bay Red Devils. Toutle Lake Fighting Ducks.

"And now my father is gone, and my mother is gone, and they're gone together, and I'm a thirty-nine-year-old orphan. I didn't even say good-bye to my father before I left the house on the day he died. I never really said good-bye to my mother before she died. I will have to live the rest of my life with a failed son's regrets. I don't even know what I'm going to do now."

As he drove off Mount Rainier and through the park, Frank knew his eulogy was inadequate, incomplete, and improvisational. He knew he would have to sit and write a real eulogy. He would fill a dozen notebooks with draft after draft. Every word would perfectly capture how much love and pain he felt for his father and mother. Harrison and Helen Snake Church deserved poetry, not the opening monologue of an indigenous talk show. Mr. Death, Frank thought, you are a funnyman, but I will not laugh. Frank sped out of the park. Ignoring the risk of speeding tickets, he drove west on two-lane highways, north on Interstate 5 through Tacoma into Seattle, east off the James Street exit, and ran red lights twenty blocks into the Central District, where he and Harrison lived on Thirty-seventh Avenue. Frank drove his government truck onto the front lawn, leaped out and raced up the front steps, struggled with the front door, threw it open, rushed into the kitchen, and saw his father sitting at the table. Harrison was drinking coffee and eating Grape-Nuts. He ate breakfast for every meal.

"You're alive," said Frank, completely surprised by the fact.

"Yes, I am," Harrison said as he studied his bloody, panicked son. "But you look half dead."

"I had a vision," Frank said.

Harrison sipped his coffee.

"I saw you in my head," Frank said. "You're supposed to be dead. I saw you dead."

"You have blurry vision," said Harrison.

One year and four days later, Harrison died of a heart attack in the QFC supermarket on Broadway and Pike. When he heard the news, Frank wondered if his previous year's vision had been accurate, if he'd foreseen his father's death. But there must be a statute of limitations for visions, Frank thought, there must be an expiration date for ESP. Beyond all that, Frank didn't believe anyone could predict the future. His supposedly psychic vision of his father's death bore some general resemblance to his real death, but the details were different. Harrison was shopping in the produce department when he coughed once, rubbed his tingling left arm, and died. "Probably dead before he hit the floor," the coroner had said. When Harrison fell, he knocked over an artfully arranged display of bananas, which was appropriate and funny, since Harrison had always hated the taste of what he called "the devil's evil yellow penis." Frank buried his father beside his mother's grave in the same Seattle graveyard where Bruce and Brandon Lee were also buried. So, hey, Frank figured his father was lying with damn good company, and if there was an afterlife, then Harrison was probably learning jeet kune do and making love to his wife, Helen, for all of eternity.

At his father's graveside, overlooking Lake Washington, Frank stood to give the eulogy he'd carefully written but found he couldn't read the words on the page. Grief turned him into an illiterate. He tried to remember what he'd written so he could recite his eulogy by memory, but he discovered he couldn't speak at all. Grief turned him into a mute. Finally, after five minutes of silence, as the assembled mourners shook with collective embarrassment, Frank finally remembered how to say four words: "I love my father."

Afterward, Frank shook the hands and accepted the hugs of dozens of his father's friends and family. He couldn't remember any of their names. Grief turned him into a stranger in his own tribe. Finally, Frank recognized an older woman, his mother's aunt Margaret Marie, who kissed him hard on the lips. She tasted like salt.

"Your father was a ballplayer," she said. "He could have played in college, you know? You should have said something about that."

Frank laughed. What kind of person offered constructive criticism at a funeral? What kind of literate mourner had the nerve to deconstruct a eulogy?

Harrison had been a very good basketball player, but he'd never been good enough to play college hoops, not even at the community-college level. He'd been a great shooter but was never much of an athlete—too short and slow and tentative—but Frank, a genetic freak at six feet six (making him the seventeenth tallest Spokane Indian in tribal history), had always been a truly supernatural baller, the kind of jumper and runner who ignored physics when he played. He'd averaged forty-one points a game during his senior year at Seattle's Garfield High School and had received 114 scholarship offers from colleges all over the country. He'd signed a letter of intent with the University of Washington and had planned to major in environmental science. But then his mother died. To honor her and keep her memory sacred, Frank knew he had to give up something valuable. He had to bury with her one of his most important treasures. So he buried his basketball dreams. On the morning of her funeral, Frank walked to the local park and shot one hundred jump shots and made eighty-five of them. He left the ball at the park, helped bury his mother that afternoon, and had not played the game since. For the first few years, Frank had almost died whenever he thought about basketball, but the acute pain turned chronic, and then it was a dull and distant ache, and then it was the phantom itch of an amputated limb, and then it was gone.

Now he was forty years old, and his life could be divided into two almost equal halves: He'd been a star basketball player for eighteen years—he was a hooper right out of the womb—and a non–basketball player for twenty-two years.

After his father's burial, Frank went home alone and stood in the quiet house. He had not yet cried for his father, and he wondered if he would ever cry, but his grief grew so suddenly huge that it pushed him to the floor. He lay on the living room carpet and wept huge and gasping tears. He screamed and wailed for ten minutes or more. He didn't know how to sing and drum, but he pounded the floor and wailed tribal vocals: *Father, way, ya, way, ha, Father, way, ya, way, ha, Father, way, ya, way, ha.* He sang himself hoarse and fell asleep on the carpet. When he woke, he crawled upstairs to his father's bedroom and lay in his father's bed. The sheets still smelled like Harrison. Frank pressed his face into the pillow and breathed in his father's scent. And then Frank gathered his father's hair, so different than Frank's graying crew cut. His father's hair was still black and two feet long on the day he died. Frank found long black hair on the pillow, in the sheets, tangled in a comb, stuck to the bathtub porcelain, clumped into a wet ball in the drain stops, and scattered in every corner of the house. Frank gathered all of the hair, rolled it into a ball, and ate it. He felt split in two, one crazy man eating hair and one rational man watching a crazy man eat hair. He chewed and swallowed the last pieces of his father's life. He felt like he was building a museum of pain, a freak show, where he was the only visitor viewing the only mutant screaming the only prayer he knew: *Come back, Daddy. Come back, Daddy.*

Frank howled. He slept. Woke and howled again. Slept again. Woke and howled until his lips and tongue were bloody. Slept again. Woke and wondered if his grief would ever end. He didn't know what to do, but he needed to love and be loved, so he opened his father's closet and stared at the basketball waiting inside. A couple times a week for many years, Harrison had gone alone to the neighborhood park to shoot baskets, so the ball was worn and comfortable, low on air. Trying to move exactly like his father, to honor his father through muscle memory, Frank picked up the ball, dribbled it around his back, between his legs, bobbled it, and knocked over a chair. Clumsy and stupid with grief, he grabbed the ball, left the house, and walked then ran to the neighborhood park. Once there, he stood at the free-throw line on the northern end of the basketball court. He stared at the iron rim with its chain net. He had not taken a shot in over two decades. He'd given up this game to honor his mother, and now he was reclaiming it to honor his father. He wanted both of them to rise from the dead. Frank dribbled the ball once, twice, three times, stepped back to the three-point line, and rose into the air for a jump shot. He missed the basket completely. Frank watched the sacrilegious air ball bounce away from him and roll quickly across the manicured grass, until it finally slowed to a stop at the tennis court on the other side of the park.

*   *   *

A week after he buried his father, Frank quit his job as a forest ranger.
He'd saved tens of thousands of dollars over the years, and the house
was completely paid for, so he wasn't worried about money. But he
was worried about being alone. For most of his life, he'd loved solitude. Walking through the deep woods, he often imagined he was
the only person left in the world, the only survivor of a nuclear war
or a smallpox epidemic. During these fantasies, Frank lived alone for
fifty years until the day when he curled into a ball at the base of a
beautiful pine and died like an old dog, whereby the human race
ceased to exist. Inside and outside of this fantasy, Frank knew he was
guilty of arrogance and misanthropy, but he compensated by being
kind to strangers and tipping really well at restaurants. He didn't have
any close friends and had probably shared more conversations with
the redheaded clerk at the university bookstore and the blond cash-
ier at the QFC supermarket than he did with anyone other than his
father. As for romance, Frank had dated a few women over the years
but found them to be too inconsistent and illogical, so he dated a
few men and found them to be even more random and frightening.
For a while, he had paid for sex with men and women, then women
only, but he eventually grew disgusted with the desperation of such
acts and, for many years, had lived as chastely as his father had lived.
All along, Frank understood that he was suffering from a quiet sickness, a sort of emotional tumor that never grew or diminished but
prevented him from living a full and messy life. At the end of every
day, Frank thoroughly washed away the human funk of the world,
but now, with his father's death, he worried that he would never feel
clean again. He needed to take control of his life. He needed to organize his grief; he needed to compose a mournful to-do list: *Bury
your father, visit your mother's grave, cry, eat hair, play basketball again,
lose weight.* Of course he felt banal. In a time of extraordinary pain,

why was he worried about something as ordinary as his body-fat percentage? He only knew for sure that he needed to keep moving, get stronger, build, and connect.

So he picked up the Yellow Pages, looked up personal trainers, and dialed the first one on the list.

"Athletes, Incorporated, this is Russell."

The next day, he walked thirty blocks into downtown Seattle (why not start training immediately?) and met with Russell, a thin and muscular black man who looked more like a long-distance runner than a weight lifter.

"So," said Russell as he sat across the desk from Frank.

"So," Frank said.

"What can we do for you?"

"I'm not sure. I've never done this before."

"Well, why don't we start with your name."

"I'm Frank Snake Church."

"Damn, that's impressive. A man with a name like that is destined for greatness."

"If my name was John Smith, you'd tell me I was destined for greatness, right?"

"Well, I'm supposed to help you be great. That's my job. Stronger body, stronger mind, stronger spirit. That's our motto."

Frank stared at Russell. Silently studied him. A confident man, Russell was comfortable with the silence.

"Are you a serious man?" Frank asked him.

"I'm not sure I understand your question."

Frank stood and walked around the desk. He knelt beside Russell and spoke to him from inches away. Russell didn't mind this closeness.

"Listen," Frank said, "I know this is your job, and I know you need to make money. And I know a large part of what you do here is sales. You're a salesman. And that's okay. You need to make a living. We all need to make a living. And hey, this job you have is a great way to make money, right? You get to wear T-shirts and shorts all year long. And you've probably helped a lot of people get healthy, right?"

Russell could feel Frank's desperation and sense of purpose, the religious fervor that needed to be directed. Russell had met a thousand desperate people, all looking to rescue or be rescued, but this Indian man was especially radiant with need.

"I keep a scrapbook of the clients who've meant the most to me," Russell said. He'd never told anybody about that scrapbook and how he studied it. If exercise was his religion, then the scrapbook was his bible, and every one of his clients was a prophet. Russell never spoke aloud of how proud he was of the woman who lost five hundred pounds and kept it off, of the man who recovered from a triple bypass and now ran marathons, of the teenager paralyzed in a car wreck who now played professional wheelchair basketball. Russell fixed broken people, and sometimes the repairs lasted a lifetime. But he could not say these things aloud. In order to be taken seriously, Russell knew he had to pretend to be less than serious about his job, his *calling*. He could not tell his clients that he thought his gym was a church. He'd sound like a crazy fundamentalist, an idiot parody of a personal trainer. He couldn't express sentiment or commitment; he was forced to be ironic and cynical. He couldn't tell people he cried whenever clients failed or quit or trained too inconsistently for the work to make a difference. So he simply repeated the tired and misleading mantra whenever asked about his work: *It's better than having a real job.* But now, after all these years, Russell somehow understood that he could tell the truth to this sad and desperate stranger.

"I remember everybody I've worked with," Russell said. "I remember their names, their weights, their goals. I remember the exact day when the quitters quit. I keep a running count of the total weight my clients have lost."

"What is it?"

"I can't tell you that. It's just for me. It's a sacred number."

"Okay," Frank said. "I think it's good to remember things that way. Very good. I admire that. So, with my admiration clearly expressed, I want you to answer my question. Are you a serious man?"

"If I said this aloud to most of the world, they'd laugh at me," said Russell. "But I think I have one of the most important jobs in the world. That's how serious I am about what I do. So yes, in answer to your question, when it comes to this work, I am a very serious man."

Frank stood and looked out the window at the Seattle skyline. With his back to Russell, he spoke. It was the only way he could say what he needed to say.

"My father died a week ago," Frank said.

Russell had often heard these grief stories before. He knew five people who'd come directly to the gym from funerals and immediately signed up for full memberships.

"What about your mother?" Russell asked.

"She died when I was eighteen."

"My mother died of sickle cell last year," Russell said. "My father was killed when I was twelve. He was a taxi driver. Guy held him up and shot him in the head."

Frank honored that story—those tragic deaths—with his silence.

"How did your father die?" Russell asked.

"Heart attack."

Frank and Russell were priests and confessors.

"Listen to me," Frank said. "I used to be a basketball player, a really good basketball player, the best in the city and maybe the best in the state, and maybe I could have become one of the best in the country. But I haven't played in a long, long time."

"What do you need from me?" Russell asked.

Frank turned from the window. "I want to be good again," he said.

Russell studied the man and his body, visually estimated his fitness levels, and emotionally guessed at his self-discipline and dedication.

"Give me a year," Russell said.

For the next twelve months, Frank trained five days a week. He lifted free weights, ran miles on the treadmill, climbed hundreds of stories on the stair stepper, jumped boxes until he vomited from the lactic-acid buildup, and climbed ropes until his hands bled. He quit smoking. He measured his food, kept track of all of the calories and the fat, protein, and carbohydrate grams. He drank twelve glasses of water a day. Mr. Death, Frank thought, I am going to drown you before you drown me. Frank's body-fat percentage, heart rate, and blood pressure all lowered. Every three months, he bought new clothes to fit his new body.

During the course of the year, Frank also cleaned his house. He removed the art from the walls and sold it through want ads and garage sales. Without ceremony, he piled up all of the old blankets and quilts, a few of them over eighty years old, and gave them one by one to the neighbors. He gathered financial records, wills, tax returns, old magazines, photograph albums, and scrapbooks, and stored them in a large safe-deposit box at the bank. After that, he scooped all of the various knickknacks and sentimental souvenirs into cardboard boxes and left them on the corner for others to cart away. One day after the movers carried away all of the old-fashioned and overstuffed furniture, other movers brought in the new, sleek, and simple pieces, so there was only one bed, one dresser, one coffee table, one dining table, one wardrobe, one stove, one refrigerator freezer, and four chairs in the entire house. He pulled up the rugs, hired a local teenager to haul them to the dump, and sanded the hardwood until the floors glowed golden and sepia. Near the end of the year, he found enough courage to give away his father's clothes and the boxes of his mother's clothes his father had saved. Frank gave away most of his clothes as well, until he owned only black T-shirts, blue jeans, black socks, black boxers, and black basketball shoes.

Frank kept all of the books, three thousand novels, histories, biographies, and essays, and neatly organized them on bookshelves he built into the walls. He read one book a day. After he disconnected the telephone and permanently stopped the mail, his family and friends worried about him and came to see him, but he turned away all visitors, treating loved ones, strangers, salespeople, religious crusaders, and political activists as if they were all the same.

Frank knew his behavior was obsessive and compulsive, and perhaps he was seriously disturbed, in need of medical care and strong prescriptions, but he didn't want to stop. He needed to perform this ceremony, to disappear into the ritual, to methodically change into something new and better, into someone stronger.

"Make me hurt," he said to Russell before every training session.

"All right," said Russell every few weeks. "I want one thousand sit-ups and one thousand push-ups, and you're not leaving here until I get them."

Sometimes Frank overtrained, ran too many miles or lifted too much weight, and injured himself. Russell would chase him out of the gym, tell him to lay off for a week or even two or three, give his body a chance to recover, to heal, but Frank kept pushing, tore muscles and dislocated joints, broke fingers and twisted vertebrae. He stopped training only when he couldn't get out of bed, and if he found the strength to crawl into a hot shower, he'd warm his muscles enough to lift what he could. At his strongest, he bench-pressed 350 and leg-pressed a thousand pounds. At his weakest, when he was injured, he could lift only paperbacks or pencils, but he'd still do three sets of ten repetitions.

"You can't keep doing this to yourself," Russell said to him again and again. "I can't keep doing this to you. It's malpractice, man. If you get hurt again, I'm quitting. I'm banning you from the gym forever."

But Russell never quit on him, and Frank never quit on Russell. Joined, they were not twins or friends; they were not lovers or brothers; they were not teachers or students; they were not mentors or apprentices; they were not monks or sinners. They remained mutable and variable, sacred and profane. Mr. Death, Frank thought, we are your contraries, your opposites and contradictions, your X factors and missing links, your self-canceling saints and self-flagellating monks, your Saint Francis and the other Saint Francis, and we have come to blaspheme your name.

Away from Russell and the gym, Frank played basketball.

Seven days a week, Frank drove the city and searched for games. He traveled from the manicured intramural courts at the University of Washington to the broken-asphalt courts of the Central District; from the violent and verbose games in Green Lake Park to the genial and clumsy games at the YMCA; from the gladiator battles under the I-5 freeway to the hyperorganized leagues at Sound Mind & Body Gym. He played against black men who believed it was their tribal right to dominate the court. He played against white men who wanted to be black men. He played against brown men who hated black and white men. He played against black, brown, and white men who didn't care about any color other than the green-money bets placed on every point and game. He played against Basketball Democrats who came to the court alone and ran with anybody, and Basketball Republicans who traveled in groups of five and ran only with one another. He played against women who endured endless variations of the same dumb joke: *Hey, girl, you can play, but it's shirts and skins, and you're running skins.* He played against former football players who still wanted to play football, and former wrestlers who wanted only to wrestle. He played against undisciplined young men who couldn't run a basic pick-and-roll, and against elderly men who never missed their two-handed set shots. He played against trash talkers and polite gentlemen. He played against sociopathic ball hogs, wild gunners, rebound hounds, and assist-happy magicians. He played games to seven, nine, eleven, and twenty-one points. He played winner-keeps-ball and alternate possessions. He played one-on-one, two-on-two, three-on-three, four-on-four, five-on-five, and mob rules, improvisational, every-baller-for-himself, anarchist, free-for-all, death-cage matches. He played against cheaters who constantly changed the score, and honest freaks who called fouls on themselves. He played against liars who bragged about how good they used to be, and dreamers who would never be as good as they wanted to be. He played against Basketball Presbyterians who refused to fast-break, and Basketball Pagans who refused to slow down. He played against the vain Allen-Iverson-wanna-be punks who dribbled between their legs, around their backs, and missed 99 percent of the ridiculous, driving, triple-pump, reverse-scoop shots they hoisted up but talked endless and pornographic trash whenever they happened to make even one shot. He played against the vain Larry-Bird-wanna-be court lawyers who argued every foul call and planted themselves at three-point lines and constantly called for the ball because they were open, damn it, more open than any outsider shooter in the history of the damn game, so pass the freaking rock!

Frank played so well that he earned (and re-earned) a playground reputation and was known by a variety of nicknames: Shooter, Old Man, Chief, and Three. Frank's favorite nickname was Oh Shit, given to him in July by a teenage Chicano kid in MLK, Jr. Park.

"Every time the old Indio shoots and makes one of those crazy thirty-footers," the Chicano kid had said, "his man be yelling, 'Oh shit, oh shit, oh shit!'"

Frank was making a comeback, though he hated that word as much as Norma Desmond had hated it, and just like her, he preferred to call it his return. After all, over the course of the year, a few older players had recognized Frank and remembered him as the supernatural Indian kid who'd disappeared from the basketball world two decades ago.

On the basketball courts of Seattle, Frank was the love child of Sasquatch and D. B. Cooper; he was the murder of Charles Lindbergh's baby, the building of Noah's Ark, and the flooding of Atlantis; he was the mystery and the religion and the outright lies.

During one legendary game at the University of Washington Intramural Activities Building, Frank caught the ball in the low post and turned to face Double O, the Huskies' power forward. He was a Division I stud slumming among the gym rats, a future second-round draft pick destined to be eleventh man for the Cleveland Cavaliers, which didn't sound glamorous but still made him one of the thousand best basketball players in the world.

"Oh Shit, you better give up the rock," Double O taunted. "I ain't letting you win this game."

Frank faked the jumper and dribbled right, but Double O, five inches taller and seventy-five pounds heavier, easily pushed Frank away from the key.

"Oh Shit, you're an old man," taunted Double O. "Why you coming after me? I ain't got your social security check."

Frank dribbled the ball between his legs, behind his back, then between his legs again. He didn't know why he was bouncing the ball like a madman. There was no point to it, but he wanted to challenge the trash-talking black kid.

"Oh Shit, you got yourself some skills!" shouted Double O. "Come on, come on, show me the triple-threat position. That's it. That's it. I am so bedazzled, I cannot tell if you're going to shoot, pass, or drive.

Oh man, you got them fun-da-men-tals. Bet you learned those with the Original Celtics!"

Distracted by the insulting rant, by its brilliant and racist poetry, Frank laughed and almost lost the ball.

"Better make your move, Old Milk," taunted Double O. "Your expiration date is long past due."

Frank faked right, dribbled left, and scored the game-winning hoop on an archaic rolling left-handed hook shot that barely made it over Double O's outstretched hands.

Frank screamed in triumph and relief as Double O howled with disbelief and fell backward to the floor. All the other players in the gym—the eyewitnesses to a little miracle—shouted curses and promises, screamed in harmony with Frank, slapped one another's hands and backs and butts, and spun in delirious circles. People laughed until they were nauseated. Nobody held anything back. Because he had no idea what else to do with his excitement, one skinny black kid nicknamed Skinny, a sophomore in electrical engineering, ran out of the gym and twenty-four blocks to his house to tell his father and younger brother what he had just seen. Skinny's father and little brother never once asked why he'd run so far to tell the story of one hoop in one meaningless game. They understood why the story had to be immediately told. In basketball, there is no such thing as "too much" or "too far" or "too high." In basketball, enough is never enough. At its best and worst, basketball is all about excess. Every day is Fat Tuesday on a basketball court.

"Did you see that? Did you see that?" screamed Double O as he lay on the floor and flailed his arms and legs. He laughed and hooted and cursed. Losing didn't embarrass him; he was proud of playing a game that could produce such a random, magical, and ridiculous highlight. There was no camera crew to record the event for *SportsCenter*, but it had happened nonetheless, and it would become a part of the basketball mythology at the University of Washington: *Do you remember the time that Old Indian scored on Double O? Do I remember? I was there. Old Chief scored seven straight buckets on Double O and won the game on a poster dunk right in O's ugly mug. O's feelings hurt so bad, he needed stitches. Hell, O never recovered from the pain. He's got that post-traumatic stress illness, and it's getting worse now that he plays ball in Cleveland. Playing hoops for the Cavaliers is like fighting in Vietnam.*

In that way, over the years, the story of Frank's game-winning bucket would change with each telling. Every teller would add his or her personal details; every biographer would turn the story into autobiography. But the original story, the aboriginal hook shot, belonged to Frank, and he danced in fast circles around the court, whooping and celebrating like a spastic idiot. I sound like some Boy Scout's idea of an Indian warrior, Frank thought, like I'm a parody, but a happy parody.

The other ballplayers laughed at Frank's display. He'd always been a quiet player, rarely speaking on or off the court, and now he was emoting like a game-show host.

"Somebody give Oh Shit a sedative!" shouted Double O from the floor. "The Old Indian has gone spastic!"

Still whooping with joy, Frank helped Double O to his feet. The old man and the young man hugged each other and laughed.

"I beat you," Frank said.

"Old man," said Double O, "you gave me a trip on your time machine."

If smell is the memory sense, as Frank once read, then he was most nostalgic about the spicy aroma of Kentucky Fried Chicken. Whenever Frank smelled Kentucky Fried Chicken, and not just any fried chicken but the very particular and chemical scent of the Colonel's secret recipe, he thought of his mother. Because he was a child who could not separate his memories of his mother and his father and sometimes confused their details, Frank thought of his mother and father together. And when he thought about his mother and father and the smell of Kentucky Fried Chicken, Frank remembered one summer day when his parents took him to the neighborhood park to picnic with a twenty-piece bucket of mixed Kentucky Fried Chicken, and a ten-piece box of legs and wings only, along with a cooler filled with Diet Pepsi and store-bought potato salad and apples and bananas and potato chips and a chocolate cake. Harrison and Frank had fought over which particular basketball to bring, but they had at last agreed on an ABA red-white-and-blue rock.

"Can't you ever leave that ball at home?" Helen asked Harrison. She always asked him that question. After so many years of hard-worked marriage, that question had come to mean *I love you, but your obsessions irritate the hell out of me, but I love you, remember that, okay?*

On that day, Frank was eleven years old, young enough to sit on his mother's lap and be only slightly embarrassed by their shared affection, and old enough to need his father and be completely unable to tell him about that need.

"Let's play ball," Frank said to Harrison, though he meant to say, *Prove your love for me.*

"Eat first," Helen said.

"If I eat now, I'll throw up," Frank said. "I'll eat after we play."

"You'll eat now, and if you throw up, you'll just have to eat again, and then you'll play again, and then you'll throw up, so you'll have to eat again. It might go on for days that way. You'll be trapped in a vicious circle."

"You're weird, Mom."

"Yes, I am," she said. "And weirdness is hereditary."

"I'm weird, too," Harrison said. "So you got it coming from both sides. You don't have a chance."

"I can't believe you're my parents. Did you adopt me?"

"Honey, we certainly did not adopt you," Helen said. "We stole you from a pack of wolves, so eat your meat, you darling little carnivore."

Laughing, feeling like an adult because his parents treated him with respect and satire, Frank sat between his mother and father and almost cried with happiness. His chest tightened, and his mouth tasted bitter. He cried too easily, he knew, and sometimes had to fight school-yard bullies who teased him about his quick tears. He usually won the fights and usually cried about his victory.

Sitting with his parents, Frank closed his eyes against his tears, blinked and blinked and thought of the utter hilarity of a dog farting in its sleep, and that made him laugh a little. Soon enough, he felt normal, like a kid made of steel and oak, and he could breathe easily, and he quickly ate his lunch of Kentucky Fried Chicken, but only wings and legs.

"Okay, I'm done," he said. "Let's play ball, Dad."

"I'm too tired," Harrison said. "I'm going to lie down in the grass and fall asleep in some dog poop."

His father was always trying to be funny. He was funny sometimes, maybe most of the time, but nobody could be funny all of the time. And being funny was sometimes a way of being dishonest.

A few years back, Harrison had told Frank's third-grade teacher that Indians didn't believe in using numbers, that the science of mathematics was a colonial evil.

"Well," the mystified teacher had asked, "then how do Indians count?"

"We guess," Harrison had said with as much profundity as he could fake.

Okay, so maybe Harrison was funny because funny was valuable. Maybe being funny was usually a way of being honest.

"Come on, let's play ball," Frank pleaded with his father, who had flopped onto the grass with a chicken leg and a banana.

"I'm going to eat and sleep and fart," Harrison said.

"Dad, you said you'd show me something new."

"Did I promise you I would show you something new?"

"Well, no."

"Did I sign something that said I would show you something new?"

"No."

"That means we don't have an oral or written contract. We don't have an implied contract, either, because you don't even know how to spell 'implication.' So that means I'm going to eat chicken until I pass out from a grease overdose."

"Mom, he's talking like a lawyer again."

"Yeah," she said. "I hate it when he does that."

"And I can, too, spell 'implication,'" Frank said.

"Okay," Harrison said. "If you can spell 'implication,' your mother will play ball with you."

"I don't want to play ball with Mom, I want to play with somebody good."

"Hey, your mom is great. Why do you think I fell in love with her?"

"Mom, he's lying again."

"I'm not lying. Our dear Helen was a cannibal on the basketball court."

"Is that true, Mom?"

"I used to play," she said.

Frank looked at his mother. Sure, she was tall (five feet eight or so, the same height as Harrison), and she was strong (she grew up bucking hay bales), but Frank had never seen her touch a basketball except to toss it in a closet or down the stairs or into a room or out the door, or anywhere to get that dang thing out of her way.

"Mom, are you lying?"

"Have I ever lied to you?"

"You told me I was raised by wolves."

"Okay, have I ever lied to you twice in one day?"

"Mom, be serious."

"She is being serious," Harrison said. "She used to play those girls' rules. Three girls on defense, three on offense. Your mom was the shooter. Damn, I saw her score fifty-two points once. And then the coaches decided to play boys' rules. They didn't have to, but they wanted to see what your mom could do in a real game. And she scored seventy-three. I missed that one. If I'd seen that game, I would have proposed to her on the spot."

"I love you, too, sweetie," Helen said to her husband.

Frank couldn't believe it. He looked at his mother in her denim skirt and frilly blue top, with her lipstick and her beaded earrings and her scarf all matching perfectly, all of her life and spirit and world color-coordinated and alphabetically organized. How could his mother, who washed her hands twelve times a day, ever have played a game so fundamentally sweaty and messy?

"Mom, did you really play ball?"

"It was girls' basketball," she said, "so it doesn't really count."

She was being sarcastic, Frank knew, because she'd taught him how to be sarcastic.

"For the rest of your academic life," she'd told him on his first day of kindergarten, "whenever any teacher tells you that Columbus discovered America, I want you to run up to him or her, jump on his or her back, and scream, 'I discovered you!'"

He'd never been courageous enough to do it, but he always considered it. He always almost did it. He almost always ran home and told Helen how close he'd been to doing it, how he was sure he could do it the next time, and she hugged him and told him how smart and good and handsome he was. Helen was loving and crazy and unpredictable and gentle and voluble and bitter and funny and a thousand other good and bad and indefinable things, but she was certainly not a liar.

"Are you telling the truth?" Frank asked her. "Were you really a good basketball player?"

"People said I was good," she said and shrugged. "If enough people say you're good at something, then you're probably good at it."

"Okay, cool," Frank said. "Do you want to play ball with me?"

"Remember, you have to spell 'implication' first," Harrison.

"It's spelled 'D-A-D I-S A J-E-R-K,'" Frank said.

All three of them laughed. They were always laughing. That was what people said about the Snake Churches. People said the Snake Churches were good at laughing.

"Okay, okay," Helen said. "Let's play ball. But I'm not making any guarantees. It's been a long time."

So mother and son took to the court and played basketball. At first, she practiced shots while he rebounded her makes and misses and passed the ball back to her. She had a funny shot, a one-handed push, and she missed the first ten or twelve before her body remembered the game, and then she rarely missed. From ten feet away, then fifteen, then twenty, and twenty-five feet, she shot and made it and shot and made it and shot and made it and shot and missed it and then shot and made it and shot and made it and shot many times and made many more than she missed.

"Wow," Frank said to his mother as she shot. He kept saying it. It was all he could think to say. This was a new ceremony for them, for this mother and son. They'd created and shared other ceremonies. They baked cookies together; they told stories to each other at night; they made up love songs while she drove him to school; they gave silly nick-names to strangers in shopping malls; they made up stupid knock-knock jokes and laughed until milk sprayed out of their noses. But they'd never played a sport together, had never been this physical, this strong and competitive. Frank looked at his mother, and he saw a new woman, a different person, a mysterious stranger, and a romantic figure.

"Mom," Frank said. "You're a ballplayer."

Oh man, he loved her, and he felt like crying yet again. Oh, he was young and worshipful and sentimental, and he didn't know it, but his mother would always want her son to be young and worship-ful and sentimental. She prayed that the world, filled with its cruel people and crueler philosophies, would not punish her son too harshly for being so kind and so receptive to kindness.

"Mom," Frank said. "Show me something new."

So Helen dribbled the ball toward the hoop, dribbled across the key, and shot a rolling left-handed hook that bounced around the rim and dropped in.

"Oh, sweetie! I love you!" Harrison shouted from the grass and sprayed chicken and banana into the air. "That was her favorite move, son, she never missed that one! And nobody ever stopped it. Hell, I never stopped it!"

"Do it again," Frank said.

So Helen shot the left-handed hook again. She shot it twenty times and made nineteen of them.

"She's beautiful!" Harrison shouted and ran to join his wife and son on the court. "Isn't she beautiful?"

Frank wondered if this was the best day of his whole life so far, if he would ever be this happy again. Those were extreme thoughts for an eleven-year-old, and Frank, though he was that eleven-year-old, understood he was being extreme, but it was the only way he knew how to be. It was the only way he'd been taught to be.

So mother, father, and son played basketball for hours, until it got dark enough for the streetlights to blink on, until it was too dark for even the streetlights to make any difference, until Frank could barely keep his eyes open, until Helen and Harrison took their exhausted son home and put him to bed and watched him sleep and breathe, and inhale and exhale and inhale and exhale.

On the first anniversary of his father's death, Frank stepped outside to see what kind of day it was. He cursed the rain, stepped back inside to grab his windbreaker, and walked to the covered courts over on Rainier Avenue. On a sunny day, fifty guys played at Rainier, but on that rainy day, Preacher was shooting hoops all by himself; he was always shooting hoops by himself. Two or three hundred set shots a day. One day a month, he closed his eyes and shot blindly and would never reveal why he performed such an eccentric ceremony.

"Honey, honey, honey," Preacher always said when asked. "Just let the mystery be."

On that day, Preacher's eyes were wide open when Frank joined him for a game of Horse."

"Hey, Frank Snake Church, what ever happened to you?" Preacher asked. He always asked variations of the same question when he saw Frank. "Tell me, tell me, tell me, what ever happened to Frank Snake Church, what the hell happened to Benjamin Franklin Snake Church?"

Preacher hit a thirty-foot bank shot, but Frank missed it. Preacher hit a left-handed hook shot from half-court, but Frank threw the ball over the basket.

"Look at me," said Preacher. "I'm a senior citizen and I've given Frank the 'H' and the 'O.' Ho, ho, ho, Merry Christmas. But wait, I must stop and ponder this existential dilemma. How could I, a retired blue-collar worker, a fixed-income pensioner, a tattered coat upon a stick, how could I be defeating the legendary Frank Snake Church? What the hell is wrong with this picture? What the hell ever happened to Frank Snake Church?"

"I am Frank Snake Church in the here and now and forever," Frank said and laughed. He loved to listen to Preacher rant and rave. A retired railroad engineer, Preacher was a gray-haired black man with a big belly. He stood at the top of the key, bounced the ball off the free-throw line, and off the board into the hoop.

"That was a garbage shot," Frank said. "You'd never take that shot in a real game. Never."

"Every game is real, every game is real, every game is real," Preacher chanted as Frank missed the trick shot.

"That's a screaming scarlet 'R' for you," said Preacher and called out his next shot. "This one is all net all day."

Preacher hit the fifteen-foot swish, and Frank also swished it.

"Oh, a pretty little shot by the Indian stranger," said Preacher.

"I ain't no stranger, I am Frank Snake Church."

"Naw, you ain't no Frank Snake Church," Preacher said. "I saw Frank Snake Church score seventy-seven against the Ballard Beavers in 1979. I saw Frank Snake Church shoot twenty-eight for thirty-six from the field and twenty-one for twenty-two from the line. I saw Frank Snake Church grab nineteen rebounds that same night and hand out eleven dimes. Yeah, I knew Frank Snake Church. Frank Snake Church was a friend of basketball, and believe me, you ain't no Frank Snake Church."

"My driver's license says I'm Frank Snake Church."

"Your social security card, library card, unemployment check, and the tattoo on your right butt cheek might say Frank Snake Church," Preacher said, "but you, sir, are an imposter; you are a doppelgänger; you are a body snatcher; you are a pod person; you are Frank Snake Church's evil and elderly twin is what you are."

Preacher closed his eyes and hit a blind shot from the corner. Frank closed his eyes and missed by five feet.

"That's an 'S' for you, as in Shut Up and Learn How to Play Another Game," said Preacher. "God could pluck out my eyes, and you could play with a microscope, and I'd still beat you. Man, you used to be somebody."

"I am now what I always was," Frank said.

"You now and you then are two entirely different people. You used to be Frank the Snake, Frank the Hot Dog, but now you're just a plain Oscar Mayer wiener, just a burned-up frankfurter without any damn mustard to make you taste better, make you easier to swallow. I watch you toss up one more of those ugly jumpers, and I'm going to need the Heimlich to squeeze your ugliness out of my throat."

"Nope, Frank now and Frank then are exactly the same. I am a tasty indigenous sausage."

"You were young and fresh, and now you're prehistoric, my man, you're only about two and a half hours younger than the Big Bang, that's how old you are. And I know you're old because I'm old. I smell the old on you like I smell the old on me. And it reeks, son, it reeks of stupid and desperate hope."

Preacher hit a Rick Barry two-handed scoop-shot free throw.

"I can't believe you took that white-boy shot," Frank said. "I'm going to turn you in to the NAACP for that sinful thing."

"Honey, I believe in the multicultural beauty of this diverse country."

"But that Anglo crap was just plain ugly."

"Did it go in?" Preacher asked.

"Well, it went in, but it didn't go in pretty."

"All right, pretty boy, let's see what you got."

Frank clanged the shot off the rim.

"My shot might've been ugly," Preacher said, "but your shot is missing chromosomes. You want me to prove it, or you want to lose this game all by yourself?"

"Here begins my comeback," said Frank as he took the shot and missed again.

"Spell it out, honey, that's 'H-O-R-S' and double 'E.' Game over."

"Man, I can't believe I lost on that old-fashioned antique."

"Sweetheart, I might be old-fashioned, but you're just plain old."

Frank felt hot and stupid. He tasted bitterness—that awful need to cry—and he was ashamed of his weakness, and then he was ashamed of being ashamed.

"Age don't mean anything," Frank said. "I walk onto any court on this city, and I'm the best baller. Other guys might be faster or stronger, maybe they jump higher, but I'm smarter. I've got skills and I've got wisdom."

Frank's heart raced. He wondered if he was going to fall again; he wondered if lightning was going to strike him again.

"You might be the wisest forty-year-old ballplayer in the whole city," Preacher said. "You might be the Plato, Aristotle, and Socrates of Seattle street hoops, but you're still forty years old. You should be collecting your basketball pension."

"You're twenty years older than me," Frank said. "Why are you giving me crap about my age?"

Frank could hear the desperation in his own voice, so he knew Preacher could also hear it. In another time, in other, less civilized places, desperate men killed those who made them feel desperation. Who was he kidding? Frank knew, and Preacher should have known, that desperate men are fragile and dangerous at all times and places. Frank wanted to punch Preacher in the face. Frank wanted to knock the old man to the ground and kick and kick and kick and kick him and break his ribs and drive bone splinters into the old man's heart and lungs.

"I know I'm old," Preacher said. "I know it like I know the feel of my own sagging ball sack. I know exactly how old I am in my brain, in my mind. And my basketball mind is the same age as my basketball body. Old, old, ancient, King Tut antique. But you, son, you're in denial. Your mind is stuck somewhere back in 1980, but your eggshell body is cracking here in the twenty-first century."

"I'm only forty years old," Frank said. He bounced the ball between his legs, around his back, thump, thump, between his legs, around his back, thump, thump, again and again, thump, thump, faster and faster, thump, thump, thump, thump, thump.

"Basketball years are like dog years," Preacher said. "You're truly about two hundred and ninety-nine years old."

Thump, thump, thump, thump, thump.

"I'm still a player," Frank said. "I'm still playing good and hard."

Thump, thump, thump, thump, thump.

"But why are you still playing so hard?" Preacher asked. "What are you trying to prove? You keep trying to get all those years back, right? You're trying to time-machine it, trying to alternate-universe it, but one of these days, you're going to come down wrong on one of your arthritic knees, and it will be over. What will you do then? You've bet your whole life on basketball, and playground basketball at that, and what do you have to show for it? Look at you. You're not some sixteen-year-old gangster trying to play your way out of the ghetto. You ain't even some reservation warrior boy trying to shoot your way off the reservation and into some white-collar job at Microsoft Ice Cream. You're just Frank the Pretty Good Shooter for an Old Fart. Nobody's looking to recruit you. Nobody's going to draft you. Ain't no university alumni lining up to financially corrupt your naive ass. Ain't no pretty little Caucasian cheerleaders looking to bed you down in room seven of the Delta Delta Delta house. Ain't no ESPN putting you in the Plays of the Day. You ain't as cool as the other side of the pillow. You're hot and sweaty, like an orthopedic support. You're one lonely Chuck Taylor high-top rotting in the ten-cent pile at Goodwill. Your game is old and ugly and misguided, like the Salem witch trials. You're committing injustice every time you step on the court. I think I'm going to organize a march against your ancient ass. I'm going to boycott you. I'm going to boycott your corporate sponsors. But wait, you ain't got any corporate sponsors, unless Nike has come out with a shoe called Tired Old Bastard. So why don't you just give up the full-court game and the half-court game and enjoy the fruitful retirement of shooting a few basketballs and drinking a few glasses of lemonade."

Frank stopped bouncing the ball and threw it hard at Preacher, who easily caught it and laughed.

"Man oh man," Preacher said. "I'm getting to you, ain't I? I'm hurting your ballplaying heart, ain't I?"

Preacher threw the ball back at Frank, who also caught it easily, and resumed the trick dribbling, the thump, thump, thump, and thump, thump.

"I play ball because I need to play," Frank said

Thump, thump.

"And I need yearly prostate exams," Preacher said, "so don't try to tell me nothing about needing nothing."

Thump, thump.

"I'm playing to remember my mom and dad," Frank said.

Preacher laughed so hard he sat on the court.

"What's so funny?" Frank asked. He dropped the ball and let it roll away.

"Well, I just took myself a poll," Preacher said. "And I asked one thousand mothers and fathers how they would feel about a forty-year-old son who quit his high-paying job to pursue a full-time career as a playground basketball player in Seattle, Washington, and all one thousand of them mothers and fathers cried in shame."

"Preacher," Frank said, "it's true. I'm not kidding. This is, like, a mission or something. My mom and dad are dead. I'm playing to honor them. It's an Indian thing."

Preacher laughed harder and longer. "That's crap," he said. "And it's racist crap at that. What makes you think your pain is so special, so different from anybody else's pain? You look up death in the medical dictionary, and it says everybody's going to catch it. So don't lecture me about death."

"Believe me, I'm playing to remember them."

"You're playing to remember yourself. You're playing because of some of that nostalgia. And nostalgia is a cancer. Nostalgia will fill your heart up with tumors. Yeah, yeah, yeah, that's what you are. You're just an old fart dying of terminal nostalgia."

Frank moaned—a strange, involuntary, and primal noise—and turned his back on Preacher. Frank wept and furiously wiped the tears from his face.

"Oh man, are you crying?" Preacher asked. He was alarmed and embarrassed for Frank.

"Leave me alone," Frank said.

"Oh, come on, man, I'm just talking."

"No, you're not just talking. You're talking about my whole failed life."

"You ain't no failure. I'm just trying to distract you. I'm just trying to win."

"Don't you condescend to me. Don't. Don't you look inside me and then pretend you didn't look inside me."

Preacher felt the heat of Frank's mania, of his burning.

"Listen, brother," Preacher said. "Why don't we go get some decaf and talk this out? I had no idea this meant so much to you. Why don't we go talk it out?"

Frank walked in fast circles around Preacher, who wondered if he could outrun the younger man.

"Listen," said Frank. "You can't take something away from me, steal from me, and then just leave me. You have to replace what you've broken. You have to fix it."

"All right, all right, tell me how to fix it."

"I don't know how to fix it. I didn't know it could be broken. I thought I knew what I was doing. I thought I was doing what I was supposed to do."

"Hey, brother, hey, man, this is too heavy for me and you, all right? Why don't we head over to the church and talk to Reverend Billy?"

"You're a preacher."

"That's just my name. They call me Preacher because I talk too much. I ain't spiritual. I just talk. I don't know anything."

"You're a preacher. Your name is Preacher."

"I know my name is Preacher, but that's like, that's just, it's, you know, it's nothing but false advertising."

Frank stepped quickly toward the old man, who raised his fists in defense. But Frank only hugged him hard and cried into the black man's shoulder. Preacher didn't know what to do. He was pressed skin-to-skin with a crazy man, maybe a dangerous man, and how the hell do you escape such an embrace?

"I'm sorry, brother," Preacher said. "I didn't know."

Frank laughed. He released Preacher. He turned in circles and walked away. And he laughed. He stood on the grass on the edge of the basketball court and spun in circles. And he laughed. Preacher couldn't believe what he was witnessing. He'd known quite a few crazy people in his life. A man doesn't grow up black in the USA without knowing a lot of crazy black folks, without being born to and giving birth to the breakable and broken. But Preacher had never seen this kind of crazy, and he'd certainly never seen the exact moment when a crazy man went completely crazy.

"Hey, Frank, man, I don't like what I'm seeing here. You're hurting really bad here. You maybe want me to call somebody for you?"

Frank laughed and ran. He ran away from Preacher and the basketball court. Frank ran until he fell on somebody's green, green lawn, and then Frank stood and ran again.

After Preacher's devastating sermon, Frank didn't play basketball for two weeks. He didn't leave the house or answer the telephone or the door. He ate all of the food in the house and then drank only water and fruit juice. He was on his own personal hunger strike. Mr. Death, you are an obese bastard, Frank thought, and I'm going to starve you down until I can fit my hands around your throat and choke you. Frank lost fifteen pounds in fifteen days. He wondered how long he could live without food. Forty, fifty, sixty days? He wondered who would find his body.

Three weeks after Preacher's sermon, and after dozens of unanswered phone calls, Russell found Frank's address in his files, drove to the house, crawled through an unlocked window, and found Frank dead in bed. Well, he thought Frank was dead.

"You're breaking and entering," Frank said and opened his eyes.

"You scared me," Russell said. "I thought you were dead."

"Black man, you keep crawling through windows in this gentrified neighborhood, and you're going to get shot in your handsome African head."

"I was worried about you."

"Well, aren't you the full-service personal trainer? You should be charging me more." Frank sat up in bed. He was pale and clammy and far too thin.

"You look terrible, Frank. You're really sick."

"I know."

"I'm going to call for help, okay? We need to get you help, all right?"

"Okay."

Russell walked into the kitchen to use the telephone and hurried back.

"They'll be here soon," he said.

"What would you have done if you'd come too late?" Frank asked. "You know, part of me wishes you'd waited too long."

"I did wait too long. You're sick. And I helped you get sick. I'm sorry. I just wanted to believe in what you believed."

"You're not going to hug me now, are you?" Frank asked.

Both men laughed.

"No, I'm not going to hug you, I'm not going to kiss you, I'm not going to recite poetry to you," Russell said. "And I'm not going to crawl under these nasty sheets with you, either."

An ambulance siren wailed in the distance.

"Because, well," Frank said, "I know you're gay and all, and I care about you a bunch, but not in that way. If we were stuck on a deserted island or something, or if we were in prison, then maybe we could be Romeo and Juliet, but in the real world, you're going to have to admire me from afar."

"Yeah, let me tell you," Russell said, "I've always been very attracted to straight, suicidal, bipolar anorexics."

"And I've always been attracted to gay, black, narcissistic codependents."

Both men laughed again because they were good at laughing.

*   *   *

One year after Russell saved Frank's life, after four months of
residential treatment and eight months of inpatient counseling, Frank
walked into the admissions office at West Seattle Community College. He'd gained three extra pounds for every twelve of the steps he'd
taken over the last year, so he was fat. Not unhappy and fat, not fat
and happy, but fat and alive, and hungry, always hungry.

"Can I help you? Is there anything I can do?" the desk clerk asked.
She was young, blond, and tentative. A work-study student or scholarship kid, Frank thought, smart and pretty and poor.

"Yeah," he said, feeling damn tentative as well. "I think, well, I
want to go to school here."

"Oh, that's good. That's really great. I can help. I can help you
with that."

She ducked beneath the counter, came back up with a thick stack
of paper, and set it on the counter.

"Here you go, this is it," she said. "You have to fill these out. Fill
them out, and sign them, and bring them back. These are admission
papers. You fill them out and you can get admitted."

Frank stared at the thick pile of paper, as mysterious and frightening to him as Stonehenge. The young woman recognized the fear in
his eyes. She came from a place where that fear was common.

"What's your name?" she asked.

"Frank," he said. "Frank Snake Church."

"Are you Native American?"

"Why do you ask?"

"Well, they have a Native American admissions officer here. Her
name is Stephanie. She works with the Native Americans. She can
help you with admissions. You're Native American, right?"

"Yes, I'm Indian."

"If you don't mind me asking, it's a personal question, but how old are you?"

"I'm forty-one."

"You know, they also have a program here for older students, you know, for the people who went to college when you were young—when you were younger—and come back."

"I never went to college before."

"Well, the program is for all older students, you know? They call it Second Wind."

"Second Wind? That sound like a bowel condition you have when you're old."

The young woman laughed. "That's funny. You're funny. It does sound sort of funny, doesn't it? But it's a really good program. And they can help you. The Second Wind program can help you."

She reached beneath the counter again, pulled out another stack of paper, and set it beside the other stack of paper. So much paper, so much work. He didn't know why he was here; he'd come here only because his therapist had suggested it. Frank felt stupid and inadequate. He'd made a huge mistake by quitting his Forest Service job, but he could probably go back. He didn't want to go to college; he wanted to walk the quiet forests and think about nothing as often as he could.

"Hey, listen," Frank said, "I've got another thing to go to. I'll come back later."

"No, listen," she said, because she was poor and smart and had been poorer and was now smarter than people assumed she was. "I know this is scary. I was scared to come here. I'll help you. I'll take you to Stephanie."

She came around the counter and took his hand. She was only eighteen, and she led him by the hand down the hallway toward the Native American Admissions Office.

"My name is Lynn," she said as they walked together, as she led him by the hand.

"I'm Frank."

"I know, you already told me that."

He was scared, and she knew it and didn't hate him for it. She wasn't afraid of his fear, and she wouldn't hurt him for it. She was so young and so smart, and she led him by the hand.

Lynn led him into the Native American Admissions Office, Room 21A at West Seattle Community College in Seattle, Washington, a city named after a Duwamish Indian chief who died alone and drunk and poor and forgotten, only to be remembered decades after his death for words of wisdom he'd supposedly said, but words that had been written by the mayor's white assistant. Mr. Death, Frank thought, if a lie is beautiful, then is it truly a lie?

Lynn led Frank into the simple office. Sitting at a metal desk, a chubby Indian woman with old-fashioned eyeglasses looked up at the odd pair.

"Dang, Lynn," the Indian woman said. "I didn't know you like them old and dark."

"Old and dark and bitter," Lynn said. "Like bus-station coffee."

The women laughed together. Frank thought they were smart and funny, too smart and funny for him to compete with, too smart and funny for him to understand. He knew he wasn't smart and funny enough to be in their presence.

"This is Mr. Frank Snake Church," Lynn said with overt formality, with respect. "He is very interested in attending our beloved institution, but he's never been to college before. He's a Native American and a Second Winder."

The young woman spoke with much more confidence and power than she had before. How many people must underestimate her, Frank thought, and get their heads torn off.

"Hello, Mr. Frank Snake Church," the Indian woman said, "I'm Stephanie. Why don't you have a seat and we'll set you up."

"I told you she was great," Lynn said. She led him by the hand to a wooden chair across the desk from Stephanie. Lynn sat him down and kissed him on the cheek. She came from a place, from a town and street, from a block and house, where all of the men had quit, had surrendered, had simply stopped and lay down in the street to die before they were fifteen years old. And here was an old man, a frightened man the same age as her father, and he was beautiful like Jesus, and scared like Jesus, and rising from the dead like Jesus. She kissed him because she wanted to pray with him and for him, but she didn't know if he would accept her prayers, if he even believed in prayers. She kissed him, and Frank wanted to cry because this young woman, this stranger, had been so kind and generous. He knew he would never have another conversation with Lynn apart from hurried greetings and smiles and quick hugs and exclamations. She would soon graduate and transfer to a four-year university, taking her private hopes and dreams to a private college. After that, he would never see her again but would always remember her, would always associate the smell of chalk and new books and floor polish and sea-salt air with her memory. She kissed him on the cheek, touched his shoulder, and hurried out the door, back to the work that was paying for school that was saving her life.

"So, Mr. Snake Church," Stephanie said. "What tribe are you?"

"I'm Spokane," he said, his voice cracking.

"Are you okay?" she asked.

"Yes," he said. But he wasn't. He covered his face and cried. She came around the table and knelt beside him.

"Frank," she said. "It's okay, it's okay. I'm here, I'm here."

*   *   *

With Stephanie's help, Frank enrolled in Math 99, English 99, History 99, Introduction to Computer Science, and Physical Education.

His first test was in math.

The first question was a story problem: "Bobby has forty dollars when he walks into the supermarket. If Bobby buys three loaves of bread for ten dollars each, and he buys a bottle of orange juice for three dollars, how much money will he have left?"

Frank didn't have to work the problem on paper. He did the math in his head. Bobby would have seven bucks left, but he'd paid too much for the bread and not enough for the juice. Easy cheese, Frank thought, confident he could do this.

With one question answered, Frank moved ahead to the others.

Three weeks into his first quarter, Frank walked across campus to the athletic center and knocked on the basketball coach's door.

"Come in," the coach said.

Frank stepped inside and sat across the desk from the coach, a big white man with curly blond hair. He was maybe Frank's age or a little older.

"How can I help you?" the coach asked.

"I want to play on your basketball team."

The coach smiled and leaned toward Frank. "How old are you?" he asked.

"Forty-one," Frank said.

"Do you have any athletic eligibility left?"

"This is my first time in college. So that means I have all my eligibility, right?"

"That's right."

"I thought so. I looked it up."

"I bet you did. Not a whole lot of forty-one-year-old guys are curious about their athletic eligibility."

"How old are you?" Frank asked.

"Forty-three. But my eligibility is all used up."

"I know, you played college ball at the University of Washington. And high school ball at Roosevelt."

"Did you look that up, too?"

"No, I remember you. I played against you in high school. And I was supposed to play with you at UW."

The coach studied Frank's face for a while, and then he remembered. "Snake Church," he said.

"Yes," Frank said, feeling honored.

"You were good. No, you were great. What happened to you?"

"That doesn't matter. My history isn't important. I'm here now, and I want to play ball for you."

"You don't look much like a ballplayer anymore."

"I've gained a lot of weight in the last year. I've been in residential treatment for some mental problems."

"You don't have to tell me this."

"No, I need to be honest. I need to tell you these things. Before I got sick, I was in the best shape of my life. I can get there again."

The coach stood. "Come on," he said. "I want to show you something."

He led Frank out of the office and to the balcony overlooking the basketball court. The community-college team ran an informal scrimmage. Ten young and powerful black men ran the court with grace and poetry. It was beautiful. Frank wanted to be a part of it.

"Hey!" the coach yelled down to his players. "Run a dunk drill!"

Laughing and joking, the black men formed two lines and ran the drill. All of them could easily dunk two-handed, including the five-foot-five point guard.

"That's pretty good, right?" the coach asked.

"Yes," Frank said.

"All right!" the coach yelled down to his players. "Now run the real dunk drill!"

Serious now, all of the young men ripped off reverse dunks, 360-degree dunks, alley-oops, bounce-off-the-floor-and-off-the-backboard dunks, and one big guy dunked two balls at the same time.

"I've built myself a great program here," the coach said. "I've had forty players go Division One in the last ten years. All ten guys down there have Division One talent. It's the best team I've ever had."

"They look great," Frank said.

"Do you really think you can compete with them? Twenty years ago, maybe. But now? I'm happy you're here, Frank, I'm proud of you for coming back to college, but I think you're dreaming about basketball."

"Let me down there," Frank said. "And I'll show you something."

The coach thought it over. What did he have to lose? If basketball was truly a religion, as he believed, then he needed to practice charity in order to be a truly spiritual man.

"All right," the coach said. "Let's see how much gas you have left in the tank."

Frank and the coach walked down to the court and greeted the players.

"Okay, men," the coach said. "I've got a special guest today."

"Hey, Coach, is that your chiropractor?" the big guy asked.

They laughed.

"No, this is Frank Snake Church. He's going to run a little bit with you guys."

Wearing black jeans, a black T-shirt, and white basketball shoes, Frank looked like a coffee-shop waiter.

"Hey, Coach, is he going to run in his street clothes?"

"He can talk," Coach said. "Ask him."

"Yo, old-timer," said the point guard. "Is this one of those Make-A-Wish things? Are we your dying request?"

They laughed.

"Yes," Frank said.

They stopped laughing.

"Shit, man," the point guard said. "I'm sorry. I didn't mean no harm. What you got, the cancer?"

"No, I'm not dying. It's for my father and mother. They're dead, and I'm trying to remember them."

Uncomfortable, the players shuffled their feet and looked to their coach for guidance.

"Frank, are you okay?" asked the coach, wishing he hadn't let this nostalgic stunt go so far.

"I want to be honest with all of you," Frank said. "I'm a little crazy. Basketball has made me a little crazy. And that's probably a little scary to you guys. I know you all grew up with tons of crazy, and you're playing ball to get away from it. But I don't mean to harm anybody. I'm a good man, I think, and I want to be a better man. The thing is, I don't think I was a good son when my mother and father were alive, so I want to be a good son now that they're dead. I think I can do that by playing ball with you guys. By playing on this team."

"You think you're good enough to make the team?" the point guard asked. He tried to hide his smile.

Frank smiled and laughed. "Hey, I know I'm a fat old man, but that just means your feelings are going to be really hurt when a fat old man kicks your ass."

The players and Coach laughed.

"Old man," the point guard said. "I didn't know they trash-talked in your day. Man, what did they do it with? Cave paintings?"

"Just give me the ball and we'll run," Frank said.

The point guard tossed the ball to Frank.

"Check it in," Frank said and tossed it back.

"All right," said the point guard. "I'll take the bench, and you can have the other starters. Make it fair that way."

"One of you has to sit."

"I'll sit," the big guy said and stood with his coach.

"We got our teams," the point guard said and tossed the ball back to Frank. "Check."

Frank dribbled the ball to the top of the key, turned, and discovered the point guard five feet away from him.

"Are you going to guard me?" Frank asked.

"Do I need to guard you?" the point guard asked.

"I don't want no charity," Frank said.

"I'll guard you when you prove I need to guard you."

"All right, guard this," Frank said and shot a jumper that missed the rim and backboard by three feet.

"Man oh man, I don't need to guard you," the point guard said. "Gravity is going to take care of you."

The point guard took the inbound pass and dribbled downcourt. Frank tried to stay in front of the little guard, but he was too quick. He burned past Frank, tossed a lazy pass to a forward, and pointed at Frank when the forward dunked the ball.

"Were you guarding me?" he asked Frank. "I just want to be sure you know you're guarding me. I'm your man. Do you understand that? Do you understand the basic principles of defense?"

Frank didn't respond. Twice up and down the court, he was already breathing hard and needed to conserve his energy.

Frank set a back pick for his center, intending to free him for a shot, but Frank was knocked over instead and hit the ground hard. By the time Frank got to his feet, the point guard had stolen the ball and raced down the court for an easy layup.

"Hey, Coach," the point guard shouted as he ran by Frank. "It's only four on five out here. We need another player. Oh, wait! There is another player out here. I just didn't see him until right now."

"Shut up," Frank said.

"Oh, am I getting to you?" The point guard turned to jaw with his teammates, and Frank broke for the hoop. He caught a bounce pass, stepped past a forward, and hit a five-footer.

"Two for Snake Church," said Coach from the sidelines.

"That's the only hoop you're getting," the point guard said and hurried the ball down the court. He spun and went for the crossover dribble, but Frank reached in and knocked the ball away. One of Frank's teammates picked up the loose ball and tossed it back to Frank.

"Come on, come on, come on," the point guard shouted in Frank's ear as he ran alongside him.

Frank was slower than the young man, but he was stronger, so he dug an elbow into the kid's ribs, pushed him away, and rose up for a thirty-foot jumper, an impossible shot. And bang, he nailed it!

"Three points!" shouted Coach.

"You fouled me twice," the point guard said as he brought the ball back toward Frank.

"Call it, then."

"No, man, I don't need it," the point guard said and spun past Frank and drove down the middle of the key. Frank was fooled, but he dove after the point guard, hit the ball from behind, and sent it skidding toward one of his teammates, a big guard, who raced down the court for an easy layup.

"What's the score?" the point guard shouted out. He was angry now.

"Five to four, for Snake Church."

"What are we playing to?" Frank asked. He struggled for oxygen. Lactic acid burned holes in his thighs.

"Eleven," said the point guard.

Frank hoped he could make it that far.

"All right, all right, you can play ball for an old man," the point guard said. "But you ain't touching the rock again. It's all over for you."

He feinted left, feinted right, and Frank got his feet all twisted up and fell down again as the point guard raced by him and missed a ten-foot jumper. As his forward grabbed the rebound, Frank staggered to his feet and ran down the court on the slowest fast break in the history of basketball. He caught a pass just inside the half-court line and was too tired to dribble any farther, so he launched a thirty-five-foot set shot.

"Three!" shouted the coach, suddenly loving this sport more than he had ever loved it before. "That's eight to four, another three and Frank wins."

"I can't believe this," the point guard said. He'd been humiliated, and he sought revenge. He barreled into Frank, sending him staggering back, and pulled up for his own three-pointer. Good! Eight to seven!

"It's comeback time, baby," the point guard said as he shadowed Frank down the court. Frank could barely move. His arms and legs burned with pain. His back ached. He figured he'd torn a muscle near his spine. His lungs felt like two sacks of rocks. But he was happy! He was joyous! He caught a bounce pass from a teammate and faced the point guard.

"No, no, no, old man, you're not winning this game on me."

Smiling, Frank head-faked, dribbled right, planted for a jumper, and screamed in pain as his knee exploded. He'd never felt pain this terrible. He grabbed his leg and rolled on the floor.

Coach ran over and held him down. "Don't move, don't move," he said.

"It hurts, it hurts," Frank said.

"I know," Coach said. "Just let me look at it."

As the players circled around them, Coach examined Frank's knee.

"Is it bad?" Frank asked. He wanted to scream from the pain.

"Really bad," Coach said. "It's over. It's over for this."

Frank rolled onto his face and screamed. He pounded the floor like a drum and sang: *Mother, Father, way, ya, hi, yo, good-bye, good-bye. Mother, Father, way, ya, hi, yo, good-bye, good-bye. Mother, Father, way, ya, hi, yo, good-bye, good-bye. Mother, Father, way, ya, hi, yo, good-bye, good-bye. Mother, Father, way, ya, hi, yo, good-bye, good-bye.*

Coach and the players stared at Frank. What could they say?

"Hey, old man," the point guard said. "That was a good run."

Yes, it was, Frank thought, and he wondered what he was going to do next. He wondered if this pain would ever subside. He wondered if he'd ever step onto a basketball court again.

"I'm going to call an ambulance," Coach said. "Get him in the training room."

As Coach ran toward his office, the point guard and the big guy picked up Frank and carried him across the gym.

"You're going to be okay," the point guard said. "You hear me, old man? You're going to be fine."

"I know it," Frank said. "I know."